The Last of the Sinners

by

Lynn Shurr

A Sinner's Legacy, Book Ten

Cover Art by *Diana Carlile*

The Wild Rose Press, Inc.
PO Box 708
Adams Basin, NY 14410-0708
Visit us at www.thewildrosepress.com

Publishing History
First Edition, 2024
Trade Paperback ISBN 978-1-5092-5567-2
Digital ISBN 978-1-5092-5568-9

A Sinner's Legacy, Book Ten
Published in the United States of America

Dedication

For the fans of the Sinners who have read every story about their lives and loves, this fifteenth and last book is for you.

A SINNER'S LEGACY

The Children of Joe and Nell Billodeaux who fulfilled the prophecy that they would have twelve offspring, this way, that way, all ways.

1. Dean Joseph Billodeaux - Joe's illegitimate son by a one-night stand with a woman who planned to shake him down for money. He is adopted by Nell who believes she cannot have children of her own. Current Sinners' quarterback. (Wish for a Sinner, Son of a Sinner)
2. Thomas Cassidy Billodeaux - a redheaded son who enters the family through an open adoption with a teenage mother. His birth father is Joe's no-good cousin. He is a kicker for the Sinners. (Wish for a Sinner, Kicks for a Sinner, She's a Sinner)
3. Jude Emily Billodeaux - twin of Ann, conceived by in vitro fertilization using eggs purchased from Nell's sister, Emily. (Wish for a Sinner, Edie's Sinner)
4. Ann Marie Billodeaux (Annie) - Jude's quiet twin. (Wish for a Sinner, The Heart of a Sinner)
5. Lorena Renee Billodeaux (Lori) - First of Nell's little frozen babies to be born, one of the triplets. (Kicks for a Sinner, The Aussie Sinner)
6. Mack Coy Christopher Billodeaux - Second of the triplets to be born. (Kicks for a Sinner, The Bad Boy Sinner)
7. Trinity Billodeaux - Youngest of the triplets and named for the Father, Son, and Holy Ghost, smallest of the three and in need of a powerful saintly help to survive. (Kicks for a Sinner, Dream for a Sinner)
8. Xochi Maria Billodeaux - child of Joe's no-good

cousin by a young Mexican woman. She is Tom's half-sister and is adopted into the family after the terrifying deaths of her parents. Her name means "blossom" in Aztec. (Kicks for a Sinner, Sister of a Sinner)

9. Teddy Wilkes Billodeaux - a child with spina bifida abandoned by his mother at Nell's health care center and adopted by the family. He believed himself to be Joe's natural son. (Paradise for a Sinner, Never A Sinner)

10. Anastasia Marya Polasky (Stacy) - daughter of Nell's sister, Emily, and a bogus Polish prince. She becomes a ward of the Billodeauxs upon her parents' deaths but is never adopted by her own wish. She arrives on their doorstep the same day as Teddy. (Paradise for a Sinner, Son of a Sinner)

11. Edith Patricia Billodeaux (Edie) - a normally conceived child, twin of Rex. (Love Letter for a Sinner, Edie's Sinner)

12. Rex Worthy Billodeaux (T-Rex) - Edie's twin brother and future Sinners' quarterback, maybe. (Love Letter for a Sinner, Last of the Sinners)

Chapter One

Rex Billodeaux stretched out his six-foot-three torso on the lounger and put his hands behind his head. This body, the exact height as his father and two of his brothers, all outstanding football players, served him well along with the broad shoulders that made long passes possible and the narrow hips that could swivel on a dime. Taking Daddy Joe's advice at the start of his professional playing career as a quarterback when selected in the draft by the rock bottom team in the league had paid off—even though both he and his dad had tried to get him a better deal with a more promising team. But the worst team would not let him go.

So, he'd worked on elevating them to winning half of their games his first season by setting a strong work ethic and benching the slackers who didn't sign on to his program. The second year of his contract, he'd campaigned for scooping up older free agents who still had some good years left and choosing the best draft picks eager to show their stuff, despite the well-known stinginess of the owner. The third year, he'd gotten his team to the playoffs and almost to the Super Bowl but had been picked off by his older brother in command of the Sinners, a win that left Dean with a severe shoulder injury. Not that he'd wished any harm, but it had gotten him where he wanted to be, back in New Orleans, offered a fortune to play backup as his brother began to consider retirement. They'd play in tandem as he learned the moves and strengths of each Sinner.

Ah, steamy, sultry New Orleans at the beginning of May, already gearing up for summer heat. Rex took a swig from the cold beer sitting on the table by his side. He almost had it all. With his first signing bonus, he'd bought the usual big, black SUV and put his team's logo on the back, since replaced by the Sinners' famed devil's tail heart as soon as he got back to the Big Easy. He needed the big vehicle to cope with the ice and snow of his rust belt former home, but of course, he'd indulged in a classic red Corvette just for fun to tool around in late spring and the short summers up north. Unlike many football players, he didn't buy his mother a house. She already had a mansion known as the ranch and didn't need it. His dad let him have some fun but made sure he invested the bulk of his earnings.

Oh yes, he was sitting pretty with only a few more goals to attain, a Super Bowl, a house in the Garden District with a swimming pool, a tall, beautiful blonde in a modest bikini playing in the water with three rumbustious boys and steering a little girl in a swim ring and floaties out of their way as one cried out, "Marco" and the rest answered with "Polo."

None of these belonged to him yet. For the afternoon, he hung out at his sister Annie's house, awaiting the start of a family barbecue in the outdoor kitchen. Her husband, Matt Keaton, had gone off with Dean to select some awesome steaks while their wives shopped for the rest of the picnic foods. Dre, that tall blonde, had been left in charge of the children as usual He might wish she'd worn a skimpier bathing suit instead of a sports bra top and a bottom that came up to her navel and showed no cheek, but as her biggest attraction was a pair of legs that went on forever, he didn't mind too much.

He might care that one of the nine-year-olds in the pool was her son, born to her at the age of seventeen and known as Drew. Dre and Drew forever she often said and clearly hers, the only pale white duckling in a pond of colorful Cajun French ducks. He didn't mind the kid, no athlete, but as brainy as his nerd brother, Trinity, and heading toward being much more handsome. No one knew his father other than Dre letting slip that he'd been smart, a little older, headed for Harvard. The guy had no knowledge of the boy. She intended to keep it that way.

He and Andrea, once called Andi and now Dre, had more of a history between them than the unknown father. Not a sexual one. If his dad had drilled anything into his head it was always wear a rubber raincoat. He'd never done sex without a condom, though he might have enjoyed it more if that were possible. Just what other men said. Considering that forgetting that rule had resulted in Dean and the same slipup was responsible for Dean's oldest son, not to mention Matt and Annie's boy, Gabe, he did not forgot protection. No by-blows left behind in the city with more slums than suburbs for certain, though he'd had his pick of northern beauties and been very selective. Somehow, he missed southern girls, their warmth perhaps, their soft rounded edges. Not that Dre fit that description.

Traveling on her own from Indiana, she'd showed up at Matt's house in baggy clothes and full Goth makeup, her blue eyes eerie in their rings of darkness, her hair chopped off and dyed a dead black in spite of being a natural blonde. Her attitude could only have been described as hostile, especially to Annie, whom she'd hoped to displace in the household, treating his sister like an employee rather than a highly skilled NICU nurse taking care of the premature Daniel. When the truth came out about Dre's pregnancy, some had implied Matt fathered the child, but the timing had been all wrong. As for himself, he was seventeen, repelled by her appearance and downright afraid of her impending motherhood. He kept his distance.

"Marco!" Drew shouted.

"Polo!" Jenny shrieked in her shrill little girl voice. Eyes squinted shut, Drew closed in on his sort of cousin by marriage. Shunting the child behind her, Dre took evasion action.

Rex remembered another game, flag football at the ranch. Someone persuaded Dre to play on the team opposing his. Things got a little out of hand, and in his enthusiasm, he'd tackled her to the ground instead of snatching the kerchief from her rear pocket. Her Goth disguise long gone, her breasts and her hips more developed from having given birth, he'd felt right at home on top of her, way too cozy. He stood before reaching full arousal and offered her a hand up along with an apology, something like he shouldn't have tackled a mother. Those blue eyes glared at him, and she'd stomped off, angry, though he couldn't figure out why at the time. Since then, she stayed on the sidelines with the older women watching the small children. Now, he just felt like an ass who had ruined the game for her.

That wasn't his only snafu over the years. Once in his mother's hearing, he'd told her she'd look better with long hair instead of the sharp, short wedge style framing a beauty queen's face free of makeup. "You know, like

Stacy and Josee," his glamorous sisters-in-law.

He'd gotten an eye roll from his mom and a putdown from Dre. "Little boys have sticky fingers always getting in your hair." Once again, she'd left the conversation. At least, he'd learned not to comment on a woman's hair unless he had a compliment to offer.

He wondered if Dre knew how men looked at her when she passed. His college friends ogled her for years at ranch holiday gatherings. They wanted an introduction. He'd told them to keep away just as he would have done if they wanted to hit on his twin sister, Edie, protecting them both and adding that she had a son. She didn't seem to notice their interest at all as she herded the boys from one activity to another. The current game edged closer to his end of the pool.

"Marco," Drew shouted again as he planted his hands on his mother's arm, the one not protecting Jenny. He'd been it for a while and maybe she hadn't moved fast intentionally.

"You got me. I'm it."

"I wanna be it," Jenny cried.

"Nope, he got me fair and square."

Rex had to admit she was a good mother—until Dre released Jenny for only a second and sent a wave of water over his lounger. He sputtered, removing the designer sunglasses that had hidden his thoughts until blinded by the big splash and getting upright in a hurry. "Hey!"

"Hey yourself. Get in here and steer Jenny around while I'm it. Or have you forgotten how to swim while you were away? Water too cold for you up there?"

Forgotten? All the Billodeaux offspring had their lifesaving certifications and still guarded the pool in shifts when his parents held their charitable Camp Love

Letter for seriously ill or handicapped children going on in the summer. He'd volunteered last year, glad to soak up some sun after enduring another season of freezing afternoon games and sometimes snowfall in the outdated, open-air arena where his team played. Dre hadn't been there to see.

He rose to the challenge, setting his shades aside, rising from the lounger and stretching, knowing he looked so fine in a Speedo. Another wave came his way.

"Stop showing off your bod and get in here. You're holding up the game."

As he slid into the pool and took charge of Jenny, Dre turned her back to give the kids some time to scatter as she counted to ten. "We gonna win Unca Rex?" Jenny piped up already giving away their location.

Dre moved out, eyes closed, hands held out. All of them good swimmers, the boys fled toward the deeper water. Handicapped by Jenny, Rex doubled back behind Dre, a good tactic until Jen yelled, 'Here we are," instead of Polo.

Dre spun in the water, both hands held out before her. She caught him square on the chest with all ten fingers spread out on its expanse. Felt good, but maybe not to her. She withdrew them as if he were on fire, not soaked to the skin.

"Sorry, I thought I had Jenny. She wants to be it so much she thinks it's winning. I'll take over again."

"Why don't you take a break and relax on the lounger? We're going to hunt those boys down, right Jenny?"

"Yes, we win."

"I'm not sure…"

"Come on. I might be the youngest of the Billodeaux

kids, but I got stuck giving all the nieces and nephews pony rides for years. I'm a responsible guy. Boys, Jenny and I are both going to be it. Close your eyes and count to ten, Jen."

She did. "Ten, here we come ready or not."

Rex didn't cheat, but Jenny had no qualms. She peeked every so often, usually right after screaming Marco, pulling Rex's head down in order to whisper in his ear. "See Danny by the steps." He steered her that way fast, creating a wake that delighted the child. They captured Danny in a corner of the pool.

"We win!" Jenny, breaking loose and turning, stretched out her arms, floaties and all, to hug her uncle around the waist.

His tanned face thunderous like the clouds piling up on the horizon, Danny said, "She cheated."

"But I didn't. She's three. Give her a break, Dan."

Jenny held up several fingers. "Soon four."

Oh yeah, by some strange coincidence, all of Annie's kids, even her adopted son, Daniel, had been born in May. One big bash would be coming up soon for all three, sure to include ponies if his dad had anything to do with it. These boys could ride like ticks on the back of a hound dog, but three years ago, there had been a Billodeaux baby boom. He'd be drafted to give pony rides again, and so glad to be back Louisiana, that didn't bother him a bit.

Dre checked a watch she'd set aside on the same table as his nearly finished beer before she'd gotten into the water. Nothing special, but he guessed it kept time as well as his super, waterproof sports watch that cost him close to a thousand dollars.

"Okay, time to get out of the pool. Shower off and

get some clothes on. We'll be starting dinner soon." She spoke with the authority of some of his coaches when giving orders.

Despite the awws and other sulky objections, the boys swam to the steps and got out. Dre swathed each one in a large terry towel from a pile in a nearby basket. She divested Jenny of her swim ring and floaties, toweled her dry, and asked if she wanted help getting dressed to be answered with a "Nope."

"But I'm hungry now," Gabe, the huskiest of the three, complained.

"I'll see about some snacks. I think I heard your dad's car."

One hundred percent right as his brother-in-law burst onto the patio with Dean a step behind as if the running back protected him from an opponent. He carried a large package wrapped in butcher paper and string, its contents already bleeding through. Matt put it down on a prep table beside the huge grill and ripped the paper open to reveal steaks cut three inches thick.

"Would you look at these beauties. We had to stand in line for half an hour to get them custom cut." Matt selected a utensil from an array of barbecue tools hanging inside a cupboard and forked the meat onto a platter.

"Only four steaks?" Rex asked.

Dean, now wise to the ways of women and children, said, "Stacy, Annie, and Dre will want to share a steak, and the kids prefer hotdogs and hamburgers."

"Got the burgers and hotdogs all ready to go once the steaks are nearly done. Okay, who wants to help me put the garlic butter rub on the steaks?"

The children had formed a semi-circle around him.

Jenny stepped back as blood oozed off the plate and made its way down to the tiles. The boys, not wanting to show they weren't up to the task, stayed put.

Quick thinking Daniel came up with an excuse. "Dre says we need to get showered and dressed." He led his pack inside, trailing their towels.

"I guess none of them will grow up to be chefs." Matt took a bowl of his famous rub from the refrigerator and turned on the gas grill to preheat.

"Here, I'll help," Dre offered.

"No, go inside and make sure the boys don't leave their wet things on the floor. You can assist Stacy and Annie with the sides in the kitchen. They'll be along soon. It's time I taught Rex how a man cooks." He dug his hands into the rub and put a glob of it on the top steak. "Really work it in on both sides. Could get messy. Maybe you should take off that fancy watch. It won't tell you how to make a perfect steak."

Rex began massaging the meat with the butter spread, not really wanting to, but not able to back down without getting teased about getting his precious hands dirty. Dean, better known for his pizza making skills, started on the second slab while Matt took up the third. Commotion in the kitchen announced the arrival of the women and the rest of the family along with a small, fluffy dog getting up in years but still capable of dashing to the puddle of blood and lapping it up as soon as the screen door opened.

"Gross," pronounced Dean's daughter, Wynn, now a teenager, a teenager with breasts Rex noted feeling a little dirty and turning out to be as gorgeous as her mother. Strange to be her uncle with only a dozen years between them.

DJ, her slightly younger brother, was still a guy and joined right in rubbing the last steak in order to be one of the boys. As his mom, Stacy, appeared in the doorway, he held up his greasy, red hands. "Can I wash this off in the pool?"

"No way. You're right beside the sink. You can swim an hour after dinner."

"Or maybe Mati will lick them clean." DJ knelt and held out his fingers toward the dog who was more than willing to help.

"Little boys are so obnoxious," Wynn remarked.

"I'm almost as tall as you, Wynnie." He neighed like a horse.

"Enough. Wash at the sink. Wynn, help us get the side dishes ready."

"What do we have?" asked Matt as he lowered the steaks onto the grill and adjusted the heat to keep them from being raw on the inside and burnt on the outside.

"Slaw and potato salad from Stein's Deli, and two dozen of their knishes to snack on while we wait. The line was forty-five minutes long. That's why we're later than you are."

"Sounds good. Any dessert?" Dean asked.

"Edie and Ty are bringing over a giant chocolate chip cookie the kids will love. There is always ice cream, and some lovely fresh strawberries with dip."

Matt hit his forehead. "I forgot Edie and Ty were coming. We're one steak short."

"Let Ty have it. The rest of us will eat burgers."

When Stacy left, she took Wynn and Dre with her. Among the Billodeauxs even cookouts could be complicated. Good thing most of the family had retired to Chapelle and the slightly cooler ranch for the offseason, and Lorena and Jock had taken off for their home in Australia. As he watched Dre disappear, covertly admiring her long legs and tight butt, Rex swore to himself he'd be good to her and not mess up this time around.

Chapter Two

Why did Annie leave her here with *him*? She knew Rex made her uncomfortable. Despite their similar age they'd never been friends, and she couldn't really blame him for that. She'd burst in on Matt and Annie's life together in full Goth mode and hiding a pregnancy with the crazy idea that she'd have the baby in New Orleans far from her critical mother and raise it side by side with the preemie Daniel, displacing the baby nurse. She understood so little then including the complexity of caring for a baby right out of the NICU. It wasn't something a person could just wing.

Annie, dear Annie, had put up with her insults and snarky attitude, straightened her out, and taught her so much. Matt did take her in along with her son and had seen she'd gotten an education in graphic design at UNO after passing her GED test. Part of her dream had come true. She'd become a member of his family, more like a sister than a sister-in-law. She held up her part of the deal by working from home, caring for all three boys, being there when they came home from school. Many people assumed she was a nanny or an au pair. She seldom bothered to set them straight.

Dre checked on the boys before changing her own clothes. They were already in shorts and tees and had hung their swim trunks over the tub instead of dumping them on the hardwood floors. She gave them the go sign, and they stampeded back to the action. Jenny had indeed dressed herself in pink shorts, a tee patterned in blue and purple unicorns, and finished off with a white tutu around her waist. The little girl held out a pair of sneakers she'd yet to learn how to tie. Dre got down and fitted them on the small feet, double-knotted the laces to prevent tripping. She released the whimsical ballerina and went to shower and get dressed with Rex still on her mind.

Rex had spent his last year in high school as an idolized football player who took the St. Jeanne Flames to the championship. Football scholarships rained down upon him, but naturally, he'd chosen LSU, his father's alma mater, and achieved the same feat there, championship after championship. He'd gone first in the NFL draft and on to a glamorous life in a dreary city. She'd heard fans cried when he didn't take advantage of a fourth-year option.

She knew he watched her as she played in the pool with the boys. Behind his dark glasses, he probably compared her to the many women he'd dated and found her lacking in big boobs and lush hips. He'd judge her bathing suit as matronly because after all, she was a mother. He hated her haircut, not understanding how hard she tried not to be like her pageant queen sister, Melinda, her mother's darling, who had tossed her long, blonde tresses to draw the attention of men. The only reason Mellie had gone to college was to get the Mrs. degree awarded by a man with a great future, a man like Matt whom she'd soon strayed from because he wanted to be a family guy, not her escort to one gala after another.

Just walking by Rex and his pals at the Fourth of

July celebrations held at the ranch took all her courage. They'd make remarks she couldn't hear, answered by Rex with a shake of his head. Don't bother. Waste of your time. She has a kid. Truthfully, she surrounded herself with the boys as a kind of protection, a camouflage of sorts. No one looked at a woman surrounded by children. She didn't want them to.

She put on a nothing special top of deep blue with a bra and bikini pants less modest than her swimwear. Pulling on a pair of cutoffs she'd hacked off too short but having lots of fringe, she slid her feet into wedge sandals that added to her height. She wouldn't be as tall as Rex, but probably had an inch or two on Edie's shorter husband. Her short, well-cut hair style needed no blow drying, only a comb run through it. She smeared her lips with a pale gloss. Good to go. She dressed to please no man same as in her Goth days.

Drew's father had told she was unique, special, exciting—in the back of his car but not out in public. Even then, she hadn't believed it. Having sex to spite her mother simply added to the thrill. Now, she had Drew, the center of her life. Any guy who approached her needed to know he came first. In fact, when asked out in college, going to classes while Annie watched the kids, she'd used that as a test, always saying she couldn't go out Friday night because she didn't have a sitter for her son. They backed off. Maybe some other time. They didn't ask again.

She ignored Annie's gentle prodding to expand her world. But she was happy with her life as it was. Thanks to Matt she had top of the line computer equipment and enjoyed spending her days designing posters and flyers and best of all, book covers, for reasonable fees in the place set aside for her in the spacious home the previous owner called a central hall villa. Earning fifty thousand a year didn't make her rich, but she could support herself and Drew if anything went wrong with her arrangements. She hoped that never happened. Annie provided friendship and guidance and Matt a father figure. Daddy Joe and Mama Nell more than made up for a lack of grandparents in her son's life, and the Keaton children provided him with two brothers and a sister, all called cousins though they weren't really.

Time to go downstairs and pretend to have a good time. She reached the wide hall and made her way to the kitchen where Stacy ruled in Annie's stead. Stace had a habit of taking over, and Annie never seemed to mind. The potato salad and slaw already sat in bowls, the first flecked with a little paprika and the other with a pinch of parsley for color. Stacy had arrayed the knishes on a round platter, each type separated with rows of raw veggies: baby carrots, cherry tomatoes, and red and yellow sweet pepper strips. A cocktail pick stuck in each section labeled the type: corned beef and swiss, broccoli and cheddar, potato and onion, spinach, mushrooms and feta.

"Anything I can do to help?" Dre offered.

"Yes, put the knishes outside on the table. I understand people are starving—according to DJ and his cousins. As soon as we have the fixings for the burgers and hotdogs on a tray, we'll be ready if the steaks are."

She took the large platter and backed through the patio door to be immediately inundated with hungry boys old enough to read labels and say, "Yuck, broccoli and spinach." The corned beef and potato varieties disappeared at once. By the time she reached Rex still being instructed in the fine art of grilling by Matt and Dean and offered the tray to the men, only the less favored knishes remained.

Rex frowned. "Hey, all the good ones are gone."

"Grow up and set an example," Dre said as she thrust the tray toward him.

"Yum, my fav, spinach, mushrooms, and feta." He plucked one off the platter and popped it into his mouth. Lowering his voice, he said, "Not half bad."

Dean, catching on, took cheddar and broccoli. Matt paused in slicing spirals into the hotdogs because he thought they tasted better that way and were more fun to eat as he told Rex. He took one of each. Jenny, nearby, demanded her share. Bending down, Dre gave her a cheddar and broccoli.

"It's good. Like when your mom makes broccoli with lots of cheese sauce on it."

Jenny didn't seem convinced. "No, you don't spit it out." The girl swallowed, then asked for lemonade from the patio refrigerator. Crisis or at least ill manners averted.

The doorbell rang. Children surged down the hall to admit the bearers of the giant chocolate chip cookie, Edie and Ty. Ty held it up high as he made his way to the kitchen where Dre had returned for the salad bowls. "After dinner, now all of you outside," she directed.

She placed the bowls on a long table set up for the occasion and draped with a cheerful cloth of red and white checks. Annie followed behind with a basket of hotdog and hamburger rolls. Leave it to Stacy to make that fancy, too, no piles of buns still in their plastic wrappers for her. Stacy, herself, carried the tray of sliced tomatoes, lettuce, onions, pickles, and cheese for toppings with an island of ketchup and mustard squeeze bottles in its center.

"No beet root since Jock isn't here," Stacy announced, referring to her Aussie brother-in-law who always insisted on it.

"Not going to be missed," Rex answered. At a glare from Dre, he corrected his comment. "I meant the beet root, not Jock. I really look forward to playing with him."

Annie changed the subject. "All ready to go. Grab a drink from the fridge if you don't have one already and pick up a plate and utensils. Eat wherever you want."

Jenny pulled on her mom's shirt. "Molly and JJ coming?"

"Maybe later. Aunt Jude and Uncle Connor had to work today."

"I want my same-age cousins." She pouted. "Only big kids here."

No doubt those two were mother and daughter with their large, dark eyes, heads of curly black hair, and petite stature. Jude and Molly likewise with Edie most definitely another sister and an aunt, all of them taking strongly after Mama Nell's side of the family. Dre sighed. How wonderful to have kin like that.

She knew she couldn't compare to tall, blonde Stacy or Trin's wife, the fashion model, Josee, another two of a kind. Not that they implied she didn't meet their standards, though Stacy sometimes offered to take her shopping for clothes. "I rarely see you in anything but jeans and tees, and you do have the kind of body anything looks good on. I think you could model. Why don't you ask Josee—" She'd cut off Stacy right then and there. "I'm happy as I am. I can work at home and wear what is comfortable."

Dre diverted Jenny by holding out a plate. "What would you like to eat, Jen-bug?"

"A swirly hotdog."

She encased one of Matt's masterpieces in a bun and added ketchup because she knew the child so well. As sides, she chose a handful of carrots and cherry tomatoes along with some pepper strips and a few pickles from the hamburger toppings. That and lemonade would be enough to fill the little girl who wasn't a big eater. She seated her in a child-sized chair with a small table where Jenny liked to play tea party. Three spare chairs remained in case her same-age cousins did arrive.

With no more children to appease, Dre set about filling her own plate with a hamburger holding all the toppings, dabs of potato salad and slaw, and a pile of raw vegetables. Her drink of choice, diet cola. When she turned to find a space to sit down and eat, she found none. The boys had settled on a beach blanket laid out on the lawn. Stacy's family took all the seats at one of the patio tables beneath shading umbrellas, and Annie sat with Matt, Edie, and Ty at another, those last two feeding each other knishes, still honeymooning after three years of marriage. They sat close together with one of Ty's tawny, muscular arms, the one bearing a charging ram tattoo, across the back of her chair. His hazel eyes, glinting golden in the sun, were only for Edie. Must be nice.

Okay, she could join Jenny and squat on one of the little chairs with her long legs folded to the side or force Drew to make a place for her on the blanket where he sat with Daniel and Gabe. Sure, that's what every nine-year-old boy wanted, to eat dinner with his mother horning in with his pals. She headed toward the tiny table before being hailed by a voice used for audibles on the football field.

"Over here, Dre," Rex shouted over other conversations. He perched on the side of the lounger and patted the lower end. "Plenty of room, and you get to eat with the best-looking guy here." For a second, he unleased that "come have sex with me smile" endemic to the Billodeaux males, but quickly packed it away knowing that it was not appropriate for family gatherings where most everyone would be a cousin or an aunt.

As she stood there in shock, Dre noticed Annie give Matt an elbow nudge. A big-shouldered guy known as the Tank in football circles and not lacking in dark-eyed attractiveness, her husband concentrated on a steak that filled an entire plate and required the side dishes to be placed on others. She elbowed him again. "Are you going to let that go unchallenged?"

"What?"

"Rex says he's the best-looking guy here."

Matt considered his words for a moment. "Nope, if we put it to a vote, I'd win. I have a loyal wife, more kids than any of you, and Drew and Dre would agree with them. Since that's settled, why don't you sit with the second-best guy—or maybe third. Dean hasn't lost his looks. Quarterbacks don't get as beat up as running backs, and he has a solid voting block too. Ty would get Edie's vote, naturally. Yeah, you can sit with him if you don't mind fourth-rate, Dre."

Matt had put Rex in his place in a brotherly way that made her smile. "Now you've made me feel sorry for Rex, poor guy. I guess I should keep him company." She went to take her place on the end of the lounger but left plenty of space between them.

They didn't speak much. Rex had pulled over the small table by the lounger and tried to manage the over-sized steak with a plastic knife, though it did seem to be tender enough to cut with a fork. He sawed off a small piece and offered it to her on the end of the knife. "You gotta taste this. It's amazing."

"Oh, I have plenty on my plate already."

"That's not the point. When something great comes along, you make room for it. Here, I'll give you a bigger piece for yourself." He sliced through the meat with ease and held it dripping over her pile of vegetables.

"Okay. Take some of my carrots and pepper strips."

"You sound like my m—" He stopped himself. "Yeah, I should eat more vegetables. Thanks."

Silence ensued. Plates were cleared and collected for washing. Edie did the honors slicing the giant cookie while Annie scooped a dollop of vanilla ice cream on the side for any who wanted it. Stacy added a chocolate-dipped strawberry to each plate. Despite people lining up for dessert, somehow Dre found herself back on the lounger with Rex.

The doorbell rang again, and Jenny got her wish for same-age company as the doctors, Jude and Connor, arrived with their children. She imagined Molly and Jenny would be mistaken as the twins in the future since JJ already tended toward tall with his father's green eyes and light brown hair, that is if Connor Bullock hadn't shaved his off. The twins seized dessert plates and headed for Jenny's table. The adults dragged chairs from the kitchen. Why hadn't she thought to do that?

Once the children ran off their sugar highs by playing tag on the lawn with the older boys occasionally allowing themselves to be caught by the little ones, the evening grew quiet as the sun set taking much of the ferocious heat with it. As the night darkened and the air turned balmy, Jenny fell asleep on the beach blanket while the twins cuddled one each on their parents' laps.

"Time to go," Jude announced, ever the first leave a party.

"Yes, the kids need to get to bed," Annie agreed.

"But the night is still young. Anyone up for drinks and dancing at Mariah's Place?" Rex said, seemingly oblivious to the needs of young children.

Dre shook her head. "I have to help Annie with the boys and cleanup."

"No, you don't. Stacy, Wynn, and the guys will clean while I get the kids settled. Go out and have a good time for a change," Annie insisted.

"Sure, Ty and I will go with you," Edie volunteered. "We haven't visited Mariah for a while. You know how she gets if she feels neglected."

"Look, I'm not dressed for it, and my dancing is terrible." Dre sorted through any other excuses she might use. "I don't have anything to wear to Mariah's."

"Good thing I live so nearby. We're about the same size. I'll be back in half an hour. Wynn, DJ, start on the kitchen. Matt and Dean, grill area. Edie and Ty, take care of the leftovers." Stacy grabbed her car keys from her purse.

"Yes, princess," her husband answered and followed up with a mock bow.

"Oh, and Dre, put on some makeup."

As Stace sailed from the patio, Dre tried again. "It's too much trouble."

"No trouble."

"Nothing sexy!" Dre shouted after her.

In the darkness out of the circle of the porch and pool lights, Rex let his "come hither" smile run rampant. "I'd take you just the way you are. But sexy might be interesting," he whispered in her ear.

Chapter Three

Here they were at Mariah's Place, the hangout of the Sinners football players, owned by the mother of their retired kicker, Howdy McCoy. The outrageous Mariah with her huge, white wig and low-cut gowns, played godmother to all members of the team, perhaps making up for deserting Howdy as a child and only reuniting with him later in life. Something of an outsider, Dre hadn't been to the club very often and always with Annie and Matt. At least, thanks to Stacy she looked like a woman who went dancing with gorgeous guys all the time.

Back in no time as she'd promised, Stacy had gowned her in a dress not too immodest but with provocative little touches. "You aren't as big at the top as I am, but the halter is very forgiving. It wraps around what you have, and hey, no need to wear a bra. It appears to be held up by this little bow but has sturdy snaps under it. Same with the waistline, a small bow accent covering more snaps at the top of the zipper. A guy would think it's easy to take off, but it's not. Still, easy enough to get out of if you want."

"Half my back is exposed, and the slit up the front of the skirt goes to mid-thigh. How is this not sexy," Dre grumbled, unwilling to admit how good she looked in the mirror.

"Portia Ramsey, Ty's mom, calls it a sundress. It's one of her casual originals. The colors are good on you, those swirls of green, white, and blue move with your body, and you've got the legs to wear it." Stacy checked her over. "Your lipstick should be a little brighter, but otherwise, not bad. Here, an evening bag in case you don't have one. Stock your essentials in it."

When Dre seemed puzzled, she added, "An ID, comb, lipstick, tissues, and a twenty or a credit card in case the night goes sour and you need to take a cab home."

"We're riding with Edie and Ty. I am sure I can count on them."

"Do it just for practice. You won't always have backup."

"I won't need backup if I don't go out."

"Oh, I think your day has come."

Now, she stood just inside the doors to Mariah's Place, her sweating hand clutched around the strap of the small purse. The music had begun. They'd missed Mariah's signature song, "Fever," belted out after a few huffs from her oxygen tank backstage. A good band that knew how to get people up and dancing beat out a tempo not too fast or too slow. Couples circled the black and white tiled floor. All the four-top tables appeared to be occupied. They'd have to sit at the bar. But no.

Mariah might not admit to wearing green contacts, but her vision in the dim nightclub stayed sharp as ever, especially since her cataract surgery. She beckoned to the group with a red-lacquered nail. "Over here, my dears."

They moved to the table with three empty seats set to one side of the stage. Edie slid into a place and gave

Mariah air kisses. Dre started to take another, but Rex moved her over one. She opened her mouth to protest.

"That's Billy's chair. No one sits in it," he spoke into her ear, almost nuzzling it.

"Who?"

"Her long dead lover."

"OOO-kay."

"Come close." Mariah summoned the two football players. She landed a wet, red kiss on Ty's cheek and did the same to Rex. Neither wiped it off for the moment.

"So glad you're home where you belong and playing for the Sinners at last, my boy. He's been way up north and has an excuse, but you haven't been by in some time, Edie. Still no babies on the way?" No one would say Mariah exercised tact.

"When we're good and ready," Edie shot back with plenty of sass.

Mariah pinched her cheek. "Always loved this one. But you two would make beautiful children." She turned her green eyes and smoky voice on Dre. "And you are?"

Sometimes older people needed a prompt. "Imagine me with black hair and lots of dark makeup."

Mariah squinted at Dre, homed in on her blue eyes. "The pregnant Goth girl that Annie and Matt took in. You've improved. How's your boy?"

"Thriving, thank you."

"You are welcome to come visit anytime. No need to drag Rex along. I can see at least three guys sizing you up for a dance and one of them is X over there in the shadows. All of you, go cheer him up."

"X needs cheering, but he's always the life of the party," Ty said.

"He's in the dumps because Caressa can't perform

here anymore. She has to play clubs her manager contracted for her. She's been all over the U.S. of A these past few years. Has a recording contract and a new album that puts my one-time career in the shade—but she got her start here. Go on, help the man." Mariah flicked her red nails again as if to make them do her will. They took the hint.

At X-avier Hopkins' table in the far, dark corner on the other side of the dance floor, the usually lively running back seemed sunk in sorrow behind a wall of empty beer bottles. Ty slapped him on the back. "How's it hanging, bro?"

"Low and lonely. Have a seat. Con-console me." He bowed his head, cornrows gone since the last time Dre had seen him at one of Dean's pizza parties and a fluffy fro, not too big, growing in their place.

Not sure how to cheer him without knowing exactly what had gone wrong, Dre said, "I see you have a new hairstyle."

X raised his mocha-colored face. His usually sharp features seemed blurred, his cheeks hollow though he'd always been lithe, fast as missile on the football field, people said. "Old school. I used to have a bigger one when I first joined the Sinners. Carie loved it. Then I had to get all fancy with the cornrows."

"Carie?"

"Caressa. I thought she was my curvy girl, but you should see her now. That manager of hers has her so skinny I swear her voice doesn't sound the same. But he thinks her looks are more important. Draggin' her all over the country, wearin' her down to the bone like a hound with a ham hock. I guess a big contract and an album was more important than what we had together."

Edie patted his back. "X, I've seen you perform with Caressa here and once at Trin's wedding years ago. Couldn't you tell she's been in love with you for a long time. Did you ever tell her?"

"I was getting around to it. I guess I held back because I knew the guys would rag me about dating a fatty. They don't understand how good she was to hold close, how sweet inside. But women just know when you care, right?"

Edie shook her head, and Dre found herself agreeing despite her inexperience. Men could be so dense. How was a girl to know, though she was certain Drew's father hadn't cared a bit.

"You got to say the words, man." Ty, who had taken the third chair, wrapped an arm tighter around Edie.

"Then, that agent signed her and took her away, changed her."

Rex scanned the room for a spare chair, spotted one, and went off to claim it. It cost him an autograph on a napkin, but he turned down an offer to join the young ladies on a night out and returned to the conversation. "X, if anyone gives you a hard time about loving a larger woman, you let me know. I'll straighten them out."

"I'll help," Ty agreed. "Y'all know my plus-plus size granny. She's the best person I know besides this one." A hug-squeeze for Edie.

"Too late now, too late. That woman is gone. How about another beer or something stronger?"

"We have OTAs coming up soon. They may be optional training, but the coaches want us there and in shape. Speaking of weight, you need to bulk up a little. You might be the only player who ever lost weight in the off-season. Junior always needs to drop twenty," Rex said.

"Beer has lotsa calories." He raised a hand. "Another with a shot and whatever my friends want."

"This isn't going to help. You need to talk to her. Where is she playing now? There is still hope," Edie insisted.

"You tell him, baby," Ty said.

"I usually do. I'm known for telling what should be obvious to everyone, but no one else says—like Jude and Connor should get married three years ago. Look how well that turned out."

"That's what makes you a great journalist, babe."

If Ty gave Edie one more adoring glance, Dre vowed she'd go ahead and call that cab to get out of here.

The waitress arrived with X's drinks and took their orders starting with Dre. She stumbled through ordering white wine, any kind, the house wine, she guessed. Edie asked if the bar had Brownlowe Valley Chardonnay."

"Sure. We stock some Australian wines because of, you know, Jock Brown hanging out here."

"Make that two," Ty said.

"Um, could I change my order to that?" Dre fumbled.

"Got it. How about you, Rex?"

The waitress, young, attractive, and wearing a very short black skirt and exceptionally high heels that showed off her legs but must have hurt as work shoes, already knew his face and name. Figured.

Rex ordered an Irish Channel Stout in a frosted mug as X tossed back his shot. He caught the waitress's attention with a quick slash across his throat and a nod in X's direction. Even Dre knew that meant to cut off his drinking. Wise idea.

X chugged his beer and let his head loll back against his chair. "Y'all should see her now. She's pitiful, playin' at the House of Blues because it's a way bigger venue than Mariah's, her agent says. You know what Mariah's Place is? The real deal. Come wit' me and see Carie for yourself. We'll go right now and save her, drag her right off that stage and get her some help."

"Not a cool idea, bro," Ty said. "Something like that could get you kicked off the team."

Showing he'd lost all sense, X answered back, "Like marijuana got you kicked off your college team, Tyson."

Edie's hand shot out to keep Ty in his seat, but she needn't have worried. Her husband said, "It's okay, baby. He knows I haven't had a toke since I signed with the Sinners. The man is hurting and drunk."

"I'm so proud of you," Edie told him, all big eyes and sappy smile. Dre turned her head away not sure how much more lovey-dovey she could stand.

The waitress served Rex with a big smile and a dip that showed her cleavage. Dre half expected him to shove a big tip down her tight top and ask when she got off tonight. He didn't. Sure, the tip was a large, folded bill, but he put it in her hand and asked her to get the wine.

Rex turned his attention back to his drunken teammate. "I'll tell you what, we'll all go with you tomorrow night and check out the scene. But right now, you need to go back to your condo and sleep this off, X. You can't drive."

"I can walk. Not far, in Dean's old building."

"Not going to let my fastest running back get run over by a streetcar or fall into traffic crossing Canal or get mugged for his wallet on the way. Since you have the car, could you take him home, Ty, Edie? We'll hold the table."

"No problem. Come on, X." Ty heaved the man from his seat and started for the door, steering X with a heavy arm around his shoulders.

Edie paused. "Dre, why don't you dance and have some fun like we planned until we get back."

"I'd rather not. I'm not much of a dancer."

"Rex is like Daddy Joe and Dean. They all dance so well they make their partners seem great. Ty isn't bad either. He dances, and I circle him like a satellite. Go ahead. Drink that wine and get out there." With that final command, Edie, bossy for such a little thing, followed Ty and the staggering X from the club.

Rex stood and held out his arms. "I'm ready if you are."

"I won't ever be ready." Dre took a large swallow of her chardonnay.

"What Edie said is true. I can make anyone look good."

"Must be your modesty." She finished her drink and considered snatching Edie's wine.

"Must be my talent. Come on, Dre. No more stalling."

By the time they made it to the floor, the band had switched to a slow dance. She had no chance to mingle with the crowd and go unnoticed as Rex held her firmly, but not too close to his chest.

"Just follow my lead. Try to relax."

Relax with his warm, broad hand pressed against her naked back, her skirt with the slit rubbing softly against his muscular thighs. Right. But after two tours around the dance floor, she began to find it easy to be in his arms.

Must be the wine kicking in. He gave her fair warning she was about to twirl, spinning out of reach and drawn back again like iron to a magnet.

"That was fun," she admitted.

"How about three in a row?"

He spun her away, turned her three times before bringing her back. People were beginning to watch and give them more space. Every time she whirled, the slit in her skirt opened to reveal a lot of long leg. "Stop, I'm getting dizzy." An excuse, really.

"Let's try this." He raised her arm, arching high, and passed under it. Somehow, she found her back pressed against his taut chest and his cheek, lightly stubbled this time of night, rubbing against hers. Her discomfort or whatever else caused her heart to pound ended soon, maybe too soon. He reversed, and they were dancing like a couple at the prom again. The dance that seemed as if it would never end did.

The band segued into a faster number, but when Dre tried to escape to their table, Rex continued to hold her hand in an unbreakable grip. She recognized the song, "Tutti Frutti" by Little Richard, sung by a rather gravel-voiced guy who didn't attempt the falsetto bits, but not the dance Rex led her into.

"Let's go old school as X would say."

So, they rocked to the east and rocked to the west with Rex pushing her away with both arms and drawing her back, a quick twirl back and forth, more rocking and rolling, and then as the end approached, he warned her, "between my legs" and slid her nearly down to the floor and up again using only the strength of one arm. Her skirt flew into the air and settled again in one swift movement, but for a brief moment she feared her white lace panties would be exposed. Thanks to Portia Ramsey's skillful design, this did not happen. That being the climax of the dance, Dre returned to their table on wobbling legs as the band announced a break and downed Edie's wine. She felt short of breath and hot all over, perhaps the way really good sex should make a person feel. Not that she would know.

Rex followed. "You did fine out there. Lexie, bring us a bottle and another glass. We're going to need it."

He knew their server's first name. Most likely, they'd gone out already, and he'd only been back in the city for a little over two months. She brought the wine deliciously chilled and uncorked, setting it down near Rex, but Dre reached across the table and filled her glass with a little more than was considered classy.

"Hey, hey, save some for Edie and Ty." Rex poured for himself, a modest portion to be slowly sipped, not gulped as she found herself doing.

"I'm really overheated." Her face must be terribly flushed and that explained it. Thank heaven, Edie and Ty returned to join them and help empty the bottle.

"Did you get X back to his place without any trouble?" she asked.

"Sure, we pulled up in front of the building and the doorman took over. Rodrigo is concerned. This is the third time in two weeks he's had to put him to bed."

"That's awful."

But the band tuned up again, and Edie reminded Ty they'd come to dance and drew him out to the floor for a fast number. Her husband did indeed have fancy footwork. Edie in the cute yellow sundress she'd worn to the barbecue orbited around him like a bright planet did the sun.

"Ready to get out there again?" Rex offered.

"No, I think I'm finished for the evening." As soon as the words were out of her mouth, she felt a light tap on her naked shoulder, but the guy behind it spoke to Rex, not her.

"Mind if I take your girl for a spin?" one of the guys from the bar asked.

"Why don't you ask her?" Rex eased back in his chair and sipped his wine.

Dre sized the man up. About her height since she wore low heels, not bad looking, polite enough when he said, "I'm Rick. May I have the honor of this dance Miss…"

"Dre," she supplied and stood up a bit too quickly for the amount she'd had to drink. Was that her giggling over his formality? She guessed it was because Edie and Ty were still out on the dance floor beginning a slow dance with Edie nestled into her husband's chest like a bird in a nest, close and comfortable.

Her new partner led her out onto the floor and assumed that high school prom stance but with more pressure to her back than Rex had applied. She figured she'd have a red mark on her light tan so carefully cultivated when she had pool time alone. They stumbled around with him treading on her toes three times and twice for her. He kept apologizing. So did she. Relief when the music ended, and he failed to ask for another dance.

On the way back to the table, Rick did deliver a compliment, but not on her footwork. "I hope you don't mind my saying you have legs that just don't quit."

"Ah, thank you." Right now, Rex seemed like a far off safe harbor as he sat there drinking his wine and peering at them over the edge of the glass. At last they reached the table, but Rick did not retreat to the bar.

"Do you come here often, Dre?"

"No, not so much.

"Then I'd better ask you now if you are free tomorrow night."

Panic reigned. She started to bring out her usual excuse about not having a babysitter, but a better one presented itself. "Sorry, Rex and I have plans. We're going to House of Blues to see a friend perform."

Their table was definitely in a dark corner, but Rick did a doubletake. Not a lot of men named Rex out there. "The Rex Billodeaux come to play for the Sinners. Super bowl here we come." He offered his hand. "I hope you don't think I was trying to poach your date."

Rex returned a less than enthusiastic shake. "You were, but Dre is her own person. She can see whoever she wants."

"Well, good then. Maybe some other time." Rick retreated like the college guys, and exactly like them soon spread the word to his buddies that he'd danced with Rex Billodeaux's girl instead of saying, "She has a kid."

"On the way back here, he said I have legs that just don't quit after my terrible performance." Why had she told him? No idea.

"Yes, he's right about your legs, and no, he wasn't thinking of what they could do on a dance floor." His blinding smile lit up their dim corner.

Dre poured another glass of wine as she felt her fair skin flush again.

"That won't help. Blushing is a fight or flight reaction to embarrassment, and you have nothing to be ashamed of, Dre. You'd better lay off the chardonnay, or I'll have to carry you up Annie's walkway."

That image in her mind only made the rising heat worse or maybe it had decided to travel lower. She buried her face in her hands. "I think I have to flee before it's too late."

"Flee, we only just got here," said Edie said as she approached the table and filled her empty glass. "Wasn't this full when we left? Oh, well. This bottle is going down fast. Want some, babe?"

Ty shook his head. "I'm driving. One was enough."

"Don't you two ever get tired of calling each other babe and baby. You're grownups for heaven's sake." Dre fought off her embarrassment by being sharp with them.

Edie only smiled. "It's a special thing with us. Ty used to call me baby to make fun of me, but now he uses it a whole different way. When we're at home, I tell him he's my golden ram. He doesn't want me to use that in public."

"I understand. Sorry." Now, she had another reason to blush.

"That's okay." Edie patted her hand. "Annie says you don't date even though she'd gladly watch Drew for you. You really need to get out and have more life experiences. Wonderful things await. If you want, we'll loan you our Ducati motorcycle, but I think Rex should drive."

"I can't, I'm a…" She'd almost said the very words she loathed when they came from Rex's mouth. I'm a mother. A mother of a boy who had no one else if something happened to her, a car crash or a date gone wrong. Not many twenty-six-year-olds had written their wills, but hers assigned Matt and Annie as Drew's guardians and left whatever she possessed to her son. "I'm afraid of motorcycles."

"All the more reason to get on one," Edie insisted.

"Let her alone, baby sis," Rex said.

"I'm older than you by at least ten minutes, twin of mine."

"She's had enough for one night. We'll do one last slow dance, nothing fancy. You'll rest against me and relax. That's all. Dre, you really do have potential as a dancer and only need practice. It's exactly like being good at football."

"Helps to have magic feet," she retorted.

"Oh, my hands are even better, I'm told. Come on, last dance, last chance." He didn't finish the well-known line but took her hand once more.

As he held her close but gently, they seemed to glide over the checkboard squares. Her head nodded and rested on his shoulder. Her eyes closed as she trusted him to guide her. Her mind wandered to what Edie had said about her unwillingness to date.

She raised her head so abruptly that she jammed it against his chin.

"I'm seeing stars," Rex said, removing the hand from her back and rubbing the hurt, but he didn't let go.

"I'm sorry for that, but Annie put you up to this, didn't she? Taking me out."

"Edie might be able to nag me into something I don't want to do, but Annie is too sweet. No, I came up with this idea all by myself. Believe it or not, I do a lot of that. I feel bad about how I treated you in the past. It wasn't intentional, but I'm not some high school kid or a college football player too full of himself anymore."

"And I'm not a pity case."

"No, you aren't, but do you know who is? X. Everyone likes him, but none are helping him. Are you with me tomorrow night to see what we can do?"

Of all the Sinners who came to cookouts and parties at the house, X could always make her laugh. Shame on her if she couldn't put aside her differences with Rex when X needed help.

"Yes, I'm with you."

Chapter Four

She should have seen this coming. Outstanding quarterbacks were known for their quick thinking, fast feet, and good hands. Rex had it all. Before she could object to going out with him again, he'd switched directions and gotten her to agree to a mission of mercy. She couldn't use her usual excuse to get out of it either. Annie always happily took care of Drew, and her brother knew it.

Now, wearing another of Stacy's dresses, she stood in her room bedecked in a classic black gown with no slits but way shorter than she normally wore. Stace urged her into higher heels. "You don't have to worry about being taller than Rex. Even if you were, he wouldn't care. Don't you love a man that is self-confident?"

Dre didn't answer that. Word of their upcoming attempt to help X had spread through the Billodeaux grapevine like the vineyard was on fire. Annie must have called Stace early in the day because here she was with all the accessories. Stacy reached into a pocket and casually drew out a single stand of black pearls.

"These will be perfect. You have such a lovely, long neck."

"What if someone steals them?"

"You're going to a concert with three football players and Edie who is entirely capable of kicking a mugger in the nuts. No worries as Jock would say. Here's a black clutch in case you don't have one. It has a little gold chain if you want to dangle it. Remember to put your girl's survival kit inside. I'd take extra tissues on a date like this."

Of course, she didn't own a clutch, but she stocked this one with the lipstick Stacy thought she should wear, the comb, the credit card, some cash, the tissues, and an ID. All ready to go as far as she was concerned.

Drew entered the room, suddenly shy at seeing his mother all dolled up. "Are you going out with Uncle Rex tonight?"

"And Edie with Ty and X, too. It's a group date. Don't worry, I'll be home by midnight."

He ground a toe into the carpet. "May I stay up until you get home?"

"No, nine o'clock as usual. Come here and get your bedtime kiss early." Dre's son obeyed, dragging his feet a little. She kissed his forehead and wiped away a smear of lipstick with her thumb. By this time of the day, she'd usually eaten hers away.

"Shoo, Drew. We have to finish getting your mom ready. How about we do smoky eyes?" Stacy said.

Feeling more than ever that she shouldn't go on this rescue mission, she watched her little boy slink away with his head hanging. "No smoky eyes."

Stacy let out the gusty sigh of a person who was doing her best against great odds. "Then more eyeliner and a hint of gray-blue shadow. Let me do it."

Dre complied. Her own hands were shaking slightly. Rex waited downstairs. He'd gotten prime tickets down front and backstage passes for after the performance, making X swear he wouldn't rush the stage. The rest of the gang waited with him while she completed her involuntary primping. She hated women who held everyone up as if they were more important.

"Enough! I'm ready to go."

"Call as soon as you get back. We all need to know how the evening went."

"If it's not too late."

"Any time. I'll put my phone under my pillow on vibrate."

"If I get the chance."

Dre rushed out of the room but took the stairs carefully, not really used to high heels, even fairly sensible ones. No need to seek out her company. They gathered by the front door. Rex, impatient, jingled his car keys. He'd worn a tailored suit, no tie, dress shirt open at the neck. She bet he could throw on anything and look fine. Ty, a little more casual in khakis and a green sports coat that flattered his unusual hazel eyes, had his arm around Edie. She'd also worn green with a small frill along the low neckline and on the edge of her skirt along with the starry silver necklace she favored. As for X, he looked ragged. Always a sharp dresser, it appeared he'd thrown on anything handy, dark slacks and a slightly wrinkled long-sleeved shirt. Still, the man made her feel better by emitting a low whistle.

"You go, girl."

"Speaking of going, I have my Escalade out front. Enough room for everyone and any emergency. We need to move right now." Rex gestured them out the door as if they only had five seconds on the clock to make a play.

Ty went ahead and opened doors for the ladies. Dre slipped in next to Edie who'd needed a hand up, not what Ty expected, but he graciously took another seat. X with some of his former humor said, "Don't worry, Rex. I'll ride shotgun with you since I'm the only one willing."

Rex bullied the large vehicle through traffic a little lighter in the evening and flipped the keys to an attendant at the Sheraton for valet parking. They legged it a block and a half to the venue and found their way to the correct stage, one with a heart in the background and House of Blues written over it. Garish blue and purple lights filling the room created atmosphere. Their party clustered around a tiny table with cloths draped down to the floor and just big enough to hold a few drinks. Rex positioned himself next to X with Dre on his other side. Ty blocked their problem child in on the other side with Edie completing the circle that brought her back to Dre.

"I'm ordering one bottle of wine for the table. That's it until the show is over. Once we've seen Caressa backstage, we can go elsewhere or get something to eat here. Everyone understand that?" Used to commanding on the football field, Rex certainly had a game plan in mind, and Dre appreciated that, but she had no idea what position she was expected to play.

The wine arrived. Rex divvied it out among them just as the house lights went down and the stage lights went bright. The small band revealed played some light jazz to silence the audience. An emcee, wearing a jacket in keeping with the purple and flashy background, dashed to the mic and throttled it like an angry lover.

"Back in her hometown after a sensational two-year coast to coast tour, our own, our beloved Caressa. Let's give her a welcome wild as Mardi Gras!"

People stamped and whistled and pounded their tiny tables making drinks spill. Many stood and clapped. X attempted to rise with them but was muscled back into place by Rex and Ty and held there until a woman approached the mic and wrested it from the stand. Bone-thin, she wore a skin-tight red dress that showed every sharp angle of her body despite some drapery across the chest in place of bounteous breasts. Her hair hung straight and sleek, blunt cut at the shoulders, bangs across the forehead, sunken cheeks that made her dark eyes seem unnaturally large, crimson lips that opened and poured out a magical voice.

"Is that really Caressa?" Dre whispered to Edie. "Last time I saw her was at Jude's wedding, and she was a big girl."

She hadn't meant X to overhear, but he did. "See what he done to her!" He struggled to rise again. The embrace of his teammates held him in place. People at nearby tables shushed them.

That hair had to be a wig. The Caressa they knew had adorned hers with strands of multicolored beads that swayed with her body as she sang. Her skin had been a lustrous, shiny black but now appeared dry and dull. Her choice of dresses, usually boldly colored and purchased from Flo's Fabulous Fashions for Larger Ladies, had plenty of room to flare to the music. The voice had retained its special quality, but something was missing.

Dre tried to pin it down and could only come up with a lack of the joy and exuberance the woman once possessed. Still, Caressa had no trouble enchanting this audience with some blues standards and cuts from her album, songs she'd written herself. She gave the performance her all, sometimes trembling with emotion, especially when she sang her Number One hit "He Doesn't Know I Love Him"—"can't he see it my eyes, can't he taste it on my lips…" the finale of the show.

Dre found herself groping in her borrowed clutch for

a tissue. She wasn't the only one to do so. As the song faded out with the repetition of the title barely breathed into the mic, X shook free of his captors with a mighty effort, stood, and shouted before the applause could begin, "Sing "Unforgettable"."

"Oh, I haven't done that one in a long while. I need a special partner to do it right." Caressa shaded her eyes against the glare of the footlights. "Is that you, X? Okay then. Come on up here, and let's see if we still got it."

Ty glanced at Rex for guidance and got a shrug. "Let him go."

X bounded to the stage and came to her side. They gazed into each other's eyes and shared the mic held close to their lips, only their voices blending with no musical accompaniment. Dre dug a second tissue from her purse—so beautiful. Edie's large, dark eyes glittered, too, blotted with a cocktail napkin.

As the last words sounded, X placed the mic on its stand and took both of Caressa's thin, shaking hands in his. "Carie, I…"

"He's gonna do it," Ty whispered. Edie shushed him.

But X never got the words out. Caressa's hands slipped from his grip. She went to her knees. He caught her before her body hit the floor, cradled her to the ground. "Someone, call an ambulance," he shouted.

Whether any did was debatable with all the phones flashing in the audience as people captured the moment. Why had she left hers at home because it wouldn't fit in the tiny bag, Dre regretted. Because one of the others in her group would have one of course if she needed to call. Her tablemates were on the move. Rex in front with phone in hand pushed past a security guard and gained the stage. Ty ran right behind, Edie in his wake. She rushed to join them as they formed a barrier between X and Caressa and the eager photographers.

"Ambulance on the way," Rex said.

How could she help? What could she do? Dre knelt and took Caressa's wrist. She'd had plenty of experience monitoring baby Daniel's breathing and blood pressure when she'd helped Annie with the preemie child. "Her pulse is irregular, but she is breathing."

"Carie, speak to me. Don't you know I love you?" X said as he gave the woman in his arms a gentle shake, dislodging her wig slightly to reveal hair cropped down to the scalp.

"Now he tells her, when she's passed out," Ty remarked and earned a sharp elbow in the side from Edie.

Rex turned toward the bouncer advancing on him. "Can you clear the room?"

A look of recognition passed over the bruiser's face. "Sure thing, Rex." He went to the mic and announced, "Show's over folks. Take your drinks with you and go." He waved to a counterpart still on the floor to start the herding process. "Anything else I can do for you, Rex?"

"Would some oxygen help, Dre?"

"Couldn't hurt."

"See if you can find any and have someone bring the EMTs in when they arrive, Archie." He added the guy's name from the tag on his chest.

"Right away." The man scuttled off. Must be nice to be so instantly obeyed, though that power probably went with being a famous quarterback.

A small man with a pencil thin mustache and a pretentious soul patch on his weak chin arrived waving his arms and screaming, "Get away from her. This is your fault." He pointed at X with a finger bearing a nugget ring too big for it. "Caressa is delicate and only has so much energy for her shows. You extended her time on stage, so this is on you."

From his place on the floor, X growled, "She didn't used to be. There's nothing left of her, not even her hair."

"She's just having one of her spells. She'll be fine in a few minutes. I'm her agent, Rocky Flint. I know how to take care of her."

"If I weren't holding her, I'd flatten you!"

Rex glanced at Dre. "Will she be okay?"

"A faint shouldn't last this long. Really, she must be taken to a hospital and checked."

Archie returned with a portable oxygen machine and a spare set of nose prongs. "Old dude out in the hall said we could use his if we don't need it too long." He handed over the apparatus to Dre who positioned the cannulas under Caressa's nostrils, plugged them into the machine, and adjusted a low flow of oxygen.

"You a nurse?" Flint questioned. "If not, get the hell out here. If anything happens to my client, I'll sue you."

Dre flinched and stood up. She topped the agent by a good six inches and stared down on his slicked-back hair. She didn't answer, tried not to let his threat rattle her, though it did. What if she made trouble for Matt and Annie or had her son taken away because she could no longer support him?

Rex stepped between them. "Let her alone. She's helping which is more than you're doing." No pushing, no shoving, just sheer intimidation. The man took two steps back.

The EMTs arrived and manhandled a gurney onto the stage. They separated X from his Carie, checked her vitals, and removed the wig to better fit an oxygen mask over her face. With the wig cast aside, she appeared even more frail. They removed her to the gurney.

"Take her to Ochsner. I'll be responsible for any extra costs," Rex said, taking his game face off of Rocky Flint for a moment.

Flint spoke up again. "I'm her agent, and I say to put her in the dressing room. All this is unnecessary."

The medics paused, waiting for a resolution to the conflict, but saying, "She should go to a hospital immediately."

Ty took on Flint. "Don't I know you? Robart Flint used to manage amateur boxers here in the city. Yeah, they called you Robbie the Robot you were so heartless. That's when you started going by Rocky. Failed at boxing and went into entertainment agenting where the clients were easier to intimidate." One hand behind him, he waved the medics to move. Rex gave them a second nod and off they went with Flint howling, "I'll sue, I'll sue."

"Looks like you're playing out of your league again, Robart."

The agent went red-faced and took a swing at Ty who simply stepped back out of his reach. Archie, the guard, twisted one arm behind Flint's back. "None of that now. How about you go to the dressing room and calm down? I'll escort you there."

With Flint gone, X trailed after the gurney. Dre gathered up the oxygen machine and spotted an elderly man waiting anxiously by the exit door. "This yours?"

He nodded, relieved as she brought it to him. "Glad to help. The wife and I love Caressa." He glanced over her shoulder where Rex now stood. "Um, could I get an autograph for the grandson, Mr. Billodeaux?"

"More than that. I'll see you get three tickets to the Sinners' opening game if you'll give me your name and address." He signed on the notepad Edie had ever present in her purse along with a pen, tore off the page, and used the next to get the gentleman's name, Harold Drexler.

Harold went off adjusting his oxygen tube and calling out to his hand-wringing wife, "I'm fine. Best concert we've ever spent money on, my love."

Edie gazed into Ty's eyes sparking golden in the footlights. "My hero. You do know how to trash talk to trash." She linked her arm with his and snuggled into his side. Dre wished she could call Rex her hero and settle into his warmth, but that possibility was next to none.

"Oh, jerks like that hate when you use their real names. Just a diversion so we could get her out of here. That swing and a miss was only a bonus," Ty answered.

"What do you do when they call you Tyson Chicken Cluck, Cluck, Cluck," Rex said.

"Grin and say, 'Do you know how hard it is to catch a chicken on the run? You're about to find out' and walk away."

"Oh, I am so going to enjoy playing football with you on the team." Rex clapped Ty on the back as if they'd completed a successful play. "Dre, nice work, too."

She didn't get so much as a pat on the shoulder. But then, her contribution had been minor.

Archie crossed the stage and came down to join them in their huddle. "I told that bozo to stay in the dressing room for an hour to cool off. Caressa is so sweet, and he's such a dildo. Anyhow, better you be on your way before he comes out."

Lynn Shurr

"Thanks again, Archie. Here, put your full name and address on this paper. I'll send you some game tickets."

Everyone was rewarded according to the roles they'd played, and their group moved out to the sidewalk where they found X forlorn and fidgeting. "They wouldn't let me ride in the ambulance with her because I'm not a relative."

"Once she gets better, you should put a ring on it, man," Ty advised. "I know a good jeweler."

"I plan to—if she lives."

Dre made a move, put an arm around his shoulders, and said, "She will. Let's get to the hospital."

Chapter Five

The clock in the ICU waiting room did not tick but time passed as slowly as ever. The remnants of their burger takeout dinner littered a low coffee table along with the last of the cold drinks from a vending machine and a drained strawberry shake. The scent of fried onion rings lingered in the air.

It had been Rex's idea to grab something to eat on the way despite X's protests. "Look, we won't be able to see Carie for a while. It's getting late, and the hospital cafeteria is most likely closed. Dre, if you want, I'll drop you off at Matt's place. Ty and Edie, you can walk home from here if you'd rather. I'll stay with X."

"I'm going with you. There's a Company Burger not far out of the way that's open until ten," Dre answered.

"Good idea. I'm surprised you knew that," Rex said.

"Their burgers and shakes were what I craved when I was expecting Drew. It was my treat on the way home from an ob-gyn checkup, and sometimes Matt would indulge me by going out at night to get one for me." She wished she hadn't said that. It reminded them that she had a child waiting at home while they did not. "I'll call Annie and tell her I'll be later than expected. Oh, the Company Burger for me and a strawberry shake."

The men added a fried egg and bacon to theirs and bought enough fresh cut fries and homemade onion rings for the group to share. They skipped the wide offering of beers and cocktails. With the waiting room deserted as close kin slept in chairs by their loved ones instead, the occasion might have been fun and festive if they weren't waiting on word about Caressa. X had helped to fill out her admission forms since he knew her best right down to her birthday, home address, and next of kin, but the nurses still denied him access to her room since he wasn't a relative. Another notch carved into his belt of guilt over not having acted sooner. One of the less strict nurses did tell him that she rested comfortably, was receiving intravenous fluids and nourishment, but had not yet opened her eyes. Go home, she suggested. Come back in the morning. They stayed.

X did call her mother who lived a long three-hour drive away from New Orleans. Dre heard the woman's wail emit from his cell loud and clear. "What if she passes? What if my baby girl passes, and I'm not by her side prayin' hard as I can?"

"It's late, and you're too upset to drive here in the dark. Come morning, you call my mama or your pastor to bring you here. Meanwhile, I'm not going anywhere." As he disconnected, he added, "She has serious health problems of her own and shouldn't be night driving at all. I hope she listens to me."

With an old, old movie showing happy people who burst into song and dance whenever given a chance turned low on the small, high-mounted TV, they began to settle in for the night. Ty stretched out sideways on the green vinyl sofa, and Edie spooned in beside him. X had claimed a recliner early on, leaving half his hamburger uneaten. Dre wrapped the sandwich in case he wanted it later and cleared off the table only to find that Rex had claimed the other recliner leaving her with two straight-backed chairs to choose between. She guessed she could push them together, stretch her legs out, and hope to get some sleep. The chairs screeched against the linoleum as she moved them.

Rex opened his eyes. "Sorry, sorry, you take the recliner, Dre. I'll sleep on the chairs."

"As if you'd fit."

"The floor then. Believe me, I can sleep anywhere— on a bus, a plane, in a lumpy sleeping bag on the ground." He rose and adjusted the chairs farther apart. Picking up the jacket to his expensive suit that he had long abandoned to a coatrack, he balled it up to make a pillow and climbed aboard. "See, very comfy."

"Okay, if you're sure." Dre curled into the recliner and put up the leg rest. Still warm from his body and lightly scented by his aftershave, she found her own comfort zone, but didn't sleep at once like the others. She learned all three men had a light snore almost as lulling as a chorus of bullfrogs singing in the night. None would be hard to sleep with, and two were taken. What a last thought to have as she drifted away to dream of a precious baby in the bulrushes lulled by their music.

****

The waiting room began to bustle around eight a.m. though the sounds of medical carts dispensing meds started earlier than that. Dre opened her eyes to the scent of warm biscuits and old coffee that a large black woman poured out to set up a fresh pot. She recognized the resemblance to Caressa immediately.

"Ah, thanks," said Dre as she uncurled from the recliner.

"No trouble for the friends who stayed by my baby all night long."

X, fully awake, made the introductions of his half-awake companions. "Rex on the chairs, Dre in the recliner, and Ty and Edie on the couch. Wake up! This is Caressa's mama, Persephone Simeon, who must have left at five a.m. to get here so soon. Pastor Charles, I hope you did the driving."

"I did, indeed, son, sniffing those biscuits all the way. Nobody makes them better than our Sister Sephy." His belly spoke to his love of soul food in quantity and his rich, deep voice to his power in the pulpit. He wore his hair no-nonsense short above a round dark brown face, his big neck encircled with a clerical dog collar.

"I couldn't sleep after your call so I baked. Always do when I'm upset. Just warmed 'em up in the microwave. Dig right in. The coffee will be done in a jiffy." Carie's mama set a jar of honey and another of fig preserves she'd pulled from a vast purse on the coffee table beside the biscuits laid out on a clean dish towel. She added plastic knife, fork, spoon, and napkin packets saved from takeout meals to the display and a stick of butter sealed in a plastic bag.

Rex had fully blinked awake and hurried to hang up his wrinkled coat and turn the two chairs outward for the new arrivals. He twisted his neck from side to side to get rid of a crick. Likewise, Ty and Edie sprang upright from their intimate position and made room on the sofa.

"So nice of you, Miss Persephone," Edie said at once, all her southern manners showing.

"Y'all call me Sephy. The other is a family name and a mouthful."

Not holding back, the pastor opened a biscuit and applied butter and a dollop of sugary sweet figs. He carefully wrapped the thin paper napkin around the bottom to prevent fig syrup from oozing onto his black shirt and slacks. "Our poor Carie, voice of an angel when she sang in the choir. That's where X over there found her and convinced her to go to the big city, set up gigs for her until her career began to take off."

"I wish I never had. She'd be well and safe back home." X covered his face with his hands.

"Now, son, she was born to sing for more than the Lord. We'll see she gets all fixed up."

"It's that agent of hers, agent of the Devil, I say. Took her away for two years from her family and friends, used her up, wore her out." Sephy's considerable flesh trembled with anger. She contained herself. "Now y'all eat those biscuits before they go cold again."

As if that might solve the problem, none of them hesitated to eat. Dre fixed hers with honey and butter as did Edie, but the men went for all the toppings at once while the TV ran the morning news. In the midst of the feast, the day nurse poked her head into the room.

"Mrs. Simeon?"

"That's me."

"Your daughter is awake and wants to see you."

"Can I bring Pastor Charles and a biscuit for her?" Without waiting, Sephy buttered and honied one for her daughter.

"Sure, but just one biscuit for now."

As the nurse turned to lead the way, X jumped up to follow, and was again rebuffed with "only family right now."

"Tell Carie I love her, Miss Sephy."

"Everyone loves my Caressa, but I will surely tell her." She hustled her broad-beamed backside clothed in a floral print out the door.

As X began to pace, Dre said, "Have another biscuit before you pass out like Carie did. I saved the rest of your burger if you want to heat that up, too."

"Yes, Mama Dre," X answered, teasing, but it hit home.

"That reminds me I should call Annie and see if she needs me. The boys and Jenny will be up by now." She went out of the waiting room to do that.

Annie, as usual, said, "Everything under control here. The boys are creating faces on their pancakes with chocolate chips. Take all the time you need. Any word on Caressa's condition."

"Not yet. Put Drew on the phone for a minute. Hey, my honey bear. I'll be home this afternoon. Don't give Angel Mama any trouble."

"Mom, don't call me that anymore. It's embarrassing. I never give Angel Mama any trouble, almost never. Were you out all night with Uncle Rex? Does that mean you're going to marry him?"

"No, honey, we were at the hospital with a sick friend. Whatever gave you that idea?"

"A kid in our class said his mom is going to marry the guy who sleeps over at their house all the time, so I just thought maybe…"

Was her son searching for a father? She thought Matt filled the role for him. Not that Rex was really his uncle either. Those would be her two brothers who had never made the effort to meet her son. The Billodeaux family had numerous honorary aunts and uncles—and what boy wouldn't want a star quarterback for a father? She should go home as soon as possible to ease his mind but wanted to be sure Caressa and for that matter, X, were all right first.

Returning to the others, she had a second biscuit, this time with figs and dribbled some syrup on Stacy's black dress, now quite wrinkled. She'd have to get it dry cleaned or appear truly ungrateful.

Sephy returned, filling the doorway. "Good news! Our girl is being moved to a private room on another floor once a doctor checks her over. They're telling me dehydration and malnutrition, but she ate my biscuit right up. Any left for me? I didn't feel much like eating before." Just lucky for her two were left.

"This was a fine start to breakfast, Sister Sephy, but I suggest we all adjourn to the cafeteria for some grits and eggs while Carie is being moved. Might take a while," Pastor Charles suggested.

"The rest of you go. I should return home, get out of this borrowed dress, and check on Drew." Dre found the little clutch bag and withdrew her credit card. "I'll call an Uber."

"Borrowed? You wear it well," said Rex who averted his eyes and changed the subject. "I'll take you home, then drop by Dean's house to get a shower and change of clothes. Anyone else going? We can meet in the lobby in an hour and see where they've put her."

"We should change, too. We aren't exactly in hospital visiting attire," Edie said.

"Whatever that is. We'll come back in our own car," Ty agreed.

"I'm staying." X crossed his arms across his chest as if they'd try to drag him out by them.

"That's fine, son. How's an omelet sound to you? Sister Sephy, the rest of breakfast is on me. Let me show you the way." The pastor started the exodus with the rest following to the elevator and going their separate ways on the ground floor.

Rex brought his SUV around for his passengers and dropped off Ty and Edie first at their small love nest above the Korean Electronics store, the building owned by her dad.

"You know, Ty, I think the Sinners pay you enough now so you could get a house."

"My contract is up this summer, and they'll pay me more, but we're happy where we are. I suspect once it's confirmed that I'm staying with the Sinners we'll start looking around. Right, Edie?" Still tired, she nodded into his shoulder.

Because X had left the group, Dre found herself in the shotgun seat when Rex opened that door for her and helped her in on her wobbly high heels. At first, silence reigned as they crossed town to the Garden District, nothing but vehicle horns and streetcar clangs filling the air.

She liked it that way, but he had to go ruin it.

"I really did mean you look great in this dress and the one the night before."

"Even with syrup spilled down the front?"

"That could be licked off easy enough."

She'd been staring out the window watching the hotels and condos change to tree-lined streets shading single homes. Her neck jerked in a double take. She chose to ignore that comment. "Both dresses belong to Stacy."

"It seems to me you should have your own party dresses." At least, he kept his eyes on the road.

"They cost money, and I don't need them. Since I work from home, I can wear casual clothes and only need a suit or two in case I have to meet a client in person, which I rarely do. Most of my work is from good referrals and done online. Besides, I'm a mom as you so often remind me."

"So are Stacy and Josee, Annie and my mom. It shouldn't matter."

"No, it shouldn't, but it does."

"Look, when you first came here wearing all that Goth makeup you were so fierce and scary. Then you turned out to be pregnant which made you even scarier. I wondered if I'd be blamed."

"I don't see how. You kept your distance. No, that honor fell to Matt who didn't deserve it. I had to keep announcing how far along I was so they'd know it wasn't true. The guy who did the deed stayed home in Indiana until he left for Harvard. I did not tell him. No use ruining two lives."

"Is that how you feel—ruined?'

"No, this isn't the Victorian Age. I do love my son with all my heart and enjoy my work, but I am more than a mother." By now, she had her arms crossed much like X earlier, defiant. "I had to grow up quicker is all."

"And I didn't, jackass teen, smart mouth college student, but all grown up now. How about you erase my past sins, and we start over on a more mature level." He tried again. "You look great in that dress and were steady and helpful with Carie." He dared take his glance from the road now that the traffic had thinned.

"Thank you," she said trying very hard to keep even a hint of a smile off her lips. "This is my stop. I'll drive my own car back to the hospital."

"Waste of gas when we could go together since I'm staying two blocks away."

"If you drive an Escalade. We could take my old but

still good Lexus."

"Done deal. I'll walk over to Matt's place when I'm ready."

She got out of his car without assistance before he turned a hospital visit into a date, too.

Chapter Six

"Nice ride. Did Matt buy it for you?" Rex said as he got into Dre's Lexus without challenging her about who would drive. He'd changed into jeans, athletic shoes, and a black Sinners tee so snug it delineated all of his chest muscles and abs.

She'd done much the same, jeans, sneakers, and fitted top in a blue that brought out her eyes. She'd scrubbed away last night's makeup and returned to a little gloss on her lips and some blusher under her cheek bones to offset her usual paleness. Not primping for him, definitely not. She took a minute to answer his question since they'd agreed to act like adults.

How much to spill?

"This was my sister's car, new right before she died. Matt gave it to me after her funeral along with some of her jewelry. I couldn't take my mother's excessive grief, the way she blamed Matt for everything, and acted like Mellie was her only daughter. I'd begun acting out before then with the Goth stuff maybe to get her attention, maybe to hurt her like she hurt me. Part of the plan was to seduce the president of the debate team and get pregnant. He couldn't believe his luck that I was so easy—every weekend in the backseat of his car."

"A teenage guy's wet dream come true. Sorry, go on."

"Found out I was pregnant just before my sister died

in a crossfire between two gangs down here. Thank God, Daniel's life was saved by C-section. Anyhow, I never dropped my bomb on Marilyn, that's my mother."

"I don't think I ever met her," Rex remarked as they got into thicker traffic. He didn't tell her where to turn or how to drive. She appreciated that.

"Be glad you didn't. She eventually had a nervous breakdown over Mellie's death and my failure to be like her beloved daughter. Anyhow, I hocked the jewels to pay for my expenses, got into the Lexus, and drove to New Orleans thinking Matt would take me in. I'd help him raise his son, and he could help me with mine. Maybe he'd be so grateful he'd marry me when I got older. So, I show up on his doorstep unannounced and there's Annie taking care of Daniel, and Matt is already in love with her. To my shame, I tried to drive her away."

Rex laughed. "You didn't know her at all. Annie comes across sweet and loving, but she was a NICU nurse and doesn't give up on anyone. Her relentless kindness wore you down, I'll bet."

"She's the mother I never had—and Mama Nell and the rest of Billodeauxs, the family I always wanted. Annie taught me how to take care of Daniel and Drew, how to raise them. I am forever grateful." She turned into the hospital lot and cruised for a parking space.

"Me, too, the way you handled Caressa last night, so calm and competent. I think you could train to be a nurse or doctor if you wanted."

"No way. I'm happy being creative, designing fantasy covers for authors and beautiful posters and invitations for events I'll never attend."

"That's a little sad—and you not having any party dresses. Tell you what, if you do want to attend any of those events, I'll get tickets. Make up for telling my football buddies they couldn't hit on you."

She found a space she could ease the Lexus into between two huge SUVs and backed into it.

"Impressed. Most women can't do that."

"Good drivers ed teacher before I ran away from home. I want to stop by the gift shop and get a balloon bouquet before we go up to her room. Why don't you find out where Caressa is right now."

Rex stuffed forty dollars into her hand. "Put my name on the card, too."

They parted to perform their separate tasks. Dre waited for the creation of the bouquet in the most vibrant colors available, remembering how Carie had once loved bright shades, then went to find Rex in the lobby where some kind of disturbance had begun.

Rocky Flint, as red-faced as he'd been last night, got into the face of the desk attendant. "What do you mean I'm not on her guest list, that I've been banned from visiting my client. I'm her agent. I made her famous."

The woman drew back, putting more desk and space between them. Rex walked up behind the man, tapped his shoulder, and said, "You heard the lady. Beat it."

"You! You did this." Rocky balled his fist.

Cool and collected as ever, Rex answered, "I did not, but agree with it completely. I'd think better of taking another swing at me. Didn't work out well for you last night and won't this morning."

Regardless, Flint drew back his arm, only to be seized by two security guards who dragged him to the entry and ejected him into the parking lot. With balloons bobbing, Dre approached the desk. "Nicely done again."

"Oh, I saw the attendant push the emergency button

so nothing to worry about. We need to show ID to get Caressa's room number."

"I'm glad someone thought to restrict her visitors. Here, sign the card before we go up."

As they rode to the top floor, Rex said, "I do strive to hit right between my father's outrageous behavior when he was my age, womanizing and brawling, and Dean's—let's call it steady dullness. I respect the women I date and stay out of fights."

"And I respect that. Here we go." They traversed a long corridor, made a turn and entered a private suite very much like the one super model Josee had occupied after a rejected admirer splashed acid on her. At the moment, only X sat by the bedside holding Carie's frail hand. Caressa herself sat propped up, eyes open, her nearly shaved head seeming very vulnerable. Still looking very ill, only one thing had changed—the light in her large, brown eyes when she gazed at X.

"We brought some balloons to brighten your room. Let us know if we can get you anything else," Dre offered.

"My mama's cooking, but they're telling me I have to start out on small, light meals and regular healthy snacks to build myself up again. Malnutrition, how could I have let it go so far? At first, Rocky told me I had to lose the weight if I wanted to front for big names. The dance lessons and dieting got me down a hundred pounds, but then while he was planning a tour for me, I spent my time song writing and recording in Los Angeles. Twenty of those pounds came back. The Simeon women store fat like a bear in winter. Even when I received nominations for Best R&B, Best Album, Best New Artist, and Song of the Year, Rocky wasn't happy since I didn't win a one of them."

"You should have won for "He doesn't Know I Love Him"," Dre told her. "Last night there wasn't a dry eye in the place when you finished singing it with so much emotion.

"Tough year up against Adele and Carrie Underwood, but Rocky said fat girls don't win Grammys and that was the real reason. He wouldn't promote my tour until I lost more weight, and if I couldn't do it the easy way, I'd have to get lap band surgery, or he'd dump me as a client. So, I just stopped eating." Caressa shrugged her bony shoulders.

"I guess you should know Flint was downstairs trying to get up here, but security took him out," Rex said.

Dre watched the light in Carie's eyes go out to be replaced by wide-eyed fear. X squeezed her hand with great gentleness. "I'd be willing to kill that man for you."

"Having you end up in jail over me is the last thing I want. As it is, there will be lawsuits because I intend to break my contract with him and get back some of the money he withheld from me. For a while, I'm going to be a complicated mess."

"You're not a mess. Never was and never will be." X kissed the back of her hand as Sephy entered.

"Got your yogurt snack and more Ensure, chocolate-flavored, baby." Carie's mother settled on the spare chair. "Eat it all now."

About one spoonful in, Edie and Ty arrived with a floral bouquet of stargazer lilies that perfumed the room. "We stopped for these on the way or would have been here sooner," Edie said.

"Beautiful, thank you, and the balloons are so

cheerful. X told me how all of you helped me after my collapse. I don't remember any of it after we finished singing "Unforgettable." "

"Be glad of that. It was scary for everyone. We couldn't prevent the audience from taking pictures before Rex had the area cleared, but we tried to shield you by making a human wall. When your agent came out screaming and swinging, we managed to get you away. Sorry to say those first photos are all over the media today. Lots of speculation going on, but Flint is telling the press you often faint and all you need is a little rest." Edie placed the flowers on a small table.

Caressa's laugh had a bitter edge to it. "Right, a little rest. The doctor told me this morning I was a month from dying, if that. With a long rest and a gradual return to normal eating, I should have a full recovery. I'm not sure I'm up to dealing with Rocky and his constant threats of lawsuits."

"The Billodeauxs have a slew of lawyers for all occasions. One of ours will take him on and keep him away from you," Rex offered.

"That would be wonderful."

"Last night, your mama and me made a list of who could see you here. All of us are on it. Flint is not. You can expand the list as you feel up to it. You know Mariah will want in since you sang at her place so often but she's a lot of woman, so we'll hold her off for now. All the Billodeauxs will be sure to visit. We'll spread them out over time. Jude and Connor Bullock might stop by since they're both doctors. They'll make sure you are treated right." X flashed a reassuring smile at her.

"Um, if you want, I can craft a press release for you to reassure your fans and the general public. If we generate regular updates, it will help to keep the press from hounding you," Edie said.

"That would be good as long as I approve them first. I forgot you are a bona fide journalist now and not just Rex's twin."

"Okay, if everyone has had their say, I need to speak up like I should have three years ago, and I want witnesses," X announced. "Carie, I love you. When you are well enough and your hair grows back, I want to marry you." He kissed the top of her head with tenderness. "I miss those braids."

Spontaneous tears slid down Caressa's sunken cheeks. "Rocky said if I got rid of beaded braids, I could change my look on stage by wearing all kinds of wigs. When the beautician cut them off, I cried and cried. Stupid me, I put them in a shoebox that I still carry around with me."

"Hey, hey, we'll grow our hair out together until mine is a giant afro if you want. Then we can bead our hair together." He'd gotten the smile he wanted, watery though it was. "But, you haven't answered my question. Will you marry me, sweet thang?"

"Yes, oh yes."

"Hallelujah!" shouted her mother in a volume more suitable for a revival than a hospital.

"I wanted you more than some grand tour, but thought you couldn't possibly love a fat girl like me. You know that blues cut on my album, "Going down to the river—Gonna let myself drown"."

"Sure, I bought fifty of those albums and gave them to my friends. I know every word you wrote by heart."

" 'Because he's not around.' You were that man, and I was that woman. After I left here, you didn't keep in touch, didn't once come to see me perform until last night. I thought I was nothing to you."

"My fault, all my fault. I was trying to get up the courage to speak when it seemed you got your big break at last and wanted to go on the road. Marrying me would have stopped you from going."

"Maybe, but I never want to leave this city again. I'd like to be the Etta James of New Orleans, maybe have a club of my own like Mariah."

"If you just get well, we'll make that happen. I'd get you a ring now but it would only fall off your finger. When the time comes, we'll go to Schifferman's and pick out any one you want, baby." He threaded his fingers with hers and kissed their union.

"Way to go, X. You said the words in front of witnesses." Ty applauded.

"I hope you don't mind, but I recorded the proposal, it was so touching," Edie admitted. She'd also been taking notes in the book she always kept in her purse. "Someday, I'd like to write your story—but not until you say so."

"Tell me you didn't take pictures when I look so vile."

"No pictures, I swear."

Dre had kept silent all this while, the lump in her throat growing bigger each minute. Then, the tears came coursing down her face—and she hadn't brought her girl's emergency kit, only a credit card to pay for the balloons, her driver's license, and car keys. Edie, ever prepared, handed her a tissue, and a strong arm wrapped around her shaking shoulders—Rex.

"Happy tears," she claimed.

"You're fine. I got a little choked up myself."

She sniffed and blew her nose. "No, you didn't. You're just trying to make me feel better about being so foolish."

"Guys can have deep feelings, too. Right, X?"

X-avier Hopkins still bent over with his hand entwined with Carie's. His eyes were closed and might have concealed a few tears. He didn't answer.

Rex took charge again. "I think it's time we go. Our work here is done. Edie, Ty, come on."

Sephy followed them into the hallway. "Thank all y'all for helping my girl. Come back again. She needs her friends who don't just want to use her to make money. I do believe they need some time alone now. I'll ride down with y'all and catch some lunch with Pastor Charles."

They split up in the lobby. In the parking lot, Dre clicked her car fob and opened the door for Rex. As he slid in beside her, he said, "Yeah, how about some lunch? Commander's Palace?"

"We aren't palatially dressed. You know they have a dress code. They don't allow T-shirts and jeans. Besides, we've completed our rescue mission which was not a date."

"Neither is lunch on the way home. Come on, pizza or a Lucky Dog to celebrate?" he pressed. "I know where we can find a cart."

"French Quarter or Convention Center?

"Jackson Square. You park in the lot across the street, and I'll get the dogs. Everything on it?"

"Absolutely. We can take them up on the Moon Walk and grab a bench. Get drinks. Anything diet for me."

"You don't need diet, but whatever you say." He

hopped out when traffic stopped for a red light.

She turned the Lexus into a pay lot, took a ticket, and waited for him at the Moon Walk approach. He juggled dogs and drinks impressively while crossing the busy street. They scaled the steps up to the promenade overlooking the wide Mississippi River and found a seat. The view truly brought home how far below river level the city rested.

They bit into their Chicago style dogs that filled the bun end to end stuffed with a fresh pickle, tomato, relish, and peppers. A slight breeze temporarily held off the growing heat of the day. Nice. Never once had she considered throwing herself into that current, not even in her darkest hours of uncertainty about becoming a mother so young and all the responsibilities that came with a child as it grew. But then, she'd not been deeply in love with a man like Caressa. For instance, if she fell for someone like rich, famous, handsome Rex, and she knew she didn't stand a chance of keeping him interested forever. Perhaps then. Despite the heat, she shivered. No, never, she had Drew to keep her sane.

Always observant, he asked, "Chilly? I could put my arm around you."

"No and no. Just thinking of Caressa and her song."

"Won't happen now."

"Thank God."

"Say, about next Saturday…"

"I'm busy."

"I know. It's the big May birthday bash for Danny, Gabe, and Jenny. I'll see you there."

He had an answer to everything.

Chapter Seven

Rex held back at the birthday bash. With all of Annie's children being born in May, she'd decided on one big party for all three each year. Drew's name went on the cake, too, though he'd had a small celebration in January on his actual day of birth. Only family attended, but among the Billodeauxs that still meant a crowd and lots of chaos.

As usual, his father trailered in four ponies: white Princess whom all the girls wanted to ride; tough Pinto Bean, a favorite of the boys; Black Star; and the new dapple, Dottie; leaving the oldest, Brownie and Goldie behind to rest. Dean's son, Beck, now living with his dad after Ilsa surrendered custody, lined up the kids and led the animals along with Wynn. Once upon a time, this had been his and Edie's job.

Glad to be free of it, he wandered around watching Dre at work as she wiped cake-smeared faces and squeezed mustard and ketchup on hot dogs for the children. So far, she'd managed to be anywhere he was not, skittish as a filly that had never been rode. The existence of Drew proved that to be untrue, but for sure she hadn't been treated right by her teenage lover. Why, he'd bet she'd never been properly kissed.

He couldn't exactly figure out his interest in Dre other than a real desire to make up for being unkind to her in his adolescent and college years. Because she was hard to get and pushed him away? He did enjoy a challenge, but there had to be more. Admiration, perhaps, for the way she'd conducted her life while he went off to play football and have a good time. Frightening thought that after three years as an NFL quarterback maturity had set in and turned his mind from easy women to one who had character and substance. Also, very long legs and a face that deserved to be photographed. He wasn't mature enough to overlook that yet.

Today she wore her conservative bikini covered by an oversized Sinners tee, this one in red, that came down to her knees and nothing on her feet but flipflops, easily kicked off in case she had to rescue any child that fell into the pool, though other adults stood all around, most with a beer in hand and chatting with others. He'd coaxed her out on an errand of mercy sure she'd always reach out to save anyone but herself, but he couldn't think of anything near what they'd done for Caressa.

He snapped his fingers—a charity ball for some good cause. He received invitations for lots of them and usually just sent a check which was what they wanted anyhow. Usually boring affairs, some had prime steak, some tough chicken, an open bar or only champagne served on trays. But it might be interesting to go with Dre. Now to find the right one, one she'd done design work for.

He searched for her in the shifting mass of adults and children. There, standing with one arm around Drew and another around Daniel while a middle-aged man fat in his center and gray hair going bald on top took their pictures. Then, she beckoned to Gabe and Jenny to join the group for another shot. Not having been to this event in several years, Rex still recognized Dre's father, Bucky Ames, the only one of her family members who attended every year.

The man held up a camera and searched around for help. "Can anyone get a shot of all of us together?"

Rex saw his opening just as he did on the football field. "I'd be glad to help with that." He took the expensive camera and lined up a shot. "How about another one with only you and Dre?" He snapped again. "Now one without that baggy T-shirt all alone. Show Indianans what they're missing."

He'd gone too far. Dre took the camera from him. "That's enough."

Thinking of his next play fast, he said, "I bet your dad would like to see some of your design work. So would I."

"Now isn't a good time."

"Andi dear, I mean Dre, I'd like that, and I'm only in town for a couple of days. Your mother frets when I'm gone. Can't we see some now?"

"Someone has to watch the pool."

Sucking on an orange Popsicle, Edie passed nearby. "Hey, Edie, watch the pool for Dre while she shows us some of her work."

His twin shrugged. "Okay, but I don't want to be stuck here all afternoon." She kicked off her sandals and took a seat on the edge of the pool, dipping her feet into the water not far from where Beck's four half-sisters, Princess, Duchess, Countess, and Lady, cavorted. Their little brother, King David, played in the shade with his nanny on watch. "Looks like Ilsa took the day off."

"Doesn't she always?" said Dre. She nodded toward the girls in the pool. "But not their fault."

"Pretty much typical Ilsa. Have kids and let someone else raise them. Let's go to your studio and see your art." Rex steered them toward the cool interior of the house. Peace reigned inside.

"Some of the little ones are napping in Jenny's room. Quiet," Dre cautioned. They went past the kitchen where Delia refilled trays of watermelon wedges, veggies, and hamburger fixings. The maid waved as they passed. Then, up the staircase in the hallway of a house with six bedrooms, exactly right for Matt Keaton's unorthodox family.

"I'm set up in the second master or maybe mistress bedroom. The previous owners didn't get along and needed their own spaces, I guess. Drew's bedroom is right next to it which is nice for us, though believe me, he doesn't need me in the middle of the night anymore, doesn't want me inside at all. We can take a peek if you want."

Dre opened the door into an amazingly neat room for a boy her son's age, bed made, laptop on his desk next to a stack of neatly piled textbooks, no clothes on the floor. Pictures of Daddy Joe, Matt, Dean, and a very new one of Rex, all in their football uniforms, flanked one side of the desk and more unusual heroes on the other side: Bill Gates, Elon Musk with his rocket ship and the sportscar he'd sent into space, Einstein with his hair at its utmost disarray.

"All the boys are supposed to keep their rooms tidy and not make more work for Delia, but Drew excels at it. Gabe's is always a disaster, and Danny's somewhere in between the two. The kids at school tease my boy by calling him Einstein, but he considers it a compliment, especially when they ask for his help on homework—

and he has Danny and Gabe for nerd protection. I'm very proud of him, but a little worried about his adulation for Elon Musk."

"Don't worry. I'm pretty sure it's the allure of the sportscar and rocket ship," Rex assured her.

"I wish your mother would come here and get to know Drew and Daniel instead of shutting them out of her life. Whenever I suggest it she hints at another mental breakdown. That's how she keeps your brothers in line, why they don't take an interest. Maybe that will change now that she has a granddaughter to groom. She's already putting her in pageants at age five." Bucky shook his head in sorrow. He did show up every year with presents for all the boys and now Jenny. He tried.

Dre shrugged. "She's missing out on knowing some wonderful grandchildren. Her loss."

She moved on to her bedroom studio. The sitting area had been turned into her work center. She wasn't as organized as her son. Sketches, printouts, and invoices for her work littered the top of her large desk. An easel held a work in progress of a dragon coiling around a book title while being subdued by a maiden. She opened a desktop computer with a large screen and topnotch printer and filed through other book covers, mostly fantasy works showing bare-chested men with swords, ladies in diaphanous gowns, and imaginary creatures.

"How do you create these?" her father asked.

"The author tells me their vision. Then I seek out bits and pieces and put them together to make what they want. Sometimes, I do an original drawing."

"So, these half-naked dudes pose for you in costumes up here in your bedroom?" Rex asked, concerned. He pointed to a red-haired Scot wearing only a kilt and tartan over a muscular chest.

Dre laughed. "I should be so lucky. No, the models have web sites with lots of poses and costumes. When I find one that fits, I pay for the use of their image and sometimes alter the hair or eye color. I met two in person at a convention. Both were very handsome, very fit, and very gay. Or as an older writer said, 'Very sweet boys' who helped her get up and down the dais steps."

Rex had to question his feeling of relief. None of these guys outshone him in looks or build, and he wasn't the least bit gay. That made him highly competitive in case she met one who was hetero.

Her bedroom door stood open exposing a queen-sized bed covered in a multi-colored quilt and bolstered with small mix and match pillows. The walls around it held a picture gallery of the boys at various ages from babies and toddlers pushing toys around the floor, pony riding, swimming, and playing sports from Little League to soccer. Dre must hold to his mother's rule of no football before high school though all the Billodeaux males started training long before that with their granddad.

A portrait-sized photo contained a shot of Dre's father posed with her, Drew, Danny, Gabe, and Jenny exactly like the one he'd snapped just a while ago but with everyone a year younger. He suspected she replaced it every year with the latest on top. Would it be weird to make love on that bed with so many children and relatives looking on? Maybe he'd find out or maybe he wouldn't. Too soon to tell.

Her father asked if fantasy covers were all she did. "No, I created one early on for a writer friend who kept giving me referrals, and it just worked out that way, but

I do love doing them. Here are some of my custom wedding invitations and posters to various events. This one for the New Orleans Artists Alliance fundraiser is coming up soon. Since it will be held in the Besthoff Sculpture Garden, I was allowed stroll the grounds and take pictures for the publicity. I got permission from the artist to use Elyn Zimmerman's Mississippi Meander with color running down the center and the words Meander Among the Arts vertical on one side and the date and pertinent information down the other. The invitations have the same design."

"Are you going?" Rex asked.

Dre laughed in a way that implied he had to be kidding. "It's a fundraiser. Tickets are $1,000 each, and invitations go out to wealthy patrons of the art museum and anyone else who can afford it. It will be grand though—twinkling lights in all the oak trees and tables scattered among the sculptures. Small food carts will serve each table with appetizers and turf and surf, two bottles of good champagne on each. The party favors are pieces of mini art done by Alliance members. I contributed a tiny dragon painting. The silent auction of larger pieces will be done entirely online during the event but can be viewed inside the museum before the event." She spoke with a sparkle in her eyes like the twinkling lights adorning the oaks.

"They couldn't spare a free ticket for their designer. You should have asked," her father, ever the businessman, said.

She shook her head. "They paid me well and promptly which is more than I can say for some of my clients." She gestured to the pile of invoices. "Second notices I haven't mailed yet. Besides, I wouldn't know anyone else attending, not my crowd."

Rex suspected she had no crowd but decided to give her one. "I'll bet Dean and Stacy will be there and Trinity and Josee if they're in town. Maybe I'll go this year. My invitation is probably in the mail." He'd make sure they did.

Dre raised her pale brows. "When did you become a patron of the arts? I'll bet you've never gone to the sculpture garden even though it's free and open every day."

"Wrong. Mama Nell dragged all of us there once. I was the youngest and only remember a big safety pin suspended in the air and a giant skull. I was more interested in seeing if they had turtles and frogs in the pond, but my tastes have changed for the better." He unleashed his inherited killer smile on her and gazed into her eyes.

Though Dre turned away, he continued. "Come on. Go with me. Let's benefit the arts."

"I don't have anything to wear to an event like that."

"Stacy does, but I'll bet Ty's mother could whip up a dress for you. She has that fancy shop now."

"Portia's Place is couture, all handmade, one of a kind. Out of sight expensive."

"Hey, she's Edie's mother-in-law. You can get a family rate."

"You do know I'm not really family."

"Who says? The Billodeauxs claim you."

Bucky Ames' head swiveled back and forth between the two as if he watched an engrossing tennis match. When they took a breath, he spoke up. "I'll pay for the gown. I've done so little for you. Let me give you this one gift. All I want is a picture of you in return."

"You know that was Melinda's thing, fancy events, not mine."

"Time to let that go. You are your own person now and one that I am proud of. Don't deny yourself something you'd love because of her."

"Yeah, what he said," Rex chipped in. "Are we on? I'll get the tickets."

"I—I guess so. We'd better get back to the party. People will wonder what became of us, and who knows what the boys are getting up to." Dre made a hasty exit as if the air had become too rare to breathe up on the second floor.

The men lingered behind her. "Thanks for helping me with that, Mr. Ames."

"Bucky. Andi, I used to call her Andi, short for Andrea, deserves some joy in her life. Take her to this big event, but don't you toy with her affections. I know a big deal guy like you can have any woman he wants, but not my daughter unless you really mean it."

"She'd say Drew is the joy in her life, but yes, she needs to get a life beyond her son. I'm trying to help her do that. I won't hurt her. My word on that."

Chapter Eight

He'd spooked her. Rex searched for Dre and found her already in the pool, red tee shucked aside on a chair, her arms in the air leading a game of keeping a beachball in the air with Beck's half-sisters and anyone else who wanted to join the fun.

After lecturing him about his intentions like a good father, Bucky peeled off to join the boys who were playing a game of H-O-R-S-E at a portable basketball hoop. Drew had just missed a shot. Bucky grabbed the ball and said, "I used to be pretty good at this. Let's start over." He threw an easy shot and handed the ball to his blond grandson to duplicate.

Rex neither joined them nor jumped into the pool. He had other work to do. Spotting his sister-in-law Stacy sitting at a table shaded by a colorful beach umbrella and sipping a mimosa, alone for the moment, he joined her.

"Hi, Stace. Enjoying the party?"

"Enjoying that Wynn, Beck, and DJ are giving pony rides to the small children, and I have a minute of peace." She dipped a strip of green pepper into a glob of yogurt dip in the center of a paper plate. "Help yourself but get your own drink."

"I wouldn't think of stealing your veggies. I'll get a burger in a while. Say, are you going to the Artists Alliance gala by any chance?"

"We already have our tickets. Josee and I are trying

to put together a table for eight. Can we convince you to come join us? It's for a good cause as the organization provides support for struggling artists and scholarships among other good deeds. We want to influence them into helping Caressa get free of her agent. Have you had any word of how she's doing?"

"Last time I called X, he'd moved her into his condo where his doorman will keep out the paparazzi and Flint. He went back to the theater and removed all her things from her dressing room with the help of the guard who handled Rocky the night she collapsed. Then, he went to her hotel room with her mother, did the same, and paid her bill. Her mama is staying at his place, too, and following the diet the doctor gave her to build up her daughter gradually. I suspect Sephy is still baking biscuits and sneaking in sacks of beignets, too."

"Sounds good. I wish I could eat like that all the time and not get fat." Stacy dunked a baby carrot into the dip and washed it down with a sip of mimosa.

"You are gorgeous, and I think Dean wouldn't care if you were fat. I mean that tattoo he has on his backside with your name and getting a vasectomy says true devotion to me." Done buttering her up, he said, "Would you mind if Dre and I crash your table at the gala?"

"That would be great. We'd only need one more couple to fill it. Maybe Annie and Matt might…"

"No, no. If they go, I am sure Dre won't. She'll feel she has to stay home with the children."

"Yeah, and they are homebodies. Neither likes dressing up for charity events. They send money instead."

He didn't admit that was his usual way of dealing with fundraisers. "I'll track down Edie and Ty and see if

I can convince them. She's comfortable with the two of them. Can you spot her anywhere? She's so short."

Stacy moved her blue eyes, scanning the various groups. "There, behind the group of men Ty is talking to. She and Jenny are having a tea party with her dolls, some of her new stuffed toys, and real cake. That's going to be some mess to clean up."

"Good eye. Thanks, Stace." He started to move away, but she grabbed his arm.

"Are you and Dre dating now?"

"Not exactly. I've been feeling bad about warning my friends to stay away from her because she has a child and not really trying to help her with Drew. She has no social life. I'm trying to pry her out of her shell and show her a wider world. Drew is growing up fast, and he'll want to go away to college. Then what will she have left?"

Stacy gave his arm a squeeze. "Look at the youngest of Joe's sons all grown at last. Go complete your mission."

Wending his way among the groups of standing adults, he arrived at the tea party table where Jenny smashed pieces of chocolate cake into the faces of a new Steiff teddy bear and an old Raggedy Ann. Her little plastic cups held lemonade, not tea. Edie sipped hers, one pinkie raised. "Such delicious tea, Miss Jenny." That drew a giggle from her niece.

"I see you haven't lost your inner child, Sis. You used to make me sit and have imaginary tea with you and your dolls."

"Don't pretend you didn't enjoy it. Corazon always supplied me with real cookies."

"The only reason I stayed. Good times, speaking of

which would you consider going to the Artists Alliance gala and filling out a table with Stacy and Dean, and Josee and Trinity. I'm taking Dre."

His sister's eyebrows shot up into her fringe of dark curls. "Truly? How did you get her to agree with that? Ty and I have been trying to lure her out more for the past three years. She always makes an excuse."

He shrugged. "She designed the invitations, and it's a good cause that might help Caressa."

"Well, fine. I already have my invite because I'm covering the event for *New Orleans Lifestyle*—and dragging Ty with me. His mom and the senator will be there, and things are still a little stiff between them, but he has unbent a lot since Titus LeMaire married Portia and adopted his sister."

"Among ourselves, can we just say Ty's birth father instead of the senator? If it's not too much to ask of your mother-in-law, could she design a gown for Dre? Her dad offered to pay for it. Turns out she's been borrowing all her fancy dresses from Stacy and could again, but it seems she should have her own."

"Not much time for a custom design, but Portia might have something she could fit to Dre. With her slim build and long legs, she won't be hard to dress. All of mine have to be cut down close to twelve inches. I was going to wear my wedding gown, but she's making me another dress from Flo's Fabulous Fashions for Larger Ladies remnants. Anyhow, I'll call her and set up a fitting. I hope Dre doesn't balk at going."

"That's why you and Stacy will go with her, dear sister of mine."

"You owe me if I have to spend half a day in a dress shop. That's Stacy world, not mine."

Lynn Shurr

"Understood. Thanks."

He returned to Stacy who had been joined by her close friend and sister-in-law, Josee, and Mama Nell. "It's all settled. Edie and Ty will fill out our table, and Edie is setting up an appointment with Portia for a gown."

Mama Nell applauded. "Bravo! What a kind thing to do for Dre. We've all tried to draw her out, but only you have succeeded."

"It's my superpower with women, Mom."

Josee laughed, and Stacy gave him a skeptical glance. Stace said, "Just as long as there is nothing in it for you, then it is being kind."

"You doubt my pure motives?"

"Oh, yes," Josee said. "She's an attractive woman your own age, and you are a man women dream about. I sense some chemistry between you."

"Nope, no chemistry. I've hardly been near her all day." To prove his point, he hung out with the guys for the rest of the afternoon.

Chapter Nine

Dre stood on the dressing room pedestal in Portia's Place wearing her utilitarian underwear and being judged by the ring of women standing around her. At least, she felt they were as every square inch of her had been measured without comment.

"Hmm," said the most sought-after dress designer in the city. "We won't have time to do any handwork or embellishments, but I am thinking something simple, something Grecian like a few of the statues in the Sculpture Garden. She's very close to your build Stacy, but not as big in the bust which will work in her favor. She could go braless and would be very comfortable on a humid night."

"What?" Dre squeaked.

"If you are uncomfortable with that idea we'll build in some support. I'd like the back to be bare."

The famous Portia looked nothing like the two tall blondes, Stacy and Josee, nor did she resemble short, curly-haired Edie. Curvaceous with gently waving black hair down past her shoulders, dark eyes slightly slanted giving her face an exotic look, and a beautiful complexion of light tan, she had her own beauty that competed easily with the others in the room. Her full lips parted in a smile.

"Ming, bring a bolt of white silk and one of gold. Let's see how it drapes."

Her Asian-American assistant who had taken the measurements and entered them into a laptop, was also a beauty with a delicate face and form and long, black hair hanging straight to her waist. She scurried off to bring the requested material and returned in no time with the fabric.

Portia unfurled the white silk first and draped it diagonally across Dre's shoulders. Then, she twined the gold silk with it. Letting the fabric fall generously to the floor down her back, she directed Ming to cut the material with some inches to spare and gathered the pieces into a loose Grecian knot on her shoulder. She widened the pieces to cover Dre's other breast and had her assistant pin it around back into a draped bodice.

"Just a start, you understand. Perhaps a slim gold tie at the waist, golden sandals of course. How I wish you had long hair that could be styled in the Greek manner, too, but I have an idea. Ming, please bring the Grecian knot necklace from the display case."

Again, Ming went in haste and returned with the requested jewelry which Portia draped over Dre's short hair until it became a striking brow band. "*Et voila!*"

Dre took a look at herself in the mirror over Edie's shoulder. She expected to see a ridiculous woman pretending to be a Greek goddess wrapped in a flowing robe and wearing an absurd necklace on her head. That was not what she viewed. No, her reflection showed that her beauty, not flamboyant but subtle, easily compared to the others in the room. She blinked a few times. Was this truly her? Portia seemed to know how to bring out the best in her customers.

At a loss for words, she fingered the necklace that appeared to turn her into some kind of royalty. "Is this real gold?"

"Eighteen karat. Lovely, isn't it? Simple yet elegant. Your father entrusted us with his credit card number before he left town. You're to have whatever you want."

"I don't want him to go bankrupt."

The women surrounding her laughed with Portia's being especially rich and low-pitched. "I'm giving you the family rate on the gown, but I do need to make some profit."

"How about throwing in an evening bag," said Stacy.

"Considering all the business you've steered my way, sure. We can make something simple from the leftover cloth. Ming, I'd like you to oversee the completion of this project. Don't worry, she's very good."

"Of course, I didn't expect you to do it yourself," Dre rushed to say.

"I would if I weren't already slammed with other orders for this gala. Summer is usually our slow season. We'll call for a final fitting when the dress is complete. Would you like to take the necklace with you?"

"I feel like I'd need an armed guard." She lowered her shoulder as Ming carefully slid the silk off her body and left her standing in her undies again. She removed the necklace herself and handed it over. The old Dre peered over Edie's shoulder from the mirror. She hastened to get back into her jeans, T-shirt, and tennis shoes.

"Don't worry, you've got us as bodyguards, the two tall ones in on either side, and I'll bring up the rear and trip any pickpockets," Edie quipped.

By the time they reached the checkout counter, the

necklace rested in a velvet box all ready to be slipped into a Portia's Place signature bag which Stacy waved away. "It's safer to put it into Edie's beat up crossbody bag with all her reporter stuff. No thief will suspect it's in there. Off we go. Dre, you've entered a whole new world."

One of couture gowns and gold necklaces she felt totally uncomfortable with. Oh well, the necklace could be saved in case she and Drew fell on hard times to be hocked as she'd done with her deceased sister's jewels Matt had given her. She'd used the money to finance her runaway trip to New Orleans, now more her home than Indiana had been, a place where all kinds were accepted, even her former Goth self.

****

A light breeze from the river lifted her nearly weightless skirts to reveal her low-heeled golden sandals, the only part of her ensemble that Dre had purchased. Ming had delayed the final fitting of the Grecian gown until Dre bought those shoes to get the hem line absolutely correct. The rest of the dress fit to perfection, lightly lined and supplied with a shelf bra that lifted her breasts, but not too high. The one opposite the Grecian knot shoulder showed a modest crescent moon while the other stayed completely covered unlike her back, mostly bare except where the entwined gold and while silk crossed it and disappeared into the narrow waist encircled with golden cord. From there, the gown floated down to the very top of her sandals. Magical described it best.

The setting helped this illusion, the live oaks festooned with tiny white lights, the music, strings wafting from an invisible source, pieces of sculpture appearing, then disappearing into the night as she walked the pathway toward their table. Rex in his impeccable, custom-made tuxedo held her arm as if they were a top celebrity couple at the Academy Awards. The simple evening bag made from two twists of silk, gathered by gold cord, and holding all her necessities, hung from her other elbow. She kept wanting to raise that arm to make sure the necklace resting on her forehead stayed in place.

Rex paused here and there to introduce her to people he either knew or who sought him out. Would they never reach the safety of the table peopled with friends before she stumbled or made a gauche remark? There, Edie's enthusiastic wave summoned them to a sturdy folding table disguised by white linen touching the grass and flickering battery powered candles grouped in its center. Ty sat beside her in a daring burgundy tux outlined in black that matched his wife's gown of a tight black bodice above a jagged handkerchief hem with alternating panels of burgundy and ebony that swirled around her ankles. Undoubtedly, both wore Portia Ramsey originals.

Dean and Stacy sat with them along with Josee and Trinity who still managed to look like the geek he was despite his own bespoke traditional tux. No matter—that geek owned a video game development company that brought in millions. No one would dare mock him. Here she stood among real celebrities, a mere graphic designer. Rex pulled out a chair for her, but before she could sit and hide her height beneath the linens, another power couple approached.

Dean and Ty rose to shake hands with the elderly man slumped in a wheelchair, his full head of white hair nodding into a collapsed chest, being pushed by an attendant in a while dinner jacket. A stunning woman with tastefully dyed red hair, perhaps in her fifties but not showing a line or a wrinkle, stood by his side. Dean did the introductions.

"Gustave Bienville, owner of the Sinners, and his beautiful wife Barbara." Dean exchanged a weak shake of hands with the old guy better known as Gus. His wife enclosed Rex's hands with a two-handed grip top and bottom that she seemed reluctant to release.

Barbara Bienville smoothed the lipstick that complemented her hair in color with the tip of her tongue before saying, "Who is your lovely companion, Rex?"

"This is Dre Ames, the talented graphic designer who created the poster and invitation for the event tonight."

No friend of the family, no mention of her position within the Billodeaux family, which Dre appreciated no end. Here, tonight, she existed simply as a talented graphic designer wearing a Portia Ramsay original with a handsome man as her escort and a very expensive necklace on her forehead. She'd gotten a trim for her hair beforehand and asked the stylist to plaster her wispy bangs to the side in order to show it off better. Intimidating as Mrs. Bienville appeared with her sharp, green gaze enhanced with contacts and all that Botox in her face, Dre still felt beautiful and confident and hopeful that Barbara would soon move along.

Instead, the owner's wife flicked her fingers like a queen and bade all the standing men to sit. Even Trinity had risen after a poke from Josee but didn't rate a double handhold or shake of any kind. She acknowledged Stacy and Josee with a mere nod.

Rex continued standing by her side as if protecting

her right flank, while Barbara eyed her again and said, "I see you are wearing Portia Ramsey. I can always tell her style—and that headpiece. I could swear I considered buying it as a necklace in her shop not long ago. Graphic designing must pay very well." Barbara's gaze switched to Rex as if inserting something crude into their being together.

"Yes, I love her gowns, and the necklace is on loan for this evening. It was Portia's idea to wear it as a browband."

"Very charming. I prefer to buy in Paris and favor Chanel."

"Nothing is too good for my Barbie, my doll," croaked her husband. "She goes to Paris every year to shop for the best." His doll's lips flattened in annoyance.

Dre gave her a smile she tried to make as genuine as possible. "Yes, Chanel, very classic and flattering," she said of the green sheath gown highly embellished with small crystals and exposing far more cleavage than her own that went uncovered by a matching wrap. "I prefer supporting local designers and am far too busy with work to get to Paris."

Mrs. Bienville offered Dre her long-nailed hand that did not have to work for a living, as if acknowledging a worthy opponent. "Please call me Barb. I'm sure we will meet again. Come along, Gus, we have others to greet."

The attendant put the chair into motion, but Barb lingered for a moment as they passed the table. "I see you over there, Edie Billodeaux. I suppose you are covering the event for *New Orleans Lifestyle*. Please don't forget to mention that Gus and I attended. I'd love to serve on the Artists Alliance board. It's such a great cause." She moved along like the passing of a sudden chill wind.

Rex offered Dre a chair again, and she sank into it before her wobbling knees gave way. Across the table, Josee applauded lightly and whispered, "Brava, Dre. You stood up to that bitchy woman beautifully."

"By lying to her, but I doubt we'll run into each other. At least, I hope not. She hardly acknowledged you and Stace."

Stacy leaned forward. "Our pleasure, believe me. I see her at the games when we are up in the sky box, see her in the restroom. All she does is complain about being dragged to watch football every weekend for half the year because the Sinners keep winning and winning. I get a little respect because I'm Dean's wife, but she is very demeaning to the other players' wives."

Josee nodded. "She resents my success in modeling and business. She'd like Gus to turn over some of his enterprises to her, but he keeps her for companionship and leaves the business to his son and the entertaining of clients to his daughter from his first marriage."

"Did she break that up?" Dre asked.

All knowing Edie chimed in. "Strangely, no. His wife of forty-two years died of cancer, and as a still very vital man of sixty-five he began frequenting the casino. His favorite server was twenty-five-year-old Barbie as it said on her name tag. Within the year, he married her to the horror of his family. I suspect there must be a strong prenup in place for her to remain at his side for the past thirty years biding her time until he croaks. Imagine being fifty-five and living with a ninety-five-year-old man. I researched all this but can't mention it in *Lifestyle* of course. The tabloids were full of the scandal back when. How about tapping that bottle of champagne, Ty? I'm getting dry."

"From too much talking." But he did it anyhow, removing the bottle from its icy bucket, spilling not a drop as he opened the seal, coaxed out the cork, and filled each glass.

"That's why she hates being called Barbie or doll, his pet name for her. It reminds her of her low origins as a cocktail waitress having high rollers shove tips into her cleavage, a school dropout who traded on her good looks for a living. Rumor also says her mother was a prostitute, father unknown, raised in foster homes, but she's from elsewhere so that is hard to verify and not worth the effort at this point. Somehow, she showed up here and managed to marry a very wealthy man." Edie finished her champagne and glanced around. "I wonder where the eats are. I have to grab some and do my rounds, get some brief interviews. It's a work night for me."

Dre sipped her drink, enjoying the tickle of the bubbles in her mouth and the quality of the wine. "That's kind of how I showed up here, a freaky runaway with a baby on the way, and a family who disowned her. I found a home here, and so did she. Maybe she does love him or at least found some security in her life."

The glamourous Josee held out her glass for a refill. "Don't be too sympathetic. She hated you on sight. She's no problem for me. Our circles rarely intersect, but be careful, Dre. And you too, Edie."

"Oh, I'll play nice. I like my job."

"I think I am beneath her notice."

Josee shook her head. A curl fell free from her high, blonde coiffeur. The only jewelry she wore was the locket that covered the scar on her throat from an acid attack planned by a crazed ex. "Don't believe that. She despises your youth, your beauty, and your talent.

Exactly why she snubs me and barely tolerates Stacy who speaks several languages and once had her own business. She must stay on Edie's good side since she wants mention in the society pages."

"Ha! Sounded more like a threat to me, but I'll give her the plug. When are they serving the food?"

As if in answer to Edie's wish, the sibilant string music ceased. From speakers hidden in the trees, a voice welcomed all the patrons of the arts, reading off a long list of thanks for various sponsorships and contributions. Dre's name got a mention to her surprise, and her tablemates gave her a round of applause.

Edie's stomach growled audibly. "Sorry, I should have eaten before I came."

"It's her hummingbird metabolism," Ty said with fondness.

"Mine, too," added Trinity.

The speaker announced the commencement of the dinner. Light jazz with a mellow sax and a lively clarinet took over the music. Small carts navigated the pathways with servers dropping off trays of appetizers: mini crab cakes, roasted oysters, shrimp with cocktail sauce. Wedge salads and the entrée of lobster and filet mignon accompanied by asparagus and baby potatoes followed quickly. After a decent interval, dessert appeared, turtle cheesecake topped with pecans and chocolate sauce.

The music changed again to slow numbers perfect for dancing among trees and works of art. Their table paired off, and Rex held out hands to Dre. She sent him a suspicious glance.

"No, honest, no fancy surprise moves," he swore.

"Okay, then." She followed him to an open area where he guided her through the simple moves of a slow dance, adding only a soft twirl or two. Drugged by the food, the music, the sculptures, she found herself drifting closer and closer to his chest until her head rested on his shoulder. The words that came to her mind were Shakespeare's from *The Tempest*. She murmured them as other couples glided by. "O brave new world that has such people in't."

"What did you say?" Rex asked.

She repeated the phrase and told him its origin. "I think I applies to the setting and the people here tonight."

"I believe I missed that play. I remember having to read *Julius Caesar* in high school and *MacBeth*. The witches were cool."

"Yes, they were, but *The Tempest* is special."

Ty cut in on their second dance. "Edie has gone to do her job. Mind if I take Dre for a spin?"

After that, she had Dean and Trinity for partners, but the last dance with Rex. The music faded and stopped. The announcer thanked all for coming. People pocketed their small pieces of art that served as favors. Trinity stared at his, an abstract of drips and blobs. "Anyone want to trade? How about you, Rex. I like the look of that dragon. I could use it in a video game with the artist's permission."

"No way. The dragon is all mine—but the artist is standing right next to me. Dre, make him pay you big time for any rights to your art."

"I doubt that will happen."

"I have no doubt it will if he decides on a fantasy game instead of football players and models." Rex crooked his arm to escort her to the exit at midnight.

Dre remained in a dreamy mood, quiet on their drive to Matt's house where a light burned in the front window to see her home. Rex walked her to the door and leaned in. She backed away.

He blocked the door and said, "An evening like this should end with a kiss, a single perfect kiss, only one."

"I don't care for kissing."

"Why?"

"It's wet and sloppy and no pleasure having someone's tongue thrust halfway down your throat." She could not suppress a slight shudder.

"I think you just described a typical teenage boy kiss. I hope I was never that bad, but then, I had great coaching from my brothers. Tell me no one has kissed you since Drew's father?"

Too embarrassed to confess, she didn't answer. She closed her eyes and lowered her head, shutting out the glow of the porch light and the man standing beneath it. His fingers touched her chin, raised her face. His lips whispered across hers, then wandered down her neck and back again. He drew her close and pressed a little harder, outlined her mouth with the very tip of his tongue until she opened ever so slightly. When he entered, he only touched tip to tip and withdrew, yet the kiss continued more urgent than before.

Her hands moved up into his hair, raking through it, holding him in place as if she never wanted to let him go. She broke the kiss and initiated one of her own. Passion long denied escaped, applying hard pressure that he returned, leaning back against the door to keep his balance.

Deep inside the house a bell rang. Urgent footsteps hit the hallway hardwood. The door swung open, and Rex stumbled inside taking her with him. Only his great sense of balance kept them from hitting the floor in front of Matt and Annie, attired in robes and slippers but completely awake.

"Thank God!" Annie exclaimed. "We thought you were being attacked on the porch from what we could see through the sidelights. "But it's only Rex—saying good night, I guess."

"Yes, yes, that's it. Only a simple good night kiss," Dre raced to say even while noticing her carefully applied lipstick, darker in shade than usual and refreshed at the gala, smeared all over his face.

"Glad I didn't have to tackle anyone to the ground," Matt said with good humor quirking his lips.

"My fault. I leaned against the doorbell. I hope I didn't wake the kids. I'd better get going. Stacy and Dean will wonder what's keeping me. Good night, all." Rex backed away and carefully shut the door. In a minute, his car roared to life and was gone.

Dre put her fingers to her lips, sure her lipstick looked a mess, and her lips would be swollen in the morning. Annie kindly removed the necklace that had canted to the side during the embrace and handed it to her. "Did you have a good time?"

"A perfect, magical evening. I'd better get some sleep.

"We won't let the children wake you early in the morning." Annie dispensed a motherly hug and sent her on her way.

Upstairs, Dre studied herself in the mirror. She did look like a person who had been thoroughly and well kissed, but then, so had Rex.

Chapter Ten

Rex let himself into Dean's home and proceeded without noise up the staircase closest to his bedroom though he figured the three kids in their early teens slept like rocks as he had at that age. Down the hall in the master suite, he heard some stirring, Dean and Stacy getting ready for bed or whatever. Which reminded him he needed to search more earnestly for a place of his own.

He could imagine Dean sliding down one of those long zippers that always got caught in the fabric of Stacy's ice blue gown accented with silver slashes in the skirt, another Portia Ramsey for sure. As it pooled on the floor, she'd turn and help him with the studs of his tux and his cufflinks until Dean shed both jacket and shirt. He didn't go any further with that thought because it led to how easy it would have been to slip his hands into Dre's dress and fondle her bare breasts. Release that gold cord at her waist and her entire outfit would tumble to the ground. Yes, he needed to get his own place and quickly.

Stowing his tux in a garment bag, he entered the bathroom for a quick splash of water on his face and a go with the toothbrush. He'd shower and shave in the morning. He gave himself a grin in the mirror as he applied a washcloth to remove Dre's lipstick. Nice shade. She should wear it more often. He'd suspected that her aversion to intimacy came from her teen experience. He didn't have to go far to do better, but he still gave the kiss his best like he did on every play on the football field.

What he hadn't expected was her passionate response as if a wall had come tumbling down and released what was hidden on the other side. He'd bet she'd go shy again come morning, but he had a plan for their next date, another that she wouldn't turn down. She'd given him the clue. He only had to find a theater putting on *The Tempest,* irresistible bait to lure her to spend more time with him. Stripped to the briefs he wore in case any of the kids walked in on him, he got into bed, but fired up his laptop and started searching.

Playing in England of course. She wouldn't go that far from Drew for any length of time. New York City, ditto. Aha! The Alabama Shakespeare Festival in Montgomery, a drive but not too long, and best of all, playing next week into July. He'd be starting summer training camp soon and had a few voluntary sessions before that but could work around them. A little keyboard work booked two tickets to be picked up at the box office on the night of the show. He would give Dre a few days to get over the kiss, and then ask her out again.

****

"What are you doing here?" Wearing her modest bikini, Dre stood over him holding a towel against her middle as if hiding behind it.

Rex grinned and pushed up his aviator sunglasses. "Tough workout today. Matt said to feel free to use the pool to chill out. He and Annie have gone out for a late lunch. Jenny is at nursery school, and Matt told me the boys shipped out for summer camp in the mountains of

Arkansas on Sunday afternoon. We have the place to ourselves."

"Delia is upstairs cleaning," she rushed to say. "It's rare she gets to do a thorough job on the boys' rooms."

"I don't think we'll bother her if we both use the pool at the same time. Getting mighty hot out here. I was about to come up to see if you'd like to take a break, but you saved me the trouble."

"I didn't mean to. I mean I often take a break out here if I've been crouched over a computer all day."

"Go ahead. I'll join you in a minute."

She hurried to the pool's edge, pushed off in a very shallow dive and began doing laps as if training for the Olympics. He followed, soon catching up, though she moved at a good pace with her long legs fluttering and her graceful arms digging in deep. After that, he merely kept pace until she slowed in the shallow end and stood up to leave the pool.

"Let me help you out." He didn't wait for her to say no but placed his hands against her bare midriff and let them linger a beat, before hoisting her effortlessly up on the edge. He wanted to accustom her to having his hands on her body.

"I'm perfectly capable of getting out of a pool by myself." She swung her legs over and pushed up, making haste to her towel, and covering up. "I need to get back to work now."

"That was refreshing. You're a good swimmer." He took his time toweling off from head to toe and around his Speedo that hid very little. Good thing he was tired from training and the laps.

"Thanks. Gotta go."

"Before you do, would you be interested in seeing

The Tempest with me on Saturday night?"

"Where is it playing? I haven't heard anything about it."

"Oh, the Alabama Shakespeare Festival in Montgomery is putting it on. Should be good."

She shot him a skeptical glance. "That's quite a drive for someone who only knows *MacBeth* and *Julius Caesar*."

"Your comments about it at the Artists Alliance gala got me interested. I tracked it down. Sure, it's a four and a half hour drive. We could leave Saturday afternoon, catch dinner before the show, then get home around two a.m. You can explain it to me on the way back to keep me awake."

The struggle to resist and the desire to attend warred across her features, a frown, a slight smile, and finally a nod of assent. "Drew won't be home to worry about me. Let's go."

"Best part is dress is casual. We can go in jeans if we want."

"Oh, I think Shakespeare deserves somewhat better, but don't expect couture this time."

"You look good in anything."

No thanks, just an expression of disbelief on her face before she said, "I have work to do" and spun on her heels to move away.

"Pick you up at one on Saturday," he called after her. She waved a hand to show she heard and kept right on going. Didn't matter. They had a date.

Chapter Eleven

On a sunny and broiling day, they left the flatlands with the air conditioning running on high and reached the rolling hills and piney woods of Mississippi and Alabama in good time. Dre appreciated their companiable silence, cruising along trying to find a radio station that didn't play country music. After all, they'd known each other for ten years, if not very well.

She leaned back in the roomy seat of the Escalade, relaxed and happy with anticipation, pleased that she'd dug deep into her closet past all the casual tops and tees to find a flattering sleeveless, deep-blue dress with a short, flared skirt accented by a slim, white belt that she hadn't worn in years. It still fit. Other than that, all she needed was a pair of white sandals and a dash of the lipstick worn at the gala—as if he'd notice. Rex showed up in nice slacks and a dress shirt with an open collar that almost matched her gown. People in far off Montgomery would think they were a couple, and she found that she didn't mind.

"Five o'clock. Why don't you search around for a restaurant you might like and get the directions," Rex said, eyes on the road but one arm slung across the top of the seat very close to her.

She searched phone for best restaurants in Montgomery. "Oysters?" she asked.

"Nope, not this far from Louisiana. I could eat a

good steak."

"Central Restaurant has one and seafood as well. Southern fusion. Great ratings. Prices a little high."

"This is a date, Dre. I want to take you somewhere nice. Make a reservation for six o'clock."

She made the reservation, but frowned as she did as if calculating the cost of the meal. "But you bought the play tickets. I should pay for dinner."

"Don't try to make this not a date. I'm taking you out. I'm paying for everything."

"I could afford—"

"When you ask me out, I'll let you pay. Okay?"

That would be the day. Never going to happen once he got established in New Orleans, and the women started stalking him. Right now, he lived low profile with Dean's family, not going out much, training a lot. Once he had his own place, he could take anyone there, and it wouldn't be her.

He fought the traffic as they entered Montgomery and followed her directions to the Central, an attractive place with a unique menu and excellent service. Once the drinks arrived, white wine for her and red for him, their server waited patiently for their order.

"I'll have the New York strip steak, rare, with asparagus, oyster mushrooms, and the fancy potatoes. Dre, what would you like?"

She'd taken too long trying to choose something not too expensive and not too messy like the tempting short ribs in bolognaise sauce. "I thought the scallops with risotto, but the…" She lowered her voice to a whisper. "Price."

"She'll have the scallops." That settled it.

As they waited for their orders, she felt compelled

to make dinner conversation and seized on the upcoming Fourth of July celebration at the ranch. "The boys will be home from camp by then. They always look forward to it so much, the pig roast, the pony rides, the dragon boat races, the fireworks."

He considered before commenting. "I think they are old enough now not to need your constant supervision. Give them free rein to run around with their cousins, and you take it easy for a change."

"There's still Jenny."

"Annie can handle her easily. She'll be playing with all the grandkids from the Billodeaux Baby Boom three years ago and loving it."

"I guess you're right. How many grandchildren do Nell and Joe have now? I've lost track."

Rex counted on his fingers beginning with Beck and ending with Lorena's Mike. "Twenty including Shashana and Drew who they claim as their own regardless of how they came into the family. Dad will say he needs to buy more ponies."

Despite her anxieties now that Rex had declared this evening a date, Dre laughed. "The six he has should be plenty for the little ones. The eldest can all handle the larger horses, and Shashana rides old Rascal just fine despite her handicap."

"Try to tell Dad that."

"I love your father. Well, you've met mine. He tries hard on the one or two days a year he visits. My mother prevents him from doing more. I still can't believe he paid for a Portia Ramsey gown and that necklace. Guilt, I guess, but I don't want him to feel that."

"Me, I try to be like Dad and Dean on the football field and somewhere between Joe after he stopped womanizing and Mack before he stopped drinking. I guess I mean more fun than Dean but not so over the top I attract the tabloids. By the way, your father did threaten me if I hurt you." Rex's stern expression told her he meant every word.

"I guess he does care."

She would have said more, but the food arrived, the scallops nicely seared, the risotto creamy, and the steak just the right amount of red. Though she wouldn't have thought of fried pickles as a side dish, she did like them and shared a few with Rex.

When down to the last mouthfuls, Rex said, "How about dessert? We have the time. I kind of have my eye on the maple glazed beignets with candied bacon and dipping sauces. I saw a plate of those go by a while ago and saved some room. How about you?"

"Full, very full. Are you sure you trust beignets not made in New Orleans?"

"Never had them with candied bacon. We'll share a plate." He summoned their server and placed the order plus coffee as she cleared the plates. That shot the tab even higher. Dre figured she'd have to bake brownies for him or at least take him to Café du Monde to repay him.

The beignets, three of them, came large and delicious. She dipped one end in the caramel sauce and the other in melted chocolate. Totally worth the calories and the mess. As a bonus at one point, Rex leaned over and dabbed the corner of her lips with a napkin.

"Chocolate," he said. "I could think of a better way to remove that if we weren't in public."

The memory of their only kiss came roaring back making her pale cheeks color and bringing to the surface a thought she'd had earlier. She couldn't prevent herself from looking over her shoulder. "You don't believe paparazzi have started following you yet? I mean I wouldn't want Drew to see me in one of those trashy newspapers."

Rex unleashed his smile. "Doing what? Having dinner with a guy he calls uncle? Going to an art gala? Not exactly their beat."

"What about all the publicity when we saved Caressa?"

"We did something great, a big group of us. X and I got the most press. They didn't mention you or Edie by name. I think Ty was a little ticked off about not being included."

"Sure. No one knows who I am. I'm being ridiculous. We need to go. Don't know the parking situation."

She read out the directions again taking them into a vast park where they found the imposing red brick building flying both American and British flags and housing the theater. "The ticket booth is over there behind the fountain," she said.

Rex dropped her by the theater entrance, parked the car, and got the tickets. They entered through the rather grand lobby and into the theater with the lights already dimmed to settle the audience, though many still typed madly on their cell phones.

After the announcement to turn those phones off, they were transported to a ship caught in a fierce storm brought about by Prospero, the wizard inhabiting a nearby island along with his daughter Miranda and many strange creatures. Among the shipwrecked are Prospero's brother who stole his crown and sent Prospero and his then infant daughter into exile. In true

Shakespearean style, various groups from the ship wandered the island encountering Prospero's enslaved monster, Caliban, and his spirit, Ariel, who made havoc among them. The grown Miranda falls in love with the prince, Ferdinand, who is at first treated as another slave, but is eventually allowed to marry Miranda.

Dre could feel Rex restless in his seat during the long interlude of singing and dancing, and she thought she heard a sigh of relief when at last Prospero forgave his wicked brother and freed his enslaved creatures. Not as magical for him as for her.

They fought their way to the car and into the bumper-to-bumper traffic that always follows a play, finally regaining the highway and on their way home around 10:30. "You want something to eat before we get out into the piney woods?" Rex asked her.

"No, still full from dinner. How did you like the play?"

"I thought the three drunks were funny. Could have done with less dancing around, but what counts is that the theme is forgiveness. Do I have yours for the way I've acted toward you?"

"Nothing much to forgive. You were a teenage guy, and I was an obnoxious girl. I think we are both over that."

"Good. We won't make it back to New Orleans before two at best if the traffic stays light. Would you rather get a room or rooms for the night outside of Mobile? I have nothing going on tomorrow that we need to rush." He kept his eyes straight ahead, his voice very casual.

For a moment, she wanted to say, "Yes, stop. One room will be fine." But she pulled back. "We'd better go straight home. I wouldn't know what Annie and Matt would say to a sleepover."

"They shouldn't say much since they were living together and had Gabe on the way when they got married. But it's up to you. Dre, I'll always give you choices and respect them."

"Thank you for that."

She fully intended to stay awake the whole time and keep Rex alert for the long night drive, but her eyes closed, opened, closed, and stayed that way until he cut off the big engine in front of Matt's house.

"Sorry, I didn't mean to fall asleep."

"I'm good at long distance driving. Here we are safe and sound." He got down and came around to open her door and help her out of the vehicle.

Yes, a light burned to welcome her home, but she wasn't about to make another mistake like the last. When Rex leaned in for a kiss, she pushed him back.

"Okay then. Sleep well."

She shook her head, led him to the darkest corner of the porch behind a pillar, and initiated the kiss that started out much hotter than the last time. Her hands went places they had no business going, and his strayed to her breasts and buttocks, pulling her tight against him. When they at last came up for air, she said, "No doorbells or lights over here."

"Good thinking," he said and dove in for another one of equal length and passion.

When they finished, she said, "I really must go in now, but next time…"

"Glad to know there will be a next time."

They walked back into the light and opened the door very carefully. She gave him one light kiss before closing him out and tiptoed through the house. Matt snored in his massive recliner. Annie slept curled on the sofa. They still regarded her as a teenage daughter that needed looking after. Practice for when Jenny reached that age, Annie sometimes said. She'd have to tell them she'd grown up.

Chapter Twelve

Rex sat on the edge of the pool and hoped Dre would notice and come down to take a dip. He'd made plenty of noise upon arrival, a hearty welcome to Delia, but he couldn't interrupt her if she was working on a project. They were in a good place right now several days after *The Tempest* date, and he didn't want to wreck that by pushing too hard, much as he wanted to.

His cell phone rang on the poolside table. He got up, took a quick glance at the caller ID, and answered, "Hi, Mom. How are things going at Camp Love Letter?"

"Fine. Don't forget your volunteer week is right before the Fourth. The kids are counting on meeting you."

He had forgotten and right now had no wish to leave New Orleans. No use asking for a change of date. His mom could unpack a guilt trip like no other when it came to the camp for seriously ill children. "No, I didn't forget."

"Good. Have you found a place of your own to stay? We thought you might be tired of sharing space with three teens at Dean's house."

If he were being honest, he liked living a few blocks from Dre. "I grew up in a crowded house. It doesn't bother me, but I do need to get my own space before training camp. I won't have much time to house hunt after the season starts. The condos where Tom and Junior live are full up, and Edie and Ty are still honeymooning over the Korean electronics store. I'm not sure I want an entire house since I don't have a family yet."

His mother picked up on that at once. She always did. "That could change fast. I understand you are dating Dre, and she comes with a child."

So, Annie had reported him. "Just three dates, and she doesn't count the first two, only the one to see *The Tempest* in Montgomery last weekend."

"I thought you hated Shakespeare. I recall all the complaints about having to read *Julius Caesar* when you were in high school."

"It wasn't so bad. I did like saying, "*Let slip the dogs of war*." Sometimes, I use that to unnerve my opponents. Classy trash talk."

"Very chivalrous to drive Dre all the way back to New Orleans without stopping at a motel, though Annie feels things are heating up between the two of you."

"Oh, we haven't reached the boiling point yet."

"Go carefully. Unlike Sarge and Alix, she is already part of the family. Don't make people take sides if you break up."

"We aren't close enough together to break apart. Any other reason you called?"

"Your dad suggested you might want to use his old bachelor pad uptown. We don't come to New Orleans as often as we used to, but a cleaning lady comes once a week to dust and water the plants. You'd have more privacy than with any of your siblings."

"Would I have to vacate the round bed if you visit?" He meant it as a joke. His dad's lair from his womanizing days was notoriously outdated, a relic of times past, and one his mom hated and seldom used.

"We'd sleep in the Madame Pompadour room as usual."

With a crystal chandelier over the bed, blue-brocaded wallpaper and curtains, gold and white furniture apt for a French mistress, the name fit. He had no desire to sleep there but did have fond memories of spending the night in the huge round bed with his siblings, piled up like puppies under a big, furry spread. As a temporary solution to the housing dilemma, Joe's pad, not such a bad idea. "Let me check it out. Anyone down here have a key?"

"We'll let the doorman know you might be coming by to inspect the place."

"Okay, sounds good. I'll let you know. Love you, Mom."

"Love you, too." Their phone calls always ended that way, never with goodbye. Thinking deeply about the move, he missed her arrival until Dre's shadow blotted out the sun. She no longer held her towel defensively against her middle. It draped around her neck now.

"I waited a few minutes to come out. I didn't want to interrupt your phone call."

"My mother checking up on me."

"Must be nice to have a mother who cares enough to do that."

"Most of the time. Not always."

"You ready for some laps?" She tossed her towel on the lounger and moved to the pool's edge ready to make her dive.

He groaned. "Training is picking up, and I am plenty sore. Let's not make it a competition."

"I'll take it easy on you. I don't want to wear myself out either. I'm trying to get ahead on work before the boys' return."

They dove in and did leisurely laps until Delia appeared with tall glasses of iced tea and a plate of brownies. "Been in there thinkin' y'all could use a snack. Hardly got anyone to feed with our boys gone."

That lured them to the umbrella table to dry off.

"She don't eat enough," Delia claimed, though in his opinion Dre's slim body was padded in all the right places. Not like poor, skeletal Caressa.

"But I can cook. Right, Delia? Taught by the best." Dre sank her teeth into a thick, moist brownie.

"Because you was taught by the best, me." Delia's lips opened into a wide grin. "When Miz Kimberly was trying to snag Mr. Matt, she had me bake these most every day for him and claimed she'd done it herself, they's that good. Good thing I come with the house when she sold it to him and went on her way."

"I gotta agree with that." While the maid with plenty of meat on her bones talked, he'd finished one brownie and reached for another.

"I'm going in now. Let you alone. Miss Dre, you bring that tray in when you finished out here."

"She might call me Miss Dre, but Delia rules here."

"I'll miss this place when I move," he said and studied her response. Did he see a flicker of dismay on her face?"

"Oh, you've found a house. Is it across the causeway, or here in town?" She dipped her head to sip tea.

"Actually, my parents offered me Dad's old bachelor pad for as long as I want. That gives me more time to look around. It's uptown, not that far from here by car, a big condo that's a blast from the past. You need to see it."

She raised her head, shy again. "If you mean that, maybe I could come over and cook that meal I owe you sometime. Cheaper than going out."

"You don't owe me a meal. But I can be a cheap date. How about tomorrow night if that's okay."

"Ah, give me two nights. I'll have to plan a menu and grocery shop."

"That's fine with me. I'll give you the grand tour. Only one request."

She stared at him as if he'd ask her to serve in the nude. "Make these brownies for dessert."

Relief untensed her shoulders. "That's a promise."

Date number four on its way.

Chapter Thirteen

Dre insisted on driving her old Lexus over to Rex's new abode. Always better to have an escape plan. That was one reason she'd learned to cook in the first place, not taught by her mother but by a black maid in New Orleans. Food was better here anyhow. If there ever came a time when she must leave the shelter Matt Keaton had supplied for so many years, she'd get by but would hardly be able to afford a servant.

Before she pulled under the canopy of an older high rise near the river where a doorman waited, she mentally checked off all she'd brought along: bags of ingredients to make an etouffee and an asparagus salad, plus the promised pan of brownies—and an overnight bag. Okay, ready or not, here she came.

The doorman called up to the condo, took her keys to park the Lexus in guest parking, and offered his assistance in unloading, but Rex arrived within minutes. He grabbed the two bags of groceries and the small suitcase, leaving only the brownies for her to tote to the elevator and up to the top floor. A polished foyer led to a single doorway telling her the condo filled the entire space. Rex had left the door wide open in his haste to get downstairs.

He dropped her bag just inside and hauled the groceries to a spacious kitchen that appeared to have all she would need to make the meal—and breakfast with an old-timey Mr. Coffee and a toaster with four slots. She pushed that thought away and stacked her containers on the counter. Turning, she handed Rex a pint of Blue Bell vanilla ice cream. "Put this in the freezer. We'll have some with the brownies."

"Sounds good. Tour or dinner first?" he asked.

"Let me get the rice started since it takes the longest. Once I begin the etouffee I can't leave the stove." Amazed her hands weren't shaking, she slid the cold asparagus salad into the fridge, found the right sized pot for the rice, and started the water to boil.

All morning, she'd fretted over what to make, then chopped the holy trinity of Cajun cooking, celery, onion, and bell pepper, once she'd made up her mind. Crushing cloves of garlic and peeling the shrimp came next, then spices, each in its own container. She didn't want the smell of the first two items on her hands when she arrived. She added a bottle of hot sauce in case the only kind at the condo might be Joe's lethal hot and spicy mixture. Oh, and two sticks of butter figuring Rex hadn't been shopping yet. With her nerves shot fearing she'd forgotten something, Delia noticed and helped her make the brownies, a calming kitchen tradition between the two of them.

"It's gonna be delicious. Don't you worry about nothing, honey," Delia told her as they carried the bags to the car. The maid didn't comment on the overnight case already in the trunk. She generally went home at six once she'd prepared dinner, her opinion being what happened after that was "none my business." She gave Dre a comforting hug before sending her on her way.

"Okay, the rice is steaming. I'm ready for the tour."

"I feel a little steamy myself. Wait until you see this

place."

Rex led her out into the living room, not so odd with its huge, black leather chairs and sofa showing their age in bumps and sags and scars caused by hard use. The only recent touch appeared to be the immense large screen TV.

"Looks normal to me," she said.

"Yeah, it does. Next, the Madame Pompadour bedroom as my mom named it, fit for a king's mistress."

It did not disappoint with its blue brocade walls that matched the spread and curtains, gold and white French furnishings including an ornate king-sized bed full of curlicues and a small chandelier hanging above it. A bathroom of blue-veined marble adjoined the room, its tub not built-in, but boat-sized and set up on four curved legs. A step stool sat nearby to assist in mounting it. Gold-washed fixtures graced a pedestal sink and other plumbing.

"My mom says she could bathe three of us at a time in that tub."

"I believe her. Plenty of room for anything a person would want to do."

"Yep, anything." His voice seemed heated to her.

They retreated into the hall. As they approached the next bedroom, Rex requested that she shut her eyes before entering. Puzzled, she did as he began to describe the so-called Chinese Bordello Room.

"Imagine walls papered with yellow silk. Intricately carved black lacquer furniture and a frieze of erotic oriental prints showing all the ways of doing it very tastefully. Now envision a social worker checking this out as the nursery."

"Oh, dear."

"Open your eyes."

She did—and saw a cheery room painted in sunshine yellow holding three sets of bunk beds side by side and possessing a row of old-fashioned nursery rhyme prints on the walls. Jack and Jill, Rockabye Baby, Jack be Nimble, all the usual characters accounted for in a parade of childhood mishaps. "I think it's changed a little."

"When my mom got word that the social worker was on her way to check out the home for baby Dean, Mom piled all the erotic prints in the closet and replaced them with nursery rhyme folks later along with getting a crib and dressing table. All that remains is the big dresser under the window because it had plenty of storage. As the family grew and they spent more and more time at the ranch, she put in the bunk beds to house all of us when we came here to watch a Sinners game."

"Only six beds for twelve children?"

"Wait until you see Joe's Love Palace." He dismissed the hallway bathroom as ordinary and went right to the highlight of the tour.

"Here it is, where my formerly womanizing father supposedly bedded one-hundred women before settling down." Rex held out his arm toward an immense round bed duplicated on the ceiling by a mirror, the theme being the Sinners colors of red and black. "Mom didn't like sleeping here, so she put all the boys except Teddy in this bed when we visited. He had to have a low cot he could get in and out of with his wheelchair. We loved making faces in the mirror, so clueless about the real reason it was up there until we got older. Next the grand master bath, another study in the round."

It certainly was, a round sunken tub, this one with a

chandelier overhead that brought light to the black marble veined in white as did a skylight that let in the sun to nourish the ferns planted in the bidet.

"Easy to water," she remarked.

"My mom is very practical—and hated thinking of who might have used it to clean their privates after sex with dad."

"I can understand that. Plants do make it homier."

"All the towels used to be red. That's about it."

They returned to the hall and passed through the overcrowded dining area possessing a large oblong table with twelve chairs, a highchair tucked in a corner, and bar stools by the kitchen counter. "I think Edie was the last to use that highchair since I was always taller. Now, it's there for any visiting grandchildren."

"Time to start the etouffee." She found a skillet in a low cabinet, a wooden spoon in a drawer, and turned on the heat. Adding a stick and a half of butter, she started gradually mixing in flour, concentrating on her roux to achieve a light brown color. Rex watched from one of the bar stools.

"Anything I can do to help?"

"Sure. Slice the French bread lengthwise and butter both sides."

She added the chopped vegetables and let them wilt, then the spices, the peeled shrimp in its own broth, and a dash of hot sauce. "Might as well put the bottle on the table in case you want more heat."

"I might."

He also accepted the dinnerware and two ruby-toned glasses to set the table while she spread some of the garlic on the bread and shook on parsley flakes and parmesan cheese. It went into the broiler on a cookie sheet. While that warmed, she arranged her cold asparagus salad on square black plates, poured on the dressing of olive oil, Dijon mustard, and chopped shallots, shaving more parm on top. She passed the dishes through to Rex to put on the table. Bread done, she sliced it into sections and placed it in a basket. She covered portions of rice on more black plates with her etouffee and took them to the table while Rex brought the bread.

"Beer or wine?" he asked.

"Just ice water for me."

"You got it." He uncapped a beer for himself.

Dinner conversation consisted mostly of tales about the apartment and the escapades of the children crammed into it. She wished she had such great family stories, but her mother only entertained to impress and hosted the big family reunions and barbecues on her manicured lawn and nowhere else. Plenty of places for her to escape or play with cousins out of her mother's critical eye.

"I wonder why your dad didn't sell this place once the big house at the ranch was finished or just get a bigger place in the city."

Rex shook a few more drops of hot sauce on his etouffee. "Sentimental reasons, I guess. Dad stayed here when he was playing as the ranch is too far away, and mom had to make sure we all got to school in Chapelle during the season. But she brought as many of us as there were at any given time to see the home games. When it was only Dean, Tom, and the twins, they stayed here a lot. Now, I think they enjoy having the place to themselves again to do whatever they want."

"I wonder with his former reputation that she trusted him to stay here alone."

"As my dad says, once a Billodeaux man settles down, that's it for him."

"Good to known." Could she possibly be the chosen one or just one of a hundred others? Now she wished she'd had the wine, but if anything happened between them tonight, she wanted to remember every second, not have it dulled by alcohol.

"This asparagus salad is great and the bread, too."

"Thanks, nothing fancy."

"But all good."

"If you're done, I'll plate the brownies. I set the ice cream out to soften and brought along some chocolate sauce. The coffee maker is all set up to go."

"I'll clear the table, then we can have dessert on the terrace now that the sun is down. Ah, where do you want me to put your bag?" he added as casually as possible.

"The blue room, I guess." If he knew she had a secret yearning to try out the round bed, what would he do? And how about that sexy nightie, black and lacy, she'd borrowed from Annie's closet. On short Annie, it reached the ankles. On her, just above the knees with the bodice being tighter and more revealing. She hoped Annie wouldn't notice its absence until she had washed and returned the gown, but knowing Annie, she would have been glad to share. Now the question was would she have the nerve to wear it or simply sleep in the tee she wore and her panties. Neither of them had dressed up for this occasion—if it could be called an occasion.

Rex had the terrace door unlocked and opened for her when she brought the brownies. He went back for the coffee. They settled into two comfortable chairs with a small table between them and watched the reflections from the Huey Long Bridge shimmer on the water. Even

119

after dark, the Mississippi teemed with water traffic: steamboats, cruise ships, barges, and container ships all well-lit to prevent collisions in the busy port. At night, they seemed more magical than practical, especially with a fat moon looming over them. A light breeze fluttered her short hair.

The moment came when he said, "I'm glad you decided to stay over tonight. You still have the choice of staying in the blue bedroom or joining me in the round bed. I'd like to show you what good sex is all about, Dre."

"In my limited experience, it's messy, uncomfortable, and quickly over."

"Again, high school sex. If I can't do better than that throw me off this terrace." He arose and took her hand, led her inside. She forgot about the dishes and the beauty of the night but hesitated in the hall.

"Change your mind?"

"Yes, but I'd like to put on something more comfortable and brush my teeth." Did that sound so not sexy?

"Sure. Me, too. Join me when you're ready."

Hands trembling, she opened her suitcase and shook out the black nightie, took off her clothes, and let it slide down her body, cool and silky. In the bathroom, she did a thorough job on her teeth, but repaired her light makeup and lipstick. Now or never. She crossed the hall to Joe's Love Palace about to join the ranks of all who came before her.

With lights turned low, Rex had centered himself in the round bed. Bare-chested, a patch of dark hair between the muscles of his pecs, and covered to the waist by the furry, black spread, he let out low whistle. "You look as pretty as a present with a great gift inside."

She sat on the edge of the mattress, still several feet from him. He held out a hand. "Come on over."

She felt the warmth of his thigh against hers and nothing but the nightie between them, stiffened a little, but he drew her into an embrace that started with a kiss. She knew how to do this now, though they hadn't done it often. Already, she'd learned he liked his lower lip sucked, enjoyed a playful nip on the ear, and kisses that lasted long and deep.

His lips left hers and worked their way down to her breasts, sucked on her nipples through the lace as she massaged his muscled back, keeping him there, but one of his hands had strayed to the edge of the nightie and worked its way underneath where he began to stroke her center lightly. When exactly the naughty nightie was cast aside, she couldn't quite recall and did not care. They were generating their own heat. He shoved aside the spread and went down on her, brought her to her first orgasm with his tongue, held her until the shudders stopped.

"Moment," he said, and reached under a pillow for a condom quickly applied all the way up to the end of his shaft. "Ready?"

Too breathless to talk, she nodded. He mounted over her and instead of plunging in, he teased her, rubbing softly against the place where she throbbed, inserting just the head of his penis, and withdrawing again, until she gripped his firm buttocks and gave him a shove. Even in the dimness, she saw his smile flash. Up above in the mirror, she looked at a woman in the throes of passion, a woman she barely knew.

Rex picked up his rhythm. Her hips rose inviting

him to go faster. His stamina seemed endless. She came again, but he continued until he got another from her. "No more!" she cried.

"Just a little more." With a few quick, hard thrusts, he let himself go with a shout and collapsed over her for a moment before rolling to the side and cradling her. "Dre, this is what sex is supposed to be. Don't settle for less because you deserve the best."

"I think you set a very high bar tonight. I'll never forget this."

"No need to make this a memory since we can do it over and over again whenever we want."

"Do you mean it?" Could it have been as good for him as for her? She doubted that.

"Absolutely."

"Easier for you than for me. I have no privacy at my place and must be there for the boys after school. If I start making overnight visits a habit, I'll have lots of explaining to do."

"Dre, my dear, love making in the afternoon is just as good as doing it in the night. When I don't have training of course. Those two-a-days don't leave much energy for anything else. I wish I had more time to show you other moves you might enjoy, but Dean expects me at the training center tomorrow early."

"Yes, we should get some sleep now."

Rex appeared to go under the second he closed his eyes. She lay awake for some time reliving what they'd done together and had no idea when she'd drifted off.

As she woke, the first rays of the summer sun sought admission to the bed chamber through the high, small windows of the Love Palace. Rex nuzzled against her shoulder.

"We've got some time before I must leave. How about you on top?"

"I've never done that, only me on the bottom in the backseat."

"You'll be great—and I am so ready. Let me get my rubber raincoat on."

"Your what?"

"My dad's name for a condom. Always have one handy." He searched under the pillow again, found what he wanted, and applied it. "Your time to get on board."

She squealed when he lifted her and put her in place. "What shall I do?"

"Ride me, honey."

"Like this?" She pumped her thighs up and down but as the sensation increased, she found herself naturally leaning over him. She worried about her breasts flapping, about the faint silvery lines on her belly that betrayed her having given birth. No need. His eyes stayed closed, his black lashes thick enough for a woman to envy splayed beneath his lids, a faint smile on his face as if he enjoyed each movement. She let herself do the same, increasing her pace and lowering her angle until her nipples brushed again his. Faster, faster until her sweat dropped onto his lips. He licked it off with relish. His breath became hot and heavy. So did hers—and then wonderful spasms grew stronger and stronger until she clenched inside, tight around him. With two thrusts of his hips from below, he finished as well.

They lay side by side coming down off a natural high. At last, he said, "Why don't you run a bath in the round tub? I'll join you in a few minutes."

He rolled off the bed and grabbed a pair of boxer briefs before opening the bedroom door and going down the hall. She felt as if she might have to crawl to the bathroom her legs were so wobbly, but she made it. The deep tub took a while to fill. She studied an array of bath additives lined up on its edge, selected one, and dumped in a capful. Bubbles foamed to the surface and a pleasant floral scent filled the air. Perfect. She stepped into the water and sank in the froth up to the top of her breasts as if she starred in some old time movie where the body could not be revealed and sex only implied.

Rex discovered her like that as he backed in bearing a tray with two mugs of coffee and a plate of chocolate croissants which he settled carefully on the edge. "Bubble bath—my mom's favorite, though her sons preferred the one that smelled like bubblegum. I'm going to take some kidding during workouts today, but you know, I don't care." He joined her and handed over a coffee.

"You planned ahead for breakfast? How nice."

"How hopeful. I got the croissants yesterday morning believing that you'd stay, and here we are." He passed the plate to her and watched her take the first bite.

"From the coffee shop by Junior's condo. You settle in fast."

"I've known about that place for years. As for settling in, I only had to transfer my clothes. Most of my things are in storage until I find a permanent place." He swished his arm through the water. "You can't beat this place for sheer decadence."

"I'd have to agree. In that spirit, I'll have another croissant."

"Me, too."

When they finished eating, he licked the crumbs from her lips and ended that with a kiss. "I'd like to do more, but you drained me earlier."

"I did?" Her confidence took a leap upward toward the sparkling chandelier.

"You did. So, we still have bathtub and shower sex to look forward to."

"Soon?"

"As soon as we can arrange it."

Chapter Fourteen

Dre still slept when he left the bed in the Madame Pompadour room where they'd gone for a change of location and had bathtub sex in the immense four-legged tub. With all the splashing and two unmade beds, the housekeeper who came weekly would believe he'd had houseguests or maybe an orgy. Dressed for a workout, he made coffee and put cinnamon rolls warmed in the microwave on a plate for another kind of variety. By the time he returned to the blue room, Dre lay awake, naked but with the covers pulled up over her breasts.

She smiled softly as the newly awakened will do, sniffed the scents of cinnamon and strong coffee in the air, and sat up, allowing the covers to slide to her waist. She took a cup of coffee first, sipped, swallowed, then went for a deep bite of cinnamon roll like a woman whose appetite had been whetted by sex. He hoped so because they wouldn't be having any for a couple weeks.

"I have a voluntary training session today. It's a good chance to get to know the rookies, and after that I'll be leaving. Stay as long as you want, just lock the door behind you.

Her eyes went wide for a moment until she schooled her features to show indifference, hard to believe when she had icing on her lips. "So, all this is over?" She set aside the roll.

"No! No, not what I meant. Right after training, I

have to set out for the ranch. It's my week to volunteer for Camp Love Letter. You know, throw around a football with the handicapped kids, do lifeguard duty, sign autographs for the families. The camp closes for the week of the Fourth. I'll stick around for the annual barbecue, and we'll see each other there. We'll figure out a way to be together."

She licked the icing from smiling lips. "As I recall, your mom keeps all the cottages locked and set aside for heavy drinkers or illness among the guests. The bedrooms in the big house are usually full of napping children."

"I know the ranch. There are other places, but none of them have beds. By the way, I want you on my dragon boat team this year."

Wonder passed over her features. "Are you sure? I've never rowed before. I'm always on the bank with the kids. I know winning means a lot to you. The year Ty messed up you didn't take it well."

"Three years ago. I've grown up a lot since then. I know Edie will drum for me, and I'll be coxswain. Dad set up rules about the teams since we have so many athletes attending the party. A boat can only have two pros, should have at least two women, and some teens. Dean often has mostly women because he gets Lorena and Alix as his pros, then Stacy and Josee as his women. They are all in great shape. He wants to let Beck row this year, too."

"I'm no athlete and don't spend the time in the gym that Stacy and Josee do. I'd hate to make you lose."

"Hey, I've seen you do laps in the pool. You will be fine. We have Ty again and maybe X if he comes. Dad always has the old-timers who are still in good shape like

Connor Riley and his wife, Stevie. He can't ask the Rev because he'd sink the boat. Really, it's just a friends and family rivalry, and that is all it should be."

"Keep feeding me cinnamon rolls in bed, and I might sink the boat, too." She finished hers.

"There are more in the kitchen. Take them with you since they will just go stale if you don't."

"The boys come home this Sunday. They'll enjoy them."

"I love cinnamon buns, too."

He leaned in for the kiss to assure her they weren't over. As far as he knew, he hadn't made love to woman who'd given birth. Sure, she had light stretch marks on her breasts and belly and wasn't as tight inside as most of the women he'd bedded. Somehow, none of that mattered. They were about the same age, yet he'd had to teach her what love making should be. Her inexperience and enthusiasm were new, too. He didn't think he'd slept with any other woman who didn't know it all already.

Plus, she'd set aside the mess of her teenage years to build a new, responsible life and raise the child she'd created with love and without resentment. Was that called character? He hadn't found it in any other woman that he'd dated casually. A thought came to him, a little bit of self-revelation that he shared with her now.

"You know how I warned other men away from you, made a big deal about your being a mother?"

"Yes. That hurt even though I wasn't looking for a man in my life."

"I believe I might have been saving you for myself."

"I think I might have loved you all along." She'd said the words first.

He couldn't quite go that far right now. He managed,

"Same here. You know I won't be around as much as I'd like with training camp after the Fourth and then the preseason games. Hardly a break after that with away games and daily training."

She put a hand on his cheek. "Rex, I've lived nearly ten years in a football family. Our lives revolve around the game. I understand the routine. Annie and Stacy and even Edie, we're there for each other. I'm glad you didn't leave me on the shelf as long as stale cinnamon buns."

"You will never be stale to me. Look, I really have to go, and you sitting there with sweet crumbs on your breasts are too much of a temptation to jump into bed again."

"Would it be so bad if you were a tad late?"

"Only if Dean didn't notice and say, 'Where the hell have you been?' like he usually does. Then, all the other guys laugh because they do know."

"Go on then. Think about private places on the ranch. I'll see you then."

Chapter Fifteen

The boys piled off the camp bus on Sunday afternoon. As usual, Gabe and Danny were brown as the bears in the woods. Drew showed off his light tan, his blond hair nearly white from being in the sun so much. "I wore my sunscreen like you told me and didn't get burnt," he boasted to his mother.

Dre tucked her son under her arm for a side hug and didn't dare offer to carry his duffel bag. He'd reached that age where he wanted less mothering and an acknowledgement that he could tote his own baggage. That didn't stop the chatter all the way to Matt's SUV.

"They split us up in different cabins, but I had a good counselor who told us right out that no bullying was allowed in Cabin Five. Because we have a pool at home, I could swim better than most of the guys, all the way to the dive platform in the lake and back again. All three of us ride horses really good thanks to Daddy Joe. I helped some of the other kids who were afraid."

"Then, I am very proud of you. That's a good way to make new friends." Although they did consult her, Matt and Annie had decided to send the boys farther afield than usual and asked that they be placed in separate cabins, feeling the time had come when they couldn't be picked up easily if they had a nightmare or didn't like the food served. All of them needed to branch out. She'd worried. Drew's closeness to his cousins made up for his not having brothers and provided him with protection at school, but he did have to learn to manage on his own.

"I'm good at crafts, too. Wait until you see what I made for you."

She already had a small collection from past years: a twig plaque with Home Sweet Home spelled out in macaroni letters, a leather bookmark with her initials punched into it, and a little paraffin burner of cardboard coiled in a tuna can that made exactly two smores before dying out, treasures all. Once seated in the car next to her, he couldn't wait to dig out a small clay dish with a rim made of thumbprints and another in the center for good measure. All the coils of clay had been smoothed out, and it only listed slightly to one side.

"I'll put my paperclips in that. It's wonderful. Maybe I should give you art lessons."

Drew wrinkled his nose. "I don't think so. I get teased enough."

"You shouldn't let that stop you from doing something you like."

"Well, maybe you could teach me to draw dragons. That'll be cool."

"Dragons it is."

Barely home, the boys dumped their bags full of dirty laundry in the hallway and raced to put on swim trunks for a quick dip before dinner. Dre decided to join them. Jenny, left with Delia, wanted to swim, too, while wearing the three necklaces the guys had made for her out of various kinds of dried pasta painted with watercolors. While putting on her floaties, Dre explained calmly that water would ruin her beautiful gifts and set her free. She could pick out who made which. Gabe's

131

was messy and colorful but had no pattern. Danny put more thought into his and used a lot of purple because Jenny loved purple. Drew had worked out a pattern first—long, long, short, then a wheel shape like a pendant, Maybe, he'd design jewelry someday.

Keeping her eye on the kids, she did her laps and tried very hard not to think of Rex. He was what, three hours away, and called her every night at a time when the children were in bed. Mostly, he told her tales of the amazing kids at the camp and what they could do. She filled him in on some new jobs she'd acquired. They didn't resort to phone sex, and neither said what really filled their minds. They ended with Miss You.

Had she spoken too soon, too rashly? Did she really mean she'd always loved him? Surly as she was when she came Louisiana, full of attitude and challenges, it would have been difficult for him to tell that like all the girls around him, she wanted him to look her way with interest, see beneath the Goth makeup and the dumpy clothes, and discover the new person she called not Andrea or Andi, but Dre.

That desire had continued through his clumsy teen comments on her hair, his constant harping on her motherhood. Couldn't he understand that no matter what she said, she wore her hair short intentionally not to be like her beauty queen sister, that she was more than Drew's mother? Now, that time had come, and she'd blurted out the love word way too soon and was careful not to use it again even in ending a phone call.

Matt came out to crank up the grill and make hamburgers with roasted ears of corn and a pot of baked beans Delia put together before leaving. Annie brought out lemonade, buns, and fixings for the burgers. She summoned all of them from the pool to drip dry before eating. While the boys lined up for burgers, and she poured lemonade for Jenny, Annie leaned Dre's way.

"So good to have them home. It's just too quiet when they are gone even with Jenny complaining about only having brothers and no little sisters. She's trying hard, but I don't think she will get her wish."

"We do have a houseful already. Despite the little spats, it's great how well they get along together. I am so grateful you let us be part of this family."

"We had a rough start, but all is well now, and you more than pull your weight in childcare. Unless of course, you have plans to get your own place any time soon."

Was this it? The dreaded conversation that they might want her gone. "Are you trying to tell me to move out?"

Annie appeared shocked by the idea. "No, not at all. I just thought with all the time you've been spending with Rex you might be considering moving in with him."

"Into Joe's bachelor pad?" The very idea made her laugh, maybe too loud in her relief that she wasn't being kicked out. "It's way too soon to consider that. Maybe if we are still together when he finds a house, maybe then."

"Good. I feared you were moving too fast with my baby brother. I'd love to see you marry him, but give it a little time, okay?"

"That's a promise."

Now if she could only promise not to think of him day and night and long for the week to pass before they met again at the ranch. The time passed so slowly even with two new book covers to be designed and sent in for approval and the boys needing rides here and there to sports events, birthday parties, and sleepovers.

At last, they filled the SUV with supplies for a long day at the ranch: sunscreen and blankets, beach chairs, a vat of Delia's baked beans, and a triple batch of brownies cut smaller than usual to go with the barbecue spread. As always, they'd invited Delia along and told her that desserts weren't needed as Jock and Lorena always supplied a wedding cake to celebrate their anniversary.

"Mark my word, all those brownies done be gone befo' you know it. And I do like to celebrate the day with my people," she said, meaning her daughter, grandchildren, and a bunch of sisters. They waved goodbye and headed northwest to the ranch.

Dre called Rex once they made it to the highway without going back for anything forgotten. "Give us two and a half hours. We're taking the shortcut."

"Good. I thought you might make it sooner. Oh well, I'm stuck with lifeguard duty until they ring the triangle for lunch. You'll know where to find me."

Good thing she'd worn her suit under her clothes, but she didn't plan to swim, maybe just sunbathe and admire Rex in his Speedo until the big feed that always marked the occasion. As he'd said and Annie seconded, the boys were old enough to roam free and Jenny required little care. She had been told to take a day off for a change. So looking forward to it like a silly high school girl who planned to linger around a guy she had a crush on until he noticed her. She'd never been silly, only stupid in her choices. Not this time.

The boys played games on their phones. She and Annie sang "The Wheels on the Bus" with Jenny and counted cows along the way once they'd gotten out of the city, over the bridge, and passed through one rural town after another. The often repeated ride had seldom seemed so long. Finally, they drove through the open wrought iron gates of the ranch, waving to the ranch manager, Knox Polk, as he checked them off his list of invitees. After winding down the long curving drive shaded by massive live oaks, Matt parked the SUV by the barn in the line of vehicles belonging to earlier arrivals.

Dre, seated next to Jenny's car seat, released the little girl but held her back as the boys stampeded for the doors. She got down carrying her beach bag holding sunglasses, a towel, and a big tube of sunscreen. "Anyone for the pool?"

"Ponies!" the boys cried and raced to the corral with Jenny eating their dust. A queue of small children from the Billodeaux Baby Boom stood waiting for a turn. Beck, Wynn, and DJ were in charge of the three ponies this year. Two of the big red horses Joe favored stood saddled and tied to the fence for the older riders. She felt the urge to follow after them as she always had.

"Go to the pool," Annie said. "I've got this.

"And I have everything else," Matt said with his usual good nature as he started unloading chairs and blankets.

With their blessing she threaded around blankets and chairs already staking a claim to a piece of lawn, passed the big house with its white pillars, far more a mansion than a ranch house, and took the path to the pool. Before entering the gate, she paused a moment simply to admire the grandeur of Rex, all lean muscle and deep tan wearing nothing but his skimpy red suit, aviator sunglasses, and a whistle up on the lifeguard stand. Two pretty college age girls in very brief bikinis leaned against its legs as if holding it up and chatted with him, though they seemed to be doing most of the talking. He turned his head right and left, scanning the pool for trouble and noticed her on his second pass. He waved. The young women followed the direction of his greeting and faded away as she waved back.

She went to him and took their place. He jumped down and gave her a kiss long enough to brand her as his own. "There, that should head off any more leg cramps that need a ridiculous amount of massage time."

"Those two girls?"

"Yes, I supposedly saved them both from drowning. You know, I used to love this job, but not anymore, not since you."

She buried how pleased this made her. "I should let you get to work. I'll be right over there admiring you from afar with your other fans."

"I'm free after lunch. We'll go together."

She selected a vacant lounger and dragged it into a patch of shade that would disappear with the coming of noon. Taking off her tee and shorts, she slathered on the sunscreen and laid back to relax, content to wait for lunch and the dragon boat races since the view across the pool was so good.

She must have dozed behind her sunglasses because the clang of the triangle by the barbecue hut woke her. Pool people began exiting through the gate to get in line but had to step aside to make way for the traditional bearing of the roasted pig from the umu oven on its plank and borne by six young Sinners' rookies. They passed through the other gate and into the palm grove to alert strollers and volleyball players on the sand court that dinner was served.

Hastily, she put on her tee and shorts again and retied the tennis shoes she'd put under the lounger. Thank God for sunscreen and shade, her legs had only a slight pink flush from long exposure. Rex blotted out the sun looming over her and gave her a hand up.

"Give me a minute to get some clothes on and close the pool," he said.

"I think there isn't a woman here who wouldn't love to have you stay in your Speedo."

"Except my mom." He went into the locker room and reappeared in black athletic shorts and a Sinners T-shirt, his feet clad in sneakers, no socks. He locked one gate, escorted her out the other, and flipped over the sign announcing the pool to be closed until two p.m. They took their time walking to the barbecue hut with pauses for kisses up against the sturdy trunks of the oaks and behind the Camp Love Letter cottages. No rush today.

"Since I have a boat entered in the races, Trinity has pool duty this afternoon. He seldom rows. We all figured he needed some sunshine after bending over a computer in a dark room all his days."

"Did all of your team show up?"

"Yep, now that you are here. I could tell by the huge basket of Sephy's biscuits on the sides table and the garlic bread Edie always brings already sliced beside it. X and Ty must be around somewhere. I hope they saved us a seat at one of the tables."

Mentioning the boat race made her hands sweat more than the heat of the day, but she didn't flinch at the idea as they came upon the end of the line into the barbecue hut. By tradition, the aged, handicapped, and those with small children ate first. Teddy and Jessie in their wheelchairs had already passed through and sat at a picnic table with their three girls. Though neither Sarge with her missing foot nor Shashana minus a leg considered themselves handicapped, they sat with them, plates piled high. Mack held back, letting other families flow by since he could wait. Once upon a time, his volatile temper would have pushed him into line, but Sarge had tamed that.

Their turn came soon enough. Plenty of crispy roasted pork remained on one pig carcass, though the other pig had been picked clean except for the head. Plantains, yams, and white potatoes cooked with the pork still covered a platter. With an abundance of sides from avocado salad to rice dressing to grilled zucchini as well as baked beans and mac and cheese, no one would miss out on their favorites. They more than filled their plates and passed up the dessert table for now with its centerpiece wedding cake surrounded by other sweets. Dre noted that Delia's bite-sized brownies were half gone and some inroads had been made into two pans of bread pudding topped with meringue lightly browned on the tips.

"Strange not to see Mawmaw Nadine behind that table doling out her bread pudding with a tablespoon for those lucky enough to get any," she remarked.

"Yeah, but she kept her promise to leave the recipe to Junior in her will. That's his work on the table. I thought she'd make it to one hundred, that tough old bird, and she almost did. Survived Covid and then just passed away in her sleep right after the New Year arrived. Edie and Ty sure did make her happy before that with their Catholic wedding."

"Did Edie finally convert?"

"Edie? Hell, no. Nobody tells Edie what to do. I

don't think either of them go to any church very often."

"Matt is fairly devout. He takes the boys to St. Mary's every Sunday. Annie is cleaving to the Billodeaux code that the girls are raised protestant."

"So Drew is being raised Catholic?"

"I let him go with Matt because he wants to, but we haven't done the baptism and first communion thing. He can make up his own mind when he's older. Would you want a Catholic wedding and to raise your children that way?" As soon as the words were out, she regretted them. They sounded pushy, like she plotted their future.

Rex shrugged it off. "I haven't thought about it. Hey, over there. I think that's Edie standing on a bench and flailing her arms to get our attention. Looks like we have seats saved."

They moved in that direction dodging picnickers on the ground. She caught a glimpse of Matt and Annie and the kids well into their meal, children on the blanket, adults in the chairs. "Maybe I should go help out over there."

"They're fine, Dre. Come on. Take a day off."

Rex guided her to the picnic table where Edie, Ty, X, and Caressa sat on one side. Dre leaned over the table and took Carie's hands, still thin, but her face had lost some of its angular sharpness. "So good to see you here and looking better. Oh, sorry, I'm keeping you from eating."

"I haven't started on this pile of food X brought. I won't get it all down."

"Now look here," X interrupted. "One of your mama's great biscuits, the nicest piece of roasted pig I ever did see, avocado salad for your greens, some tasty baked beans, and a little rice dressing. Eat all you can."

"I'll try, but the real goal my dietician told me is to regain some of my weight but not all of it since I don't want to end up with my mother's health problems. That's what I'm going for. Besides, the best part is being here with all my rescuers. I'd be dead without you."

They murmured disclaimers for saving her life, but X intervened. "You did. Stop being so modest."

Looking at the double-sized seat on their side of the table, Dre asked in a quick change of subject, "Where is your mama?"

"She met a woman from her high school years, Precious Armitage, a pretty big lady herself. They went off to see if Joe will give them the pig heads to make headcheese."

"Okay, sounds awful."

"You been in the south this long and haven't tried a good, homemade headcheese served on crackers? I'll ask mama to send some over when it's done."

Dre tried to wiggle out of the offer. "Oh, don't go to all that trouble for me."

The others laughed and started in on their meals. Sephy joined them with a plate overflowing. "I can pick up the head when we get ready to leave. All y'all will get some."

They hit the dessert table after Lorena and Jock cut their wedding cake and posed for pictures. The brownies were almost gone, but they helped themselves to the second pan of bread pudding, yep, exactly like Mawmaw used to make.

Rex stood. "Since most of my team is here, take a rest. Be at the boats by two-thirty. The two of us are going for a ride to work off all this food. See you later." He led Dre toward the corral where the pony rides had been suspended, but the two quarter horses remained saddled in the shade near a water trough.

"We're going for a ride?"

"To a very special place not far away."

She took his word for it and mounted old Rascal, knowing his tricks because Joe had taught her to ride on this animal. Rex took Lazy Loser, a horse that never ran off or threw anyone because he'd rather graze. Rex had the ability to keep Loser's head up and his legs moving. They set off ambling along the dirt track that skimmed the edge of the bayou where the dragon boats already bobbed in the sluggish current, dipping their fierce heads up and down as if eager to run. Turning off on the lane running between a small wood and the cow pasture, Rex stopped about halfway to the next road.

"We should lead the horses in. The branches are low and there's lots of brush to skirt."

"Where exactly are we going?" Dre dismounted.

As soon as Rex got down from Loser's back, his horse stretched out its neck to eat a mouthful of small, yellow sunflowers. "None of that now. There's plenty of grass on the edge of the glade."

"Oh, a glade, is it?"

"A secret mossy glade with no security cameras around."

"I see." Dre's heart picked up a beat. Soon they'd be together again in the way she'd been craving for days. As if picking up on her emotions, Rascal head butted her into his arms. They took the suggestion well with no one except the white Charolais cattle to watch. The kiss went long and deep and often beyond the bounds of the lips. When they began to tear at each other's clothes, Rex raised his head. "I think we need to move along to a better spot."

They entered the deep shade cast by the live oaks with low growing branches swathed in swags of Spanish moss. Skirting blackberry brambles and clumps of poison ivy, they made good progress until Rex stopped suddenly and uttered, "Dammit!"

"What?" said Dre coming up behind him.

"Ty's Ducati motorcycle. They beat us to the spot. Must have taken the road past Teddy's house. Edie, if you are in there, get out. We haven't been together for weeks, and you two can do it any time."

Edie's voice replied. "You owe me one for nearly running us down on dad's stallion last time we were in here."

"Yeah, three years ago before you were married. I was looking out for my baby sis."

"I'm your older sister by several minutes. Don't need your help now."

"Come on. Have a heart, Edie. After this, I'll be in training camp, and we won't have time together."

"Ty has training camp, too."

Ty spoke up. "I'll get to come home nights during camp even if I'm too tired to do much. But we don't have to sneak around or have kids interrupting. I promise to make it up to you tonight once we're home."

"Oh, okay, fine." The other couple broke through the brush surrounding the glade still buttoning up and lugging a blanket.

"Would you leave the blanket? I was in such a hurry I forgot about moss stains. And maybe you could give mom and dad a hint that the glade is in use."

"Humph, anything else I can do for you? Bring wine and pillows? Don't worry about our parents. They won't leave their guests for any more than a quickie in their bedroom. You'd think they'd be too old for that by now." Edie shoved the blanket into her brother's arms.

Ty kissed the top of her head. "I hope we never get too old, just like them." He wheeled his motorcycle carefully along the path broken by the horses wide enough to keep it from being scratched. Edie followed with reluctance in every step.

Rex tied the horses to the ring of bushes surrounding the private spot. Loser began to munch on the greenery as they pushed their way inside where thick moss carpeted the floor of the forest and a single beam of light penetrated the shade of the overhanging magnolia trees that shed their cones and red seeds on the ground. Edie had brushed these aside saving them some time. Rex flared out the blanket. They were on it in seconds.

Not much clothing to discard, two tops, two pairs of shorts and shoes, and their swimwear beneath. Stretched out in that beam of light, she wondered out loud, "Do you mind my stretch marks?"

"Hardly notice them." He proceeded to show her by kissing each breast and going lower to give her hips the same treatment, and being in the vicinity, went lower to prepare her with a few strong licks of his tongue, stopping only to apply the condom from his shirt pocket.

He made all things magical, this special almost enchanted place, his fine body now rising over her. "Why me?" she murmured.

"You feel—right." He brought her own scent to her lips and stilled her voice until they both cried out loud enough to scare the crows that had gathered to watch. The sunbeam moved, leaving them in shade and a light doze. The horses shifted. The crows returned to protest their presence, making enough racket to rouse them.

"Jesus, we need to get to the boats. We're in the first heat."

"That's how I feel—in heat. But, yes, the race. I'm so relaxed I'm not nervous anymore."

"You'll be great. Let's go."

Dressing in haste, Rex helped her to mount the patient Rascal and pulled Loser's head away from some tender leaves. He led them out on the path they'd made coming in and picked up the pace to a trot once on the dirt lane. Ahead the area around the boats now swarmed with people shrugging into life vests and being checked off crew lists by Joe. Lines of guests gathered on beach chairs to watch or sat on the bank of the bayou for a closer view.

"About time you got here. Edie is already behind the drum and the rest of your crew is in place," Joe said with a gesture toward their boat. X and Ty waved in a knowing sort of way.

"The horses?"

"DJ, take the horses back to the barn. They won't like all this noise and crowding," Joe ordered.

"But I'll miss the race," his grandson whined.

"Not if you're quick. Go on, ride Rascal. We'll wait until you return to sound the cannon."

That taken care of, Dre latched her life preserver and Rex put on a larger size. He helped her into place on the boat and made sure she held the oar correctly before he took his place to guide them to victory. She had no time to introduce herself to the young woman next to her who resembled one of the girls mooning over Rex at the pool. Her partner said, "You are so lucky," as the boats maneuvered into position, not so easy in the awkward vessels.

They were up against Dean and his crew of stalwart women and teens. When DJ came racing back from the barn, Joe raised his arm. When he dropped it, a miniature cannon sounded, and the rowers dug deep into the brown waters to the beat of the drums.

The first strokes were slow and measured as the crew adjusted. Rex signaled for an increase of speed. The drums picked up the pace in both boats. Dre paddled as hard as she could as the water frothed mocha colored about them. In the other craft, Annie pounded harder on the drum. Annie here? Who was watching the children? She nearly missed a beat. Matt of course, an experienced father good with the kids. She heard Jenny's shrill cry. "Row, row, row your boat, Mama. You, too, Auntie Dre."

"Go, Mom!" Drew's voice, easy for her to single out. She oared until her arms burned. The sweat beaded on her forehead and dribbled down her cheeks. Beside her, her counterpart in Dean's boat, Lorena, seemed to row without effort next to Alix, yet neither pulled ahead. She prayed for the bend in the river that signaled the end to appear before she shamed herself. At last, they passed under a rope hung high that marked the finish. The drumming ceased. She collapsed over her oar as someone shouted, "Dead heat."

Rex steered to the shore. She remained seated as other rowers scrambled up the muddy bank, and Ty helped Edie from her perch. Then, Rex was there, arms out, raising her up and out on wobbling legs and helping her out of the life vest. "You did great. I knew you would."

She had to admit to clinging to him, two sweat-soaked bodies glued together. "What does dead heat mean?"

"We tied. One of us must race the winner of the second heat. That would be Dad against Mack."

"Oh, God, no!"

"Come on. Let's get some water and shade, and you'll be good to go. You can do anything you set your mind to."

Despite the football style pep talk, she doubted that. Another pair of arms wrapped around her waist. "That was so cool, Mom. Can I row in your boat next year?" Drew asked.

Rex gave her some room. He smiled at her son. "Let's see your muscle."

Drew did a bicep curl. For a nine-year-old, he managed to raise a small bump. Rex gave it a squeeze. "I'll buy you some light weights, and you'll be ready next year. You can work out with your mom, build that upper body strength. How about getting your mother and me some water?"

The boy raced away to the blanket where Annie lay stretched out flat surrounded by young boys radiating heat. Jenny cooled her with a paper fan. They followed and arrived as Drew took dripping, icy bottles from a small cooler and handed them to him. "We came prepared like they told us at camp."

"Appreciated. Mind if we sit with our opponent, Dre?"

"Who?"

"Angel Mama," he said, using the term for his sister that Daniel had coined as a toddler.

"I'll soon be a real angel if I keep doing this. Getting too old," Annie groaned. "Next year, I'll get Wynn to take my place."

"Who do you suggest to replace me?" Dre said.

"I will!" her son offered as she folded onto the blanket.

Rex sat beside her. "They're lined up for the next heat. Let's see who we have to beat, Joe's old-timers or Mack's crew. Mack has Sarge and Jock. Wow! Jude is drumming for them. Never thought I'd see that. She's usually so bah-humbug about any special day. Not much of a team player."

Annie raised herself enough to see. "She's mellowed a little with motherhood. My guess is she's setting an example for Molly. What I can't believe is Teddy drums for Dad without wearing his braces because once his boat overturned and the braces pulled him down. I know he has great upper body strength and swims well, but that takes courage."

The race ran close, but Mack's team prevailed by a flick of the dragon's extended tongue. The boats did their slow, clumsy turn against the current and returned to the mooring spot. Joe hopped to shore and gestured to Rex and Dean. Rex bounded to his feet to answer the summons.

"He's in such great shape." Dre sighed. "Look at me. I'm destroyed. Whatever does he see in me?" she asked, a question directed more at herself than the occupants of the blanket.

She got an unexpected answer from Matt who cradled Jenny between his legs. "Maybe a woman of substance who built her own career and is already a loving and wonderful mother."

"I couldn't have done it without you. You put me through college and gave me and Drew a home."

147

Lynn Shurr

"I paid for your brothers' educations, too, exactly as I said I would despite my falling out with your family. You've always more than earned your keep."

"You're pretty, and you draw beautiful things and can cook, too," Drew said with eagerness to bolster his mother.

Annie gave a limp wave of her hand. "What they said. Rex is lucky to have you in his life."

The compliments ended when Rex jogged back to the blanket and announced, "We're going to break the tie with a coin toss. Dad says it's getting too hot for two more heats." He returned to join Dean as his father announced the decision in his audible-calling voice. Rex went for tails and lost. He shook hands with his brother before returning to their group.

"Sorry about that. It's the luck of the draw. Dean and Mack get an hour to rest their teams, then they'll go at it again."

Annie moaned. "I think I need longer than that to recover. As I recall no subs unless someone gets hurt— or dies. We've come close to that a couple of times before you arrived on the scene, Dre."

"I think I might have jinxed our boat by praying you'd lose the toss, Rex," Dre admitted.

"Well, *my* prayers weren't answered," Annie said.

Rex shrugged. "It's only a game."

"So is football."

"As you should know, football is a way of life."

"I do know," Dre answered. "It dominates the offseason, too. You'll soon be in training camp, then traveling for the preseason games."

"We'll find some time." Surrounded by nine-year-old boys, he left out any details.

Annie took the hint and ran with it. "Dre, why don't you stay and help with the cleanup. Rex can bring you home afterward."

"Good idea, but we might be late, very late," Rex agreed.

"Sounds good to me," Dre said as casually as possible.

How she got through the next race she did not know. Mack triumphed, despite a tired drummer, and received the traditional leis and the small tiki statues that went to the winners. The ice cream feast followed, homemade sundaes, cones, or cups, to cool everyone down. Few left before the spectacular fireworks lined up along the cane field road across the bayou were ignited and filled the clear summer sky with splashes of red, white, and blue, and showers of gold and silver.

Then, the crowd began to thin with people picking up their leftovers and containers. She noted Delia's bean pot had been wiped clean and all the brownies eaten. Sephy bid them goodbye, toting her biscuit basket now filled with a well-wrapped pig's head and directing X to be careful with a bulging bag of the remaining foods for Carie.

Rex helped stow the boats and picked up chairs. She assisted Knox Polk in gathering trash to be burned in a bonfire and aided Nell and Corazon in storing any victuals not claimed by others. All done, Nell handed Rex a huge bag of provisions, gave him a kiss and an "I love you, my youngest one. It's late. The two of you need to be on your way." She added a kiss on Dre's cheek, thanked her for the help, and waved them down the lane.

Dre fell asleep on the long three-hour drive while the indefatigable Rex stayed behind the wheel. By the time they arrived at the bachelor pad, she found herself revived and ready for anything, anything at all.

Chapter Sixteen

The round eye of the mirror over the bed stared down on two thoroughly spent lovers. Both lay faces up. Dre, one arm draped across Rex's chest, could feel the beat of his still wildly excited heart.

"Did you teach me a new position tonight?"

"I don't know what that was, but it included two laterals and ended with a very successful quarterback sneak. Score, big score. Was it the same for you?"

"Two scores for me and a couple of extra points. Too bad I don't remember all the moves." Dre laughed, tired but elated.

"Writing it down would have interrupted the play."

"Time?" she asked.

"Oh, we must have gone at it for an hour."

"No, the real time."

Rex consulted the sports watch he rarely took off. "Three a.m., and my blood pressure is finally going down."

Dre bolted upright. "I need to get home. The boys will wonder where I've been all night."

"Matt and Annie won't. Tell the kids it got late, and we stayed the night at the ranch. They're nine. They'll accept that."

"But that's lying to them. Come on. Get up and drive me home." She gave him a shove in the right direction, but he hardly budged.

"Wait a few more minutes."

"Okay, but I am getting dressed now. No coaxing me back into bed." She gathered her clothes wherever they'd been flung.

Springs groaned, and Rex rolled out of the covers. He drew on a pair of jeans commando, unfurled a T-shirt over a chest that was a shame to cover, and shoved his feet into a pair of handy loafers. "Ready."

"So easy for you." Dre combed her short but thoroughly mussed hair into place. Together, they left Joe's pad and took the elevator downstairs in a sleeping building. The night doorman startled from a doze but brought the car around personally. He received a big tip for his service.

Crossing into the quiet Garden District, Rex double-parked in front of Matt's pillared mansion and escorted her to the door as usual. And as usual, kissed her long and hard. "Sure I can't convince you to come back with me for the rest of the night?"

"Not this time, but there will be lots of others in the future. Once the boys are back in school, plan on some afternoon delights if you can get a break in training. That's the advantage of being with a woman who is her own boss—long lunch hours."

"One day a week won't be enough. But for now, good night."

Dre put her key in the lock and tiptoed up to her bedroom.

****

The next thing she knew, the first hot rays of a summer day flooded through the windows whose drapes she'd failed to close. Someone knocked urgently on her door. Had anybody been hurt—Drew, Rex?

"Hey, Mom, hey, Mom! Blueberry pancakes for breakfast. Delia wants to know how many you want?" Drew shouted.

"Um, two, I guess. Let me get a shower first, okay?" she answered without inviting him in. Right now, she was grateful that she'd taught him at an early age to knock before entering. The aroma of sex clung to her hair, her body, and the discarded clothes. He wouldn't recognize that scent for a few years, she hoped.

She had to get her act together or miss breakfast with the boys before they scattered to friends' houses or simply wanted to spend all day in the pool where she'd be expected to serve as lifeguard for part of the day until Annie took a turn. Matt and Dean would already be training along with Rex who might not be as sharp as usual on just a few hours of sleep. Her fault, his fault, their fault, or no one's fault.

She did know the football player's life, having observed Matt doing it and Annie accepting it. As she washed her hair twice, she reviewed what she could expect: only one day a week when the men didn't practice, long weekends alone when the team flew to out of state games and back again, tired men, sometimes grouchy men when they'd suffered a loss. Not that Matt had ever taken a poor performance out on his wife or the children, only a brooding reluctance to talk about it if he'd fumbled a ball or missed a crucial hit on the opponent. She hoped Rex managed his temper in the same way. Here she was, dreaming of a life together when he still avoided saying I love you.

Out of the shower and after combing her no-nonsense hair into place, Dre brushed her teeth and skipped any makeup. She slipped into underwear, shorts, and a tee, shoved her feet into flipflops, and made her way still dead tired to the breakfast table, grateful for Delia who had poured her orange juice and kept two pancakes warm for her. If she and Drew were on their own, they'd dine on cold cereal most likely.

Annie regarded the tired face she'd seen in the mirror upstairs. "Late night?" she inquired with a knowing look.

"Ah, yes. Long drive home." There, she'd done it, lied, but the boys, arguing over possession of the blueberry syrup, took no notice. Jenny in her booster seat asked for help cutting up her flapjacks.

At the height of the summer heat, the kids decided on a pool day and wanted to invite friends to join them. Annie vetoed that. "A lot of your friends are probably on vacation right now. Maybe next week. Are you working on anything today, Dre?"

"I should catch up on a few things."

"That's fine. I'll do pool duty this morning, and you can take the afternoon shift."

"That works for me."

She finished that excellent breakfast and returned to her room while the boys washed their faces and hands and got into their swimming gear. Halfway through her emails, she fell asleep in her office chair and awoke with crick in her neck and one foot asleep, but at least she wouldn't doze off later when watching a pool full of active children. After accepting a light lunch of chicken salad in a tomato blossom, she put on her suit and took up her post while the children polished off peanut butter and jelly sandwiches with apple slices at the picnic table and waited for another round in the water.

Rex arrived late in the afternoon as she steered

Jenny around in another game of Marco Polo exactly as he had two months ago, yet everything had changed between them. Her heartbeat kicked up and throbbed even more as he stripped off his shirt and dropped his shorts revealing the red Speedo. She called out to the children, "How about a snack break? Uncle Rex and I are going to swim some laps."

As the children surged dripping from the water, Rex drew close. "Laps are not what I had in mind."

"Can't do anything more. Annie is at the NICU helping mothers of premature babies to learn their care and Delia has gone shopping. Matt isn't back yet. Probably having a post training beer with Dean. Let me get their snack. That will buy us a little time to talk."

"Yeah, talk, that's a great substitute."

She ignored him and fetched a tray of watermelon slices, knowing a seed spitting contest would soon ensue, and she'd be the one to clean it up. She didn't care so long as she had a little free time with Rex. They entered the water knee deep and stood very close. With a quick glance at the kids who'd already begun spitting, Jenny included, she gave Rex a quick brush of the lips and whispered, "I can't get last night together out of my mind."

"Me, either. Dean said my mind wasn't in the game today. You know where it was. When can we get together again?"

Before she could answer, he kissed her longer and harder than he should have in front of the children. The spitting contest stopped. Young heads bumped together in a huddle. Whisper, whisper, glance their way, more whispers.

"Now we've done it. Here comes Drew. A while ago

he asked if we were getting married because a friend of his's mother was marrying the guy who slept over at their house."

"I haven't slept here—but I'd like to."

"Hush," she said, proving she'd lived in the south since becoming a mother.

Drew walked to the edge of the pool, squared his thin, sunburned shoulders, and looked them almost in the eye since they stood at a lower level. He brushed his blond hair out of his eyes, shuffled his feet, and cleared his throat. "What are your intentions toward our, I mean, my mother, Uncle Rex?" The very serious question came out thin and squeaky in a voice that had not yet begun to change.

Rex handled it better than she did as she had a great desire to sink underwater. He simply raised his brows and suppressed a slight smile. "Entirely honorable, I promise."

"Oh, good, I guess. So, are you getting married?"

"Right now I need to tell you we are dating, getting to know each other better. It's a little soon for marriage. Okay with you if I take your mom out on Friday and Saturday night this week so we continue learning about each other?"

"Ah, sure, but don't you know each other well enough already? I mean you knew my mom since before I was born."

"We were very young then. Now we're older and more serious."

"Okay. But what about me?" Drew asked, finally getting to what really bothered him.

"I'd be a lucky man to have you for a son and your mother as my wife if everything works out. By the way,

I brought that set of light weights along, but left them in the house. You need to get into condition for next year's boat race."

"Gee, thanks, Uncle Rex. I will."

Dre read her son's eyes, his joy, his eagerness to have Rex as his dad. She couldn't mess this up. "Go win the seed spitting contest for me. We want to swim now."

She pushed off toward the deep end. Rex followed. As far from the kids as they could get, both pulled up and treaded water. "I think we both learned children always know more than we think they do. Asking about intentions sounded more like Daniel than Drew. Danny is always the mediator and a little older, but they are all into this together."

"What will happen if we change our minds about getting more serious?"

"Oh, Danny will pat Drew on the back as if he just missed a field goal and tell him sometimes things don't work out. Jenny will cry, and Gabe will punch you in the gut."

"Then, I better be very careful. I think I can take a shot from Gabe, but I can't stand it when little girls cry."

She placed a hand on top of his head and pushed him under. When he came up, he wiped the water from his eyes, and kissed her again. "Now that we are out as couple, we might as well make the most of it. And I set up two more nights we can be together."

"You do realize I can't stay overnight."

"No problem. We'll get takeout to save time—unless you want to dine out."

"Takeout on Friday, but a real dinner on Saturday, best of both worlds."

"I'll be ready, very ready since Dean doesn't make

us work out on Saturdays."

"Hey," called Gabe. "If you two are done fooling around, can we get back in the pool?"

"Sure thing." They stroked back to the shallow end.

Half glad that they'd been honest with Drew, but half afraid what would happen if they broke up because this was lust, not love, Dre almost dreaded the weekend.

Chapter Seventeen

They had their wild weekend. Pizza and beer consumed in the round bed one night and dining at the Court of the Three Sisters on crab cakes and having bananas foster for dessert Saturday, followed by a leisurely stroll down Bourbon Street with all its lights and diversions on display from the guy dressed as Homer Simpson sitting on a garbage can to a frozen statue of Andy Jackson, and more than one barker claiming all the pole dancers were college girls.

At one point, a trolling paparazzo caught them in an affectionate clutch. Dre imagined the headline in the gossip rag. "Rex dating Cousin?" Then, the article would go on to explain that in no way were they related by blood and expose her name, odd living arrangements, and the way she made a living. The incident ruined the balmy night for her until they got back to Joe's place and made the incident go away.

The picture did turn up on a slow week for scandal with copy as she'd predicted. It gave a little boost to her business she did not expect, but the majority of the potential clients wanted to meet in person, most likely to draw her out about Rex and their relationship. All but two faded away once she explained she only worked online. She did resent that the reporter dredged up old stories about Matt being the possible father of her child, easily disproved because she'd been pregnant when she arrived in Louisiana. Thank heaven, his sole reference to Drew was that she had a nine-year-old son without mentioning his name. The blip on the notoriety scale faded away fast.

Training camp started the following week, mandatory for all the Sinners players. Rex toiled at the Ochsner Sports Performance Center in Metairie doing two-a-days and straggling back to the apartment to fall into bed at night, but not before calling Dre. Only the rookies stayed together at a hotel near the Center for a more thorough indoctrination. Seasoned players went home and slept in their own beds with wives and girlfriends, lacking the energy to do anything else.

In the brief interval between the end of training camp and the first offseason game slated to be out of town, they did manage a few intimate moments, staying in, ordering out, and making heavy use of both beds and baths. Knowing the boys were watching, they agreed on no overnights. Family get-togethers were rare after the Fourth once the juggernaut grind of the playing season began. By Christmas, she hoped Rex might take the next step and make her a true part of the Billodeaux family along with Drew. She would not push or use the L word again until then.

The first regular game against their perpetual arch-rival, the Falcons, came up fast. Dre took her usual spot in the Billodeaux sky box where the women with small children gathered. Since the Billodeaux Baby Boom, a whole troop of three-year-olds rampaged around the box and ate off a special buffet of kid friendly foods featuring pigs-in-a-blanket, chicken nuggets, fruit cubes, baby carrots, and juice boxes beside more adult fare and drinks.

"Her" boys begged to be allowed into the fifty-yard-line box with Daddy Joe. They were old enough now. They'd be good. The extra seat where Auntie Lorena used to sit was up for grabs now that she had to monitor little Mikey. Aunt Edie took up so little room they could squeeze in beside Beck and DJ since Wynn wanted to stay with the rest of the women. All good arguments, the final winner being Drew's earnest plea to be able to watch Uncle Rex play close up. Permission granted. She did, however, escort them through the throngs of people on the ramps to the safety of Joe's protection. As she left, he repeated the rules of the box——no talking or squabbling during the game, no requests for hot dogs or drinks which could be had upstairs, but lots of cheering their team on, understood? She watched her guys nodding solemnly as she reached the first level and made her way upward to the quiet confines of the boxes only the rich and large companies could afford.

She'd worn jeans, running shoes, and a Sinners' black tee with Rex's number on the back, typical dress for a game if not wearing a costume like so many did in New Orleans. Once her Goth days were done, she no longer cared to call attention to herself, not when it might embarrass her son. But in the airier atmosphere of the upper corridor, she did flap her arms a little to cool down after her exertions.

Of course, she ran directly into Barb Bienville just entering the owner's box and attired as if going to a fancy ladies' luncheon. At least, she'd shown some team spirit by dressing all in black with a token touch of red in a silk scarf draped artfully around her neck. Her long red hair curled perfectly about her shoulders. She eyed Dre from head to foot and said, "I often wish I could fly away from these games week after endless week, but Gus insists we mustn't miss a one no matter how far away."

"Oh, I find them exciting, Mrs. Bienville."

"Barb. I'm not that much older than you, Dre Ames."

Only twenty-five years or so, Dre thought, but put on a pleasant smile. "I'm flattered you remembered me, Barb. Last time, we were at the art gala in semi-darkness."

"I'd remember anyone there with Rex Billodeaux. You two are quite the item now, all over the scandal sheets."

"Only once. Slow salacious news week, I guess." She kept her smile plastered in place.

"What I would give for a young lover like that. Is he good in bed?"

While she wanted to reply, "Better than you'll ever have," she choked that down. "No more time to chat. I don't want to miss the kickoff." She fled to the refuge of the Billodeaux box and sank down in a seat next to Stacy after grabbing a cold drink from the bar.

"You seem flustered, Dre. Anything happen between here and there?" Stace said with a nod at the field where the boys cheered the entrance of the team through their devil's mouth blowup and clouds of dry ice simulating steam.

"I ran into Mrs. Bienville."

"Always unpleasant and catty. She can't stand anyone younger and more beautiful than she is. Be careful or she'll send her huntsman out to bring back your heart in a box or gift with you a fruit basket full of poisoned apples."

"She asked me if Rex was good in bed. I told her I

didn't want to miss the kickoff and fled."

"That's a question I'd never ask with Rex being my brother-in-law, and besides I know the answer. All the Billodeaux men are, including Teddy in his wheelchair. While I'd ordinarily say don't flee from a predator, you did the right thing. Avoid her whenever you can, but you might have to suffer her company at team events."

"Assuming I will be going to team events."

"After you marry Rex, then you get to endure mandatory appearances at all of Barb's parties."

"Y'all know something I don't. Rex doesn't think we understand each other well enough yet to move ahead." Had she actually used y'all, a word she despised? Yes, she had been in the south too long. It had slipped out so naturally. Perhaps, she should go back to Indiana and clean up her grammar for a while, letting Rex alone to make up his mind about their relationship.

"That's just what he told the boys to take the heat off," Annie said. They'd told her all about Drew's questions about his intentions after she got home. "I think that was so sweet, and Rex handled it well."

"He is good with kids, again like all the Billodeaux men, but that doesn't mean what he said isn't true."

All wise Stacy simply answered, "Bet you a twenty you two are engaged by Christmas."

"I'd love to let you win that bet." They turned their gazes back to the field.

Warmups done, coin tossed, Tom Billodeaux trotted out to do the kickoff, sending the football deep to the ten-yard line, a good start. The game proved to be a defensive battle with no score as the clock wound down to halftime. Both quarterbacks had been sacked several times and gotten up shaken. Each time Dean ended up under a three-hundred-pound tackle, Stacie shuddered. Dre could feel it in the arm that rested next to hers.

Rex subbed in for a few plays while his brother went into the tent to be run through the concussion protocol after a vicious hit. Back on the field, Dean lobbed a long one straight into the end zone to put up a score in the last seconds. Stacy and Dre stood, cheered, and clapped as did the cadre of three-year-olds who had no idea what went on. Stacy pressed against the glass and waved as the team left the field for halftime. The crowd continued to scream and chant Dean's name, almost drowning out the wail of a siren drawing near.

Out in the corridor, feet thudded. Doors slammed open. Stacy raced to the door of theirs. "What if Dean collapsed in the locker room?" she told Dre, hot on her heels.

Denizens of the sky boxes who were out and about for a leg stretch or a restroom break plastered themselves against the walls as a gurney and EMTs erupted from the elevator and headed straight for the owner's box. Holding back the tide of toddlers trying to escape their room, Dre answered, "Not Dean. Someone in the Bienville box."

With Annie and Xo helping from inside, she managed to close the door without crushing little hands. She waited with the rest to see the outcome, not a long time at all, as a gray-faced Gus rode the gurney to the elevator. Eyes closed, chest not heaving for air, the old man exhibited few signs of life other than being covered with a sheet to his chin and not over his face. Following in her high heels, Barb, dry-eyed and somber, clipped along behind the medics. As the elevator closed, Dre could have sworn the woman sent a slight, smug smile her way.

"Did you see that?" she asked Stacy.

"I did. Barbie is getting her payoff for thirty years of service to Gus Bienville at last."

"You think he's dead?"

Jude, who had managed to scrape off her twins and make it into the corridor before the gurney got away, answered. "Oh, yeah. Gus has been whistled down by the great ref in the sky."

The aide, who usually accompanied Gus everywhere, turned as he waited for the elevator's return. "Please, go about your business and enjoy the rest of the game. Gus would want that. Thoughts and prayers, people. We'll have an update on his condition later." The doors slid open, and he slipped away,

"I'd call time of death at the start of halftime. The guy doesn't want to upset the crowd—but it is what the old man would approve of if he was still with us," Jude said rather coldly as she set about opening the door to the suite. Before going all the way, she shouted, "Line up for juice boxes!" to clear her way.

Xochi, who had the most children and experience with feeding them, stood behind the caterer's offerings making up small paper plates with one sausage roll, one nugget, a couple of tater tots, a single carrot, and a cube of cantaloupe surrounding a small puddle of ketchup for dipping. She doled them out to the children, saying, "You can have more when you finish this."

Jude, making good on her promise, poked straws into juice boxes. Annie arranged the little ones in a circle on the floor to eat. The older boys returned from their grandpa's box to heap what they wanted onto larger plates, hitting both the kiddie stuff and the adult fare of mini-muffulettas and barbecued shrimp on skewers, leaving the raw oysters on ice alone. Dre and the other mothers settled into their own seats with their choices just as the second half began.

Teddy Billodeaux's mellow announcer's voice filled the air. "Ladies and gentlemen, fans of the Sinners, our beloved team owner Gus Bienville has been taken to the hospital, possibly suffering a heart attack. Let's observe a moment of silence to send up prayers and best wishes for his recovery. Then, honor him by supporting his team in this close game against a fierce opponent. Thank you."

Into the silence, Jude muttered from her spot on the other side of Dre, "That man's a gone pecan."

Her twins ran over to show their empty plates. "More nuggets please, Mama."

"Ask Auntie Xo. The game is about to start."

The Sinners received. The return team ran the ball back to the thirty-yard line. Dean took it from there, moving his men along ten yards at a time with short, sharp passes all the way to the end zone where the progression stalled. The Sinners had to settle for one of Tom's precisely placed field goals. Ten to nothing, but not much of a lead.

Stacy downed an oyster dabbed with hot sauce from its shell. She took a deep breath. "My husband is playing hurt. I know they pumped him full of pain killers and bandaged something to keep him going at the half."

Jude agreed. "I'd say his right side is bothering him, so no long passes or trying for a run himself. And stop slurping those oysters. You know how many people I treat every year for eating bad ones?"

"No idea." Stacy ate another.

Dre wondered if she had what it took to be a football player's wife, knowing about the injuries and the danger of many concussions. Dean had played a long time without significant injuries and won four Super Bowls, but now as he slid toward forty more occurred, the one requiring shoulder surgery most recently.

"Would you like him to retire?" she asked Stace.

"Oh, yes. We've talked about it. He wants one more ring, and I told him he has enough expensive jewelry. They do hate to quit."

Out on the field, their rivals ran the kick back nearly to the goal until Ty with a burst of speed took the carrier down on the ten-yard line. That failed to stop a touchdown in two more plays. Score ten-seven.

Dean took the field again, tried to run the ball when none of his receivers appeared open, and went down hard. As he rose, he spent a time out for a brief conference that resulted in Rex being called in to finish the game. When the two men passed on the field, Dean gave his little brother a pat on the back and pointed to the crowd. "Rex!" he shouted. The fans took up the chant as the game resumed. Rex, Rex, Rex!

"Do you think he'll go to the locker room?" Dre asked.

"Oh, hell, no. My man will sit on the bench, give advice, and cheer the Sinners on until the last second. That's just the way he's built. I won't know what's wrong with him until we get home."

Which didn't keep the commentators from speculating. Sprained ankle, broken ribs, both?

Rex threw long passes, found holes to run through thanks to his offense, and carried the pig skin across the line for a touchdown. He delivered that ball into the hands of the ecstatic Drew in Daddy Joe's box. Dre felt her heart go out to encompass both of them.

Rex scored another with a pass into the end zone late in the fourth quarter and put the game away twenty-four to seven. Amid the cheers and the handshaking and the reporters rushing to get an interview, Teddy's voice stilled the crowd.

"We are grieved to report that team owner, Gustave Bienville, has passed away. We dedicate this game to him, the man who brought the Sinners to the Dome as an expansion team so many years ago and lived to see them become a major force in the league. Arrangements for a memorial service will be announced at a later date. Go forth and raise a glass to his memory."

Although the mood turned from jubilant to somber in a minute, the interviews went on as the crowd dispersed into the French Quarter, many to do just that. Dre asked Stacy, "Are we still going to Mariah's Place tonight?"

"I don't think Dean is up to it. Maybe tomorrow evening. They'll have a team meeting Monday and the afternoon off. By that time, we might know the fate of the Sinners."

"What do you mean?"

"The owner is dead. His family has been squabbling for years over ownership of the team, but old Gus never gave a clue as to what he'd do. I guess we'll know when the will is read."

"What do you think the team is worth? Can't someone buy it, maybe Joe?"

"I don't think even Joe can come up with five billion dollars. Yeah, that's what a team like this is worth."

Chapter Eighteen

Stacy organized a phone tree among the Sinners' players inviting them to meet at Mariah's Place on Monday evening for a special tribute to Gus. Mariah promised a free champagne toast, though Gus was more of beer man, and a special musical performance. She'd close the club to the public.

Rex and Dre walked into the perpetual twilight of the bar to standing room only. X had arrived early, pushed two four-tops together, and guarded the chairs as closely as he did a football in his grip. Ty and Edie who lived close by were already seated. Matt and Annie, who had followed Rex and Dre, slid into two of the seats, and they took the last, all but one remaining vacant. Nearby, Joe and Nell sat with Dean and Stacy—which meant that Rex's parents were staying over in the old bachelor pad until after the funeral on Friday—and Dre would not. His folks wouldn't mind, but Dre refused, always with Drew in mind. He'd miss their stolen hours together.

Rex poked at X that the man had spent the afternoon getting his hair done, braided into short dreads with bright beads inserted here and there. "That's going to be uncomfortable under a helmet."

"Worth it, totally worth it. Wait until you see."

Waitresses passed the champagne glasses. Dressed in a low-cut black sequin gown without the signature slit up the front, very conservative for her, Mariah lost no time mounting the stage before the drinks were consumed. She raised her flute of wine and made it short and sweet. "To Gus Bienville who brought the Sinners to New Orleans. Now, a special musical tribute by our own Caressa."

Caressa appeared in the gold choir robe she'd used for Jude's wedding and performed an Ave Maria so moving one or two of the tough guys on the team dabbed at their eyes with cocktail napkins. Once more, she'd bedecked her head with beaded strands. Her face had rounded out, and the joy in her eyes shone clearly again as she sang. Finished, she dropped the robe and exposed a black dress with a full skirt that swirled around her restored hips, cut low enough to show softly rounded brown breasts.

"Now I'm going to perform a medley of Gus Bienville's favorite songs with a very special ending." As she swung into the first number, the deep gores in her skirt opened to display scarlet slashes, black and red, the Sinners' colors.

"She looks good, X. Now I understand your new do. Matching hair, huh."

X leaned in to answer Rex. "Hers are a wig. I found the shoebox with the hair that bastard cut off when we cleaned out her dressing room and had it made for her to wear until she doesn't need it anymore. Now, hush up and just listen to her sing."

Dre's hand moved to give X's arm a squeeze. That simple gesture tossed Rex into deeper water, the what ifs. What if X hadn't insisted on rescuing Caressa? He would have lost her forever. Life could end in minutes like the heart attack that brought Gus down. Why hadn't he told Dre he loved her? He had to admit he liked her freshness and openness to new experiences, the fun they had sneaking around, but wasn't it time he got serious? He glanced at Dre who swayed slightly to the music and recalled teaching her to dance in this very spot. At that time, he wanted to make amends for past treatment, but it turned out to be the start of something more. She felt his gaze and answered with a smile before turning her interest back to the stage. He signaled the waitress to bring him a stiffer drink than the depleted champagne. What if—what if he lost her before speaking up?

As the medley wound down, Caressa gestured to X to come to the stage and perform "Unforgettable", the song they'd joined voices in many times. Though they stared into each other's eyes for the duration, Carie flipped the ending by saying, "Gus, you were unforgettable, too."

The team stood to applaud, but the show wasn't over. Caressa and X, hands clasped, took a bow, but clearly that song hadn't been about Gus because X dropped to his knees.

"Carie, this might not be the right time or place, but I want all my friends to witness my love for you. I can't wait any longer now that you are healed. Will you marry me?" He presented a ring, not a big, honking flashy yellow diamond like Stacy wore, but one perfect for Caressa, a large ruby circled with small diamonds, deep red and sparkling all at once.

"I think I'm going to faint again," Carie said.

"No you don't, woman. Not before you answer me. I want to be here to catch you for the rest of our lives."

"Yes, yes! I just didn't expect this tonight."

He slipped the ring on her finger, an apparent perfect fit, and stood. "Okay, guys, let's turn this into a happy occasion. Order some drinks and toast to us. I'm paying."

He led his new fiancée from the stage to the chair he'd been guarding the whole evening. Dre, Edie, and Annie exclaimed over the ring. Stacy came over to get a closer look. "I thought you were going to wait until she was well enough to go ring shopping together."

"Couldn't wait. You know, Leslie at Schifferman's. He knew exactly what would suit her. Unless you want something else, Carie babe?"

Caressa shook her head sending those beaded braids swinging. "It's perfect."

Buying jewelry for women, not his strength. Rex stuck to red roses and nice dinners for his dates, but he couldn't help noticing that only Dre's long, artistic fingers were bare of rings. All the others bore diamonds, Annie and Edie's smaller than Stacy's big yellow rock but right for their small hands. Dre deserved her own. He must make time to seek out Leslie, then plan the moment he'd present the ring to her. Life only lasted so long, and he'd been wasting it.

Chapter Nineteen

The team stayed late at Mariah's and drank long. Not too sure of himself to get Dre home safely, Rex sent her back with Annie and Matt who left early to pay off their babysitter. Training the next day wasn't exactly a Cajun barbecue considering the sore heads, but Gus would have expected them to sweat out the alcohol. Coach Buck sure did. He rode the players hard all week always reminding them this season was dedicated to their former owner—but who owned the team now? What happened next? The question lingered like a timeout for an injury in the back of every mind.

Then, Barbara Bienville, the questionably grieving widow, required each and every Sinner to attend a rehearsal for the outlandish funeral Gus had outlined in detail and expected her to carry out inside the Dome. They'd stayed after practice on Thursday as the funeral director informed them that the team would run out onto the field in full black gear through the steaming devil's mouth as if beginning a game, then take seats placed on either side of the fifty-yard line and stow their helmets beneath their chairs. His chosen pallbearers, allowed to dress in black suits, were all five quarterbacks who had served the team over the years: Art Golden, Joe Billodeaux, Rex Worthy, Dean Billodeaux, and Rex himself, included because Gus hadn't planned on dying during his first season. They'd escort the coffin draped in a red Sinner's banner, to a position under the goal post. Art Golden in a wheelchair would follow the more able-bodied. He'd position himself on one side of the remains along with Joe and Rex Worthy while Dean and his brother plus the widow stood on the other side. The man's two grown children were to be placed at the head of the coffin.

After the National Anthem sung by Caressa, everyone would take a seat. Teddy had been delegated up in the booth to read a lengthy eulogy outlining Gus Bienville's rise from a luxury car dealer to a real estate magnate, to a man whose wise investments earned him the wealth to bring an expansion football team to New Orleans. He'd be lauded as a generous owner who brought the best players on board over time to win nine Super Bowls and hoped for a tenth in the year of his death. Following a short religious ceremony, then on to the football game style refreshments catered by the Dome staff, hot dogs, chicken wings, barbecued shrimp skewers, and plenty of free beer. Attendees could record their memories of Gus in a private booth. Anyone with season tickets or a box received an invitation to attend, the whole thing to be filmed for posterity.

On Friday, all went off according to plan, but Rex standing by Barb heard her mutter, "Tacky, so tacky, no dignity at all. That was Gus." His children never ceased glaring in her direction despite her impeccable all black mourning outfit, maybe a little tight in the rear and set off with stiletto heels, but flattering with her red hair, and a ruby pin large enough to be considered ostentatious. Might have been worse, Rex figured, though he could have done without her strong, almost gagging perfume in his nostrils.

Between stumbling over his parents in the bachelor pad and more than once returning from practice to find them in the round tub together or locked in a bedroom, plus the long rehearsal, he hadn't gotten a chance to slip away through the impressive doors of Schifferman's to purchase a ring for Dre. She sat in the fifty-yard line seats with Stacy and Edie, Trinity and Josee, while other members of the family occupied the box on this historic occasion, but he could hardly propose at this kind of event anyhow.

As the LSU marching band, hired for the occasion, played Gus off to his rest, Barb leaned against him. "Please help me to the limo, Rex. I'm afraid these shoes weren't intended for walking on artificial turf."

With their red soles and ice pick heels, they appeared as sharp as the team's colorful cleats, but he offered his arm as any gentleman would. As the chauffeur held the door for her, Barb hung onto this hand. "Ride with me. I am so alone."

She cocked her head toward the Bienville children and grandchildren piling into another vehicle. He tried and couldn't think of a good excuse to deny her and so rode to the vast Metairie Cemetery where Gus had squeezed an elaborate classical tomb into Millionaire's Row upon the death of his first wife. Rife with columns and angels, the stone football topping it instead of a cross did seem a little out of place, but Gus had added that after the Sinners won their fifth Super Bowl, bragging that the sepulcher was roomy enough for both wives, his kids, and grandkids. Now that he'd seen it for himself, Rex had to agree.

The final ceremony remained private as the priest did the ashes to ashes, dust to dust part, and the family laid red roses on the coffin placed on its bier in the middle of the tomb. All the while, Barb clung to him as if he were family. In fact, assuming so, the undertaker thrust a rose into his hand, too. He laid it respectfully among the others and murmured, "So long, Gus, you were a legendary owner."

As they left the cool darkness of the tomb, he heard the daughter sniff, "Looks like Barb has picked out her next husband." The heavy bronze doors clanged shut.

No way, no how, never. Still when Barb asked him to open the champagne in the limo, he did. She wanted to steady her nerves, she claimed, and had no desire to return to the after party in the Dome or to her huge, empty condo. Could they go to his place for a short time?

"Um, I'm staying with my parents right now, and they expect me to join them in the sky box for a last salute to Gus." His flesh prickled the way it did when he anticipated being sacked.

"How sweet. How young." She clutched her stemmed glass with fingernails tipped in bright red, Sinners' colors after all. "You are about the same age I was when I came to New Orleans to seek my fortune. I found it with Gus who was a vigorous sixty-five at the time and missing female companionship. The first twenty years were a blast, the last ten, not so hot. I've been waiting a long time for my inheritance. I expect to be a very rich widow."

He wanted to say she'd earned it, but that seemed crass. He settled for an understanding nod and hoped the Friday traffic back to the Dome wasn't too thick. To make sure there was no misunderstanding, he rapped on the limo window and made sure the driver knew where to drop him off. In the meantime, he refilled Barb's glass and his own. "To Gus," he said to remind her of her very recent loss.

They parted at the VIP entrance. He hightailed it up to the sky box where the party continued, giving old Gus the sendoff he wanted. Dre, where was Dre in this chaos of kids, brothers, and sisters? She sat at the window overlooking the now empty field, a plate of food in her lap, a worried expression on her face. He pushed through the toddlers racing around the room, past the bar where Jude and some of his other siblings toasted the dead team owner, and down to a seat next to her. He went in for a kiss, and she started to respond, then drew back.

"Perfume? Where have you been?"

"Oh, yeah, the widow wore some scent strong enough to make my eyes water. On film, it will look like I'm crying for Gus. She asked me to help her to the limo because she'd worn ridiculous shoes. Then, she asked me to ride with her to the cemetery since the rest of the family snubbed her. I did feel a little sorry for her, but I'm here now." He left out Barb's suggestion that they go back to his place. He went in for the kiss again. Their lips touched.

"Champagne? You've been drinking champagne with her?"

"On the way back, she asked me to open the bottle and didn't want to drink alone. Only two glasses. I'm not drunk."

"No, you aren't. I'm being ridiculous. But, that woman is a predator. Please be careful around her."

Many women would have parleyed the entire incident into an argument, maybe even a breakup. But Dre fretted about him, Mister Cool in the Pocket, Master of the Field. It touched his heart. He had to make the time to get that ring and soon.

Smiling, he said, "With luck, Gus left her his place in Paris, and we won't have to see her again." He sincerely hoped so. He finally got his kiss.

Chapter Twenty

But Saturday morning, the team flew off to an away game on the west coast and played on Sunday night. Dean and Rex did all they could to stabilize their men, but the events of the previous week and the uncertainty of their future kept minds from the game. No owner or his widow in a sky box to cheer them on. A team they should have defeated easily came within a field goal of taking the win. The Sinners had been saved by Tom's very accurate toe in the last seconds.

They flew out Monday morning, had a brief team meeting, basically a pep talk about getting their heads in the game and honoring Gus, before being released for the afternoon. He wanted to spend that afternoon with Dre since his parents had decamped for the ranch after the funeral, but the ring had to come first.

Tired as he was, he dragged himself to Schifferman's and stood before the intimidating glass doors with their scrolled S's. He thrust them open and strode past the cases of watches, pearls, and colored gems, wedding place settings and silver cups and rattles for babies as if stiff-arming tacklers all the way to where a small man with a tidy silver mustache waxed on the ends waited behind a matte black counter.

"How may I assist you, sir?"

"A ring, an engagement ring." His voice faltered before the legendary Leslie appearing exactly as his brothers had described the man.

Leslie allowed himself the slightest smile. "An important decision to be sure." The man rested pale, manicured hands on the countertop. "You are Rex Billodeaux of course, but who might the fortunate lady be?"

The clerk didn't seem like the kind of guy who followed football, but his recognition of the new quarterback was easily explained. "You greatly resemble your brother, an early client of mine. If you would describe your future fiancée I will do all I can to help you choose the perfect ring."

"She's tall and slim, blonde, and blue-eyed. Her fingers might be as long as mine but much thinner, artist's hands. She isn't very girly but could be if she wanted. Something simple but elegant, I think."

"Would this be the graphic artist, Dre Ames?"

"Yes, how did you know?"

Again, that slight smile graced Leslie's lips. "I read both the society pages and the scandal sheets. One never knows who will walk into the store. I like to be prepared. I admit I've been anticipating your visit and have put several selections aside. One moment while I get them from the safe." He vanished behind a black curtain like a magician about to perform a spectacular illusion and returned with three rings, laid them out on velvet.

"First, an emerald cut diamond ring with baguette shoulders, 3.19 carats, set in platinum. The second, an old emerald cut with tapered shoulders, 5.38 carats, set in gold. The last, a 2.5 carat stone with baguette cut diamonds along the shoulders set in platinum." Leslie waited with patience as his customer pondered.

Prices ranged from $45,000 to $167,900. The cost

didn't matter at all, neither did the number of carats as far as Rex was concerned. Relying on Leslie's reputation, he didn't worry about color or clarity or being cheated. "Why all emerald cuts?"

"Emerald cut rings are sophisticated and timeless. They are favored by celebrities and those with good taste such as an artist."

"The first one, could it be altered to add one of these, ah, baguettes across the top? Dre has a son I'd like to adopt. I want that stone to represent him."

"Certainly. Schifferman's offers the finest of alterations. Of course, the price would be adjusted upward, and the work will take some time. Payment in advance, but we do guarantee satisfaction with the final design."

"Then, I'll take this one." He withdrew a credit card with a platinum color that matched the ring and waited while the charge cleared. "Do you know how long it will take to make the change?"

"I do not, but we will call as soon as the ring is finished. Is there a hurry?"

"No, no hurry." He didn't want Leslie to think he'd gotten Dre pregnant, though these days, it was no longer a big deal. Mostly, since Gus had died, he had a pervading feeling that no time should be lost before he proclaimed his love to Dre, but another few weeks would hardly matter. Tomorrow, he'd make sure they had time together.

Chapter Twenty-One

Dre knew the drill. She'd lived for ten years with a football player's family and did not complain about his long training sessions that killed their afternoons together or weekends when he had to travel for games and didn't see her at all. He did call and often imagined her along with Annie and the boys watching him play on television. When he flashed that famous smile into the camera after a touchdown, it was for her, he'd said and meant. Lots of women pretended otherwise in their fantasy worlds, judging by some of the social media posts he'd seen.

The Sinners played their next game after the passing of Gus at home, a tough match against a good opponent that they'd pulled off with a last-minute touchdown which X had brought about by leaping over a fallen tackle after a handoff from Dean. On the bench, Rex noted a promising sign up in the owner's sky box. The Bienville children, aged seventy and sixty-five, had filled it with grandchildren and great-grandchildren, all cheering for the team. No sight of Barb who had always worn bright red gowns to show up against the glass when the cameras turned her way. If Edwin "Ned" Bienville and Paula Bienville Chapman inherited the team, the future looked sunny as a New Orleans summer's day. Meanwhile, they had to play their best until their fate was settled by the reading of the will.

Since the game had aired at noon, players had some time to rest and relax afterward. He took Dre on one of their date nights at Mariah's after they had dinner with his parents and a bunch of siblings and grandkids at Brennan's on Royal Street. Well-filled with satsuma lacquered duck, and cane-syrup-braised beef cheeks, followed by the signature bananas foster flamed at their table, they had no need of bar food and ordered a bottle of wine at the night club where Caressa did a short set of songs, still pacing herself after her breakdown. She joined them and the hero of the day, X, at their table when she finished.

"So nice to see all my saviors here together." She included Edie and Ty in her glance. "You know, I think this is what I want, a club like Mariah's where I can sing what I wish, write my music, and discover new talent. No more traveling for me."

X kissed the hand bearing her engagement ring. "We're gonna make that happen, babe."

"What worries me is that X, Ty, and me all signed fat three-year-contracts this past summer. Will the new owner honor those or want to renegotiate everything to cut costs?" Rex took a sip of wine and decided he needed something stronger. He ordered a bourbon on the rocks.

Ty nodded. "We have a potential Super Bowl team sitting right here in Mariah's. If the contracts aren't honored, some of the guys will split, and there goes Dean's fifth ring."

"And my first. Yours, too, Ty."

"I think it's a good sign that Ned and Paula were up in the owner's box, right?" Dre said.

Rex downed his bourbon. "We better hope so. I think we'll call it a night. Enjoy the rest of the wine. You ready to go, Dre?"

"Absolutely."

The group shared knowing glances, and X piped up, "Off to the bachelor pad, huh?"

"My folks should be on their way to the ranch by now, and I have to get Dre home by midnight according to Drew. I think that boy is already training to be a girl dad. So, no time to waste. See you at team meeting."

They wasted no time on the way to the apartment, kissing at stop lights and stroking above the waist. It had been more than a week since their last time together. Keys flipped to the concierge and a quick elevator ride upward landed them outside the condo door and already shedding clothes that made a trail to the round bed and its mirrored ceiling.

Dre inhaled the scent of clean sheets as she hit the covers. "I think your mom changed the linens before they left."

"It's the least they could do. While they stayed here, I never knew which bed would be available when I came home. So, are you sure you can't stay the night?"

"Even though Drew will be asleep well before midnight, I can't break his trust. You are right. We should be going slow and not rush this relationship."

"Well, I'm in a rush right now. Condom?" He nodded toward the night table closest to her hand, and she tossed him one from the drawer. "I envy my parents. They don't have to mess with these things anymore." He fumbled getting it on in his haste.

Dre took over, smoothing it over an urgent erection. "I love doing that."

"So do I. Let's see what I can do for you."

"I think we got a good start in the car."

His hand slid into her silky bikini briefs, and he found the moisture he anticipated but didn't stop with that. He took the time to insert a finger and move it in and out while massaging an eager clit until she pushed the hand away and urged him inside. Neither of them took a long time coming. They leaned back as Dre relaxed in his arms.

The only thing he hadn't taken off was his fancy sports watch. "Best aerobics exercise in the world," he commented. "We'll have time for another before the Cinderella hour."

"Can't wait," Dre replied, a little drowsy.

"Oh well, then. Let me oblige." Despite some protest, he brought her along again with his hands and mouth.

"I love—that, too."

He noticed the catch in her words, wanted to tell her the time neared when he'd say the words she wanted to hear. Leslie seemed to be taking his good old time with the ring design, but to call him would be an insult to the man renowned for his good taste. Soon, Dre, soon, he thought as she nestled just above his heartbeat.

Chapter Twenty-Two

Another road trip to play the Giants in New York loomed ahead. Another weekend with Dre lost, but they'd see each other on Monday night. The Sinners remained victorious. Waiting for them upon their return—the news that the will would be read on Tuesday. Personally, Rex had better information, a call from Leslie that the ring had been returned from the designers for his approval.

He took himself to Schifferman's after team meeting and a light practice session. The doors no longer intimidated him. He strode past the cases of jewels and tables of dinner settings where perhaps Dre might want to display her choices for their life together in the near future straight to Leslie who waited with that slight smile on his lips.

"I think you will be pleased." The ultimate salesman flipped open Schifferman's signature black silk box and presented the ring.

It didn't resemble the one he'd chosen very much. The central stone still shone in the same place, but the side baguettes had been reset to frame it vertically which balanced the horizonal diamond at the top. The platinum band seemed thicker.

Leslie spoke. "By making the side baguettes vertical, not only is the arrangement more pleasing, but it allows for the addition of more stones—should your union be blessed with children. However, if you wish any changes…"

"No, no. It's better than the first. Thank you. I hope I will be bringing it back a time or two. She's going to love the whole idea, assuming she accepts me."

"Little doubt of that I am sure. A man who thinks of her child is a good man." Leslie sighed and said with a hint of reproach, "I have so enjoyed serving the Billodeaux family. Of course, your brother Mack bypassed Schifferman's."

Rex felt he had to explain. "Mack has always been a loose cannon. He married a woman who didn't want an engagement ring."

Leslie pursed his lips. "That is a rarity, but perhaps later for an anniversary. I do hope I am still here to celebrate the next generation of Billodeaux buyers."

"They wouldn't go anywhere else."

"Shall I put it in a bag?"

"No, I think I feel safer with it zipped into my inside pocket. Now to decide on a perfect place and time."

Leslie served up a wise smile. "Any place and time can be perfect. Do not delay too long."

"We have a Monday night game coming up that will allow a little more down time. Before then, I think."

"My best wishes to both of you."

He left with the ring a burning presence inside his Sinners' jacket. Where to hide it until the right time came? Not in the night table drawer for sure where she'd find it among the condoms. Certainly not in his SUV of a brand often broken into or stolen. Finally, he put it under the mattress of the top central bunk in the bedroom they never used. Good enough for now. When she came over that night, Dre had no idea how close they were to being engaged.

He pondered how to make the occasion special for her. It threw him off in practice the next day. He fumbled two handoffs. His perfect spiral passes went high and sank low. He covered his distraction by saying catching those balls amounted to good training.

Two choices for a proposal came to mind. Real estate agents had been dogging him since his arrival in New Orleans with spectacular homes for sale. He'd narrowed the choices down to places in the Garden District near to Matt and Dean's homes since he wanted Drew to be close to his cousins, but he'd yet to view any of the houses. If he took Dre along and she showed a preference, he could propose there and tell her this is where they'd live. But with a realtor looking on, not so romantic.

The obvious choice was Mariah's where they'd had their first dance together when he still thought he merely opened up her life to new possibilities. He hadn't expected to enjoy her company so much, hadn't meant to fall in love with her. Yet, he hated to imitate X's recent proposal. Maybe he could change it up, get Dre out on the dance floor for a slow one and arrange for Mariah to gradually clear the floor until only they danced in a spotlight with Caressa singing softly in the background. He'd get down on his knees and proclaim himself before his friends and family that he loved her and wanted her to be his bride. Yeah, that sounded good.

A football hit him in the side of the helmet. Fortunately, it was only being lobbed back by the receiver of his last pass and did no harm except for some harmless mockery from other players. "It's good practice," one of them chortled.

Coach Buck blew his whistle. "All right, all right. Cut it out. We're all on edge today." He checked a watch so old-fashioned that its only extra functions included a stopwatch and an inset with the day of the year. "They're reading the will right now. You got another hour of practice, no slacking, then hit the showers. We might have word by the time you towel off, so stick around instead of running home."

Rex applied himself to not slacking, but more than gladly trotted off to the locker room after the last of the drills. He had a towel wrapped around his loins when the general manager walked in and drew the attention of team.

Mitchell Michener cleared his throat twice, not a good sign from a man who routinely gave players who didn't make the cut their walking papers. Sweat dewed his receding hairline and settled in his wrinkled brow, but that might have been because of the heat and moisture in the air since he wore a conservative summer suit and with flashy red necktie. The man took off his stylish glasses and wiped them with his pocket square before putting them on again, but he did not meet a single eye.

"The new owner of the Sinners wishes to have a word with you."

Must be Ned because he doubted Paula would show up in the locker room. Rex breathed deep with relief— until Barb Bienville, wearing deadly black, clicked in on her icepick heels and chilled the air. Several players rushed to pulled up their pants, but he was too far from his and just stood there nearly naked as she raked her green eyes over the men as if judging livestock.

"My late husband has seen fit to leave the Sinners

and all its assets to me. As I did not get a share of the business, the house in Palm Springs, the condo in New York, or the pied-a-terre in Paris, but only our apartment in New Orleans, I find myself in want of funds."

"Pied-a-what?" Huddleston, the muscleman among the safeties, questioned.

Ty, who had drawn on a pair of shorts and a T-shirt, whispered, "A little place in Paris."

"That's what she wants, not a football team?"

"I guess."

Barb shot a sharp glance their way. "I intend to sell the team to the highest bidder no matter who it is or where it is."

Always the last off the field, Dean walked naked out of the showers with a towel slung over his shoulder. Showing the same speed and coolness he displayed as a quarterback he made a quick turn and secured the towel around his waist before confronting the new owner.

She eyed him and said with a smirk on her red, red lips. "I see it's true that your wife's name is tattooed on your ass."

"Yes, and proud of it." He stood tall for the team. "If Rex and I could meet more privately with you, perhaps tomorrow, we might be able to give you good reasons to reconsider selling."

"I doubt that. But fine, one o'clock at my place. Don't be late. Bring your best arguments." She turned and stalked out as if stabbing each one of them in the heart with her heels.

"Gentlemen, I'm sorry about this intrusion. She insisted. As you must have figured out, your jobs and mine depend on what Mrs. Bienville does next." The GM loosened his tie as if he were choking. He shoved several of the antacids he always kept in his pocket into his mouth.

"Get me figures on how much the team generates each year in ticket and merchandise sales and whatever else might convince her to relent," Dean said.

"Will do. You'll have it tomorrow morning. Until then, don't panic. We'll work this out." Said as if he didn't believe it, Michener followed Barb out the door.

"We're counting on you, Dean," X said.

"I'll do my best. We all love the Sinners and this city. We have to defend them as hard as we do a goal line. I'll let you know how it goes as soon as I can."

Chapter Twenty-Three

In a display of business brinksmanship, Barb had left them the code to the private penthouse elevator at the desk. At precisely one p.m., Dean and Rex arrived at her door, opened by a maid, and were left to sit for forty-five minutes. At least, the chairs were comfortable and the décor sports memorabilia since Gus had owned the place before Barb insinuated herself into his life. After turning down offers of water or coffee from the maid, they surveyed the glass cases full of game balls, each labeled by event, admired framed jerseys including Joe's famous lucky seven, and an array of Super Bowl rings as stunning as any display in Schifferman's. The view alone was priceless of the Mighty Mississippi, busy with boats, and the old Huey Long Bridge that would be brilliantly lit at night.

Rex stared out the large window at the river surging by and remarked, "She has a fortune in stuff right here in this room that would sell for millions. And she's pissed over not getting the place in Paris."

Dean shook his head. "I have the feeling Barb is a person who will never be satisfied—or happy with what she has."

They heard the staccato of her heels against the tiled flooring. "Speak of the devil and here she comes," Rex said. They turned in the direction of the hall door.

Barb entered like an empress, red hair coiffed high, still firm throat throttled with diamonds, still dressed in stark black but rather low cut. "So sorry to keep you waiting. I had a fitting with Portia Ramsey today that ran over. It is so hard to re-schedule with her. Sit and show me what you have to offer." The last phrase was issued as sharply as a command to a dog.

Barb folded herself into a wing chair as if it were her throne and arranged her long legs for maximum effect. If she possessed any broken or varicose veins, her tinted stockings hid them. She held out her hand for the portfolio Dean clutched.

Rex knew his brother had read the materials over and over as if preparing a game plan. "As you can see, the Sinners have a net worth of four point five billion dollars. Of that, one billion point ten are revenues made from ticket sales, merchandise, and other monetizing of the team's popularity. All that would be yours year after year. If we win the Super Bowl this year, those figures will go even higher. If you sell the team, it's a once and done for your income. Please consider that."

"Oh, I have. My financial advisor received three bids for the team since word got out yesterday. All are in the five billion dollar range." She regarded her long nails that appeared to have been filed to a sharp point. "I had them painted gold before returning home. Of course, you can't guarantee me the Super Bowl. It's an ill kept secret that your skills aren't what they used to be, and you will be retiring at the end of this season—because that wife of yours wants you to, old man." Barb dug her nails lightly into Dean's outstretched hand. "Isn't that correct?"

Rex grimaced at the insult to Dean's talent, still way above most quarterbacks as he edged toward forty. Dean never responded to trash talk and continued on, his game plan fully under control.

"We discussed it together and came to the decision that I will retire next year. I want to go out on top, not as the quarterback that stayed on too long and faded away.

That's why I urged Gus to make Rex an offer no one could refuse. He has a year to work with me and the team and then lead them on to more glory—for the new team owner. Another advantage is that several other highly paid players might also retire. That leaves room under the salary cap to acquire the best of the drafts picks and top men around the league who go free agent. What a dynasty you could build. I'd offer my advice on those choices freely to see the Sinners stay in New Orleans."

Nicely played. She removed her nails from Dean's hands and left little pressure marks behind. He needed to say something to support his brother.

"Not only money brought me here. I've dreamed of playing for the Sinners as long as I can remember and of living in this great city. I pledge I will do my best to carry on where Dean left off and keep the Sinners the most lucrative team in the NFL."

"Great city," Barb huffed. "Full of snobs who called me the trophy wife and that cocktail waitress Gus picked up. My advisor also tells me that moving the team elsewhere will sink a large part of the economy here from Dome income to the smallest T-shirt shop. I can do that. Make them all hurt."

"If it's access to society you want, I could talk to Stacy about nominating you to various boards and seeing that you are invited to prestigious events."

"Could you get me into the Krewe of Rex ball?" she queried about one of the oldest and most prestigious of the many Mardi Gras associations. "Ned belongs but won't invite me."

"Possibly," Dean answered.

He knew his brother had once been their Grand Marshall as had Daddy Joe who loved heading the parade while Dean did not. Then, she asked the impossible.

"Could I be their Mardi Gras queen?"

"Everyone knows their queen is nearly always an eighteen-year-old deb, so no, sorry."

"You are boringly honest and probably the most whipped man in the NFL. Stacy this, and Stacy that. No fun to deal with at all. You've had your say. You may go." Barb flicked her taloned hand toward the door.

The men stood, Rex burning to issue some stinging retort, but held in check by his brother's calm. Dean left the portfolio on the coffee table. "When can I tell the team your decision?"

Barb issued a laugh as sharp as her nails. "When I am good and ready. Get out. No, not you, Rex, only your much older brother."

As if she weren't that many years and more older than Dean, fifty-five Rex had heard though she didn't look it. At a nod from his brother, he took his seat again.

"I'll wait for you in the lobby."

She stopped Dean halfway out the door. "No need. I'll see your baby brother gets home safely. This might take a while." She turned her attention back to Rex.

"What is it you want, ma'am?"

"Don't ma'am me. I'm not your mother. I told you to call me Barb."

"Yes." The ma'am almost came out again. "Barb."

"I recall how kind you were to me the day of the funeral, taking my arm, riding with me in the limo—but scurrying off to be with your family and leaving me alone. No more of that. I want your complete attention and total devotion to my welfare, my plans—and I might consider keeping the team in New Orleans. We'll see how it goes this weekend. I need a companion to a charity affair on Saturday night. With you at my table, people will beg to sit with us, not merely Gus's decrepit friends who always tried to cop a feel of my breasts and behind when he wasn't looking."

"I'm sorry about that." Maybe he was a little. Women should be treated with respect. Just ask his mom. "I'd like to help you out, but we have a home game on Sunday, and I'm in training. I have to be in by midnight." Preferably with Dre in his bed. They wouldn't go out or stay up all night since they still honored Drew's curfew as well. Not much longer now. He smiled, knowing that. He'd settled on Monday night at Mariah's. After he left here he'd go to the club and set the arrangements for their engagement into place.

"Poor boy, you don't understand. You will do whatever I ask of you, whenever, or the Sinners are on their way out of town. Think of how Mariah's Place will suffer when she has no more football players hanging around drawing the fans and tourists. Think of never playing in the Dome again because there will be no team. Keep me happy, and you keep the Sinners here."

"I'm not sure I can do that. It's unethical."

"Another small detail. If you report me to the NFL for coercing you, I'll make a deal to sell the team before you drag me down. So, we'll see how much you can please me this weekend before I make up my mind. Do you understand? It's all up to you, Rex. One hint that you aren't enthralled by being with me, and you and the Sinners are gone. You'll tell no one about our arrangement. Sign this now or the offer is off the table." She shoved a nondisclosure agreement in front of him and offered a Mont Blanc pen.

He signed.

"Keep the pen to remember this day. Now, shall I have my driver take you home?"

"No, I brought my own car." Rex stood. He hadn't been so wobbly since he took a helmet to the head. Without saying another word, he went to the door, the elevator, the lobby where Dean waited.

"What happened up there?"

"Nothing really. She said I'd been kind to her after the funeral and asked me to take her to a charity event on Saturday night because she has no companion." He hoped his voice sounded even and sincere.

"Well, okay, if it will keep the Sinners in the running to stay here. It can't hurt, right? Just don't drink and get to bed early."

Dean had no idea. This could hurt worse than the time Mack had a bone sticking out of his leg after a bad takedown, but no one would see the injury.

Chapter Twenty-Four

Directives came all week from Barb to his private number: what to wear to the gala (his custom tux), when her driver would be by to pick him up (seven), what kind of corsage to bring (orchid), and yes, she'd have him home by curfew. Sounded like a prom date to him. If only it were. She'd probably tire of him quickly he kept telling himself.

He continued to talk to Dre every night but cancelled their Friday evening at Mariah's. "I'm feeling a little off tonight. And tomorrow, Barb Bienville wants me to take her to a gala. I can't miss that or Sunday's game, but I'd rather be sharing my germs with you."

"How thoughtful of you. With a house full of kids over here, we'd better not take any chances of sharing an infection. We'll plan on a few hours at Mariah's on Monday if you are better."

"Sure." At least, she wouldn't be surprised to see him with Barb on the society pages Sunday morning. He might be able to endure his predicament until it ended if he could still hear Dre's voice and be with her when not on call by the team's owner.

That hope ended the second he slid into the chauffeured Cadillac beside Barb and presented her with the orchid corsage, not one of those big, purple horrors she'd dictated, but flat, white blossoms that relieved the swath of black sequins she wore. Like some callow youth, he eyed her breasts mounding out of her neckline and wondered where to pin it. In high school that had been easily solved by one worn on the wrist. None of his dates had shown such a large amount of flesh.

Barb prompted, "High on my shoulder, silly boy. I expected you to be more sophisticated."

As he pinned the flowers into place, he said, "Women my age usually don't wear corsages. They're more for Mother's Day."

As she sucked in her breath, he almost stuck her. "You won't be dating anyone your age. Give me your phone. Open it to your calls."

He did. No big deal. He called his folks sometimes and Dre a lot. He kept the numbers of good restaurants and other team members. It wasn't as if he had a drug dealer on there. Then, he understood.

She checked off all the calls to Dre and deleted them along with Dre's number from his contacts list. Not that it mattered. He knew it by heart.

"There, I've blocked Dre Ames entirely to save you the trouble. I'll bet you thought a woman of my age didn't know how to do that. You won't be seeing or calling that pathetic mother of a child with unknown parentage who lives off of Matt Keaton anymore or the Sinners are done in this city." She tucked the phone deep into his pants pocket.

"Dre Ames does not live off of Matt. She runs her own business and pays her own way. He put her through college just as he did her brothers, and she made the most of the opportunity."

"It might have been nice to have someone take care of me like that instead of working as a casino cocktail waitress. At least, I didn't get pregnant."

"No, you met Gus and have lived a life of luxury ever since. You have no reason to be jealous of Dre."

"Don't I? You'll break it off with her entirely as of now or bye-bye Sinners."

Rex declined to answer. He stared into the darkness of New Orleans lingering beneath the bright lights of Canal Street until they reached the distinguished Roosevelt Hotel and were dropped off at the red carpets leading into the building. Playing his part, Rex held out his arm to assist Barb up the steps and into a wide gilded hallway bedecked with potted palms. He knew the way to the ballroom.

"Stacy had her wedding reception here," he remarked.

"I don't want to hear about that fake princess. Let's find a table near the front. I want to show you off." She guided him to a space as yet unoccupied since they were a trifle early. Most of the guests still lingered at the open bar or gathered in clumps of well-dressed men and glittering women.

"Would you like me to get you a drink?"

Barb scanned the room. "No, open the bottles on the table."

"The servers will be by to do that soon."

"I want some now," she insisted like a child craving chocolate milk.

Grateful that the cork in the red wine gave way easily, Rex took on the champagne next, careful to ease out the cork as Jock had taught him in order not to lose a drop.

Barb frowned. "It must be flat since it didn't explode. Cheap ass charity."

"It doesn't if you do it right." He poured a small

amount into the proper glass where it bubbled and fizzed and took a sip. "It's fine, middle of the road, neither cheap nor expensive. That leaves more to go the Crippled Children's Fund of New Orleans."

"As if I care about crippled children. Very well then, pour."

He filled her glass.

"Not drinking?"

"Game tomorrow. Champagne gives a killer headache."

Barb raised her hand into the air, no flab on that bare, toned arm, and waved it as if summoning a predatory bird to land upon it. Evidently, their discussion of wine had ended. She attracted not one, but two women of a certain age dressed in bright plumage, either joyous divorcees or merry widows because no husbands followed them. The more aggressive of the two shoved into the seat next to Rex. The other sighed and sat by Barb.

"My friends, Carol and Sharon. This is Rex Billodeaux, quarterback for the Sinners and my *dear* companion. Watch out for Carol. She has straying hands."

Carol, her short hair dyed red as a stoplight, giggled as if she'd already consumed quite a bit of free champagne. "It's true. I can be a little handsy."

Rex jumped when she pinched his thigh. Barb said, "Hands on the table, Carol. He's mine, and I don't want him bruised like yesterday's bananas."

Black-haired Sharon, too far away to join in the action, smirked. Her red lipstick had begun to seep into the smoker's lines around her mouth. "I'm sure his banana is very firm and at the peak of ripeness."

Saying nothing, Rex managed a good sport sort of grin as the women cackled. Should be a cauldron in the center of the table instead of wine bottles, a basket of rolls, and a single red rose in a vase. Their laughter drew more of their ilk like crows to carrion. Soon their table had been filled by three blondes of various shades hiding gray hair and one who had the honesty to go all the way silver. That one was Mary. She had more flesh on her bones than the others, lots more.

He didn't catch all their names because the servers came around opening wine bottles and distributing rather ordinary salads dressed up with croutons and truffle shavings. That gave him a chance to stay silent while he ate, but the women chattered on in a conversation loaded with sexual innuendo like the stuffed baked potatoes that followed, cheesy and studded with bits of bacon. The main course of a small lobster tail and a filet wrapped in bacon accompanied by pencil-thin asparagus capped with hollandaise sauce came next. The meal ranked above average for charity events, and he'd attended many, but the coven ate very little except for salad, lobster, and veggies, drained the wine, and cried out for more. Throughout, he felt he was the central dish, not the filet mignon. Carol elbowed him so many times at each off-color remark, he figured there would be bruises after all.

As gone gray Mary, who had eaten every bite of her dinner, dug into the usual cheesecake dessert that the others ignored, the MC for the event mounted the stage and silenced the band playing low key dinner music.

"Thank you, thank you, generous citizens of New Orleans for caring about our crippled children."

"How many of them could there be in this day and

age," Barb grumbled.

"Our very own board members will be passing among you to collect your generous donations as we enjoy a performance by the outstanding Caressa who has donated her fee to our cause."

Over the smattering of applause, Mary said as she wrapped Sharon's filet in a linen napkin and deposited it in a large handbag, "That girl almost starved herself to death, but she's pudging right up again. I think her size makes her voice better. There are dangers in being too thin, you know." She turned toward blonde number three. "If you don't want that my poochie would appreciate it." Mary scored another filet before Caressa made it to the mic.

Thankful that Barb had placed him in a chair with his back to the stage in order to show off her conquest, he didn't turn around until she made him do so. She slung a possessive arm around his shoulder and snuggled in. He glanced up to see the astonishment on Carie's face before she put on her wide stage smile and greeted the audience. Soon she swung into her first song, swinging her beaded braids and swaying her rounded hips. No blues tonight, only upbeat songs to encourage the donors. A board member soon arrived at their table.

Each of the blondes took out a discreetly folded check from their tiny handbags and placed them in a basket held by a young woman who accompanied the eager leader, an elderly distinguished woman with white hair piled high on her head. Rex recognized her from many charitable events as Betty Bigler, a childless heiress who devoted herself to good works. She looked at the remaining tablemates expectantly.

"Elise is one of our huge successes. In a wheelchair

at six and now after several surgeries able to walk," Miss Betty declared to encourage them.

Mary delved deep into her bag and fished out a check slightly stained by steak juices. Rex opened his wallet app and typed in a figure. The basket holder gave him a shy smile and transferred the amount to another phone.

"Thank you so much, Mr. Billodeaux. I attended Camp Love Letter in my childhood. Your parents are so wonderful to do that for kids like me, or like I was."

Miss Betty smiled approvingly. "Yes, we nominated her family to attend the camp. Do say hello to your parents for me. I'd hoped to see them here. As for your brother, Mack. He's a saint. He plans to adopt another child we sent to the camp and see the boy gets all the medical help he needs."

News to Rex. Especially to hear his most devilish brother referred to as a saint. He hadn't been one very long, but his wife kept him in line. The entire family expected Mack to slip up, but no, he'd hung strong. He had to question if what he was doing for the team amounted to hanging strong or simply hanging himself but could not decide.

Barb fumbled with her checkbook trying to fill in an amount with a tiny gold pen that matched the long nails getting in her way. Rex leaned over. "Let me help you with that." He added another zero to her amount. "Sign it."

She glared at him but pasted on a smile as she presented the check unfolded.

"Oh, my, Mrs. Bienville. How much you care about others. Perhaps, you'd like to chair this event next year," Miss Mary gushed.

Barb arched her brows and her lips but kept her eyes on Rex. "If I am still in the city of course."

"Where else would you be? We would hate to lose you. Well, we must move on, Elise." She glided on low heels like a girl who'd once gone to finishing school to the next table.

Elise leaned in. "Could I get an autograph for my dad, please?"

"Sure." Rex signed on one of Barb's deposit slips since he still held her checkbook.

"Thanks. I have to go. Mrs. Bigler has no idea how to do phone transfers or work the credit card gadget." She caught up easily.

Caressa finished her set with a standing ovation. Rex wished he didn't tower over most of the guests, but he couldn't ignore her fine performance.

The MC returned. "The band will continue to play for another hour for those who want to dance, and the bar is still open. Please don't drink and drive. We have cabs waiting for those who want to leave. We don't want to lose any of you wonderful donors. Thank you and see you again next year."

Rex checked his watch. "We should be leaving. I have to rest for the game tomorrow."

"Oh, yes, the game that you'd better win for me. Forgive me, ladies, I have to tuck Rex into bed. Do join me in my private box in the Dome tomorrow."

The three blondes agreed to share a cab and followed them out, arms intertwined to hold each other up. They had a short wait until Barb's driver steered the Caddie to the curb. Barb restrained herself until they got inside before she attacked.

"A hundred-thousand dollars! Are you insane?"

"I might be, but you have to think large if you want to break into high society. You already have a committee assignment for next year."

"How much did you give?"

"Ten thousand, but I'm only a paltry football player."

"Not for what Gus paid to get you. I plan to get my money's worth."

"Just drop me off at my place so I can get some sleep. I'll play my heart out for you tomorrow."

He knew he'd pushed her too far when she drew one of her sharpened nails down the side of his face until blood welled out of the scratch. "We're far from done tonight. Surely you didn't believe going to a fancy dinner is all there is to our agreement. We'll go to my place, and when I am done with you, you can go home to Joe's apartment. I would like to see it one day, however."

He blotted the blood with his handkerchief. "My parents are coming in for the game and will stay over."

"Another time. Ah, here we are."

She led him by tugging on the bow tie he'd loosened in the back of the vehicle thorough the lobby, up to her penthouse, into the trophy room and beyond to a sitting room that appeared to have been crafted to her taste. The room contained numerous places to lounge on soft, velvety surfaces, most of them black as if she were a diamond being shown off at Schifferman's. A small bar sat to one side. The view of the bridge gleamed, its reflection captured in the waters of the Mississippi.

"Drink?" she asked.

"No, thanks. Game tomorrow."

"Game on tonight." Barb slid a wide door open to reveal a hallway that split into two luxury suites. She entered the one on the left. "Mine," she said. "Make yourself comfortable."

He sat uneasily on a stool belonging to a makeup table littered with powders, small pots, and the potions Barb used to maintain her looks. Above it, a huge oval mirror framed in gold reflected the king-sized bed covered in jewel-toned satin cushions that added color to a black bedspread of the same shiny material. Barb drew back the covers—red sheets.

"Gus was obsessed with the team colors, Sinners black and red everywhere. I indulged him because I'm stunning in and on both. You look ridiculous over there. Come." She patted the mattress. He forced himself to rise and move forward out of the pocket of safety.

"Strip for me. Do you know how long it's been since I slept with a young man?"

"Thirty years." He made it a statement, not a question. No brainer that Gus had a prenup that hinged on her fidelity. He took off the tie and laid it on a nearby chair, a golden thing with a black cushion and feet like claws. He put his shoes under that chair, balanced on a leg to take off one sock, then the other, as slowly as he could.

"Shit, this isn't strip poker. Let me at the goodies." Barb peeled back his jacket and tossed it away, disposed of the cummerbund, and tore open the stiff, white shirt without removing the studs. They scattered everywhere and sank into a deep, pale gray carpet. He'd need to buy a new set. She spared his gold cufflinks, a present from his mom, by putting them on the night table. If she could see him now.

Shirt off and down to his slacks, Barb wasted no time getting into his pants and soon left him standing there naked. She eyed him with distinct displeasure. "Such a beautiful body but no arousal. We'll fix that. You do me next."

"Do what?"

"Undress me of course." She turned her back to him and leaned into his body. "Open the clasp on my neck."

He had to dig through her clutter of diamonds to find and unfasten the catch. The black sequined sleeveless gown slithered down her body like a snake shedding its skin. She wore no underwear. As it passed her hips to pool on the floor, she rubbed her bare buttocks against his crotch. He began reciting the Sinners' playbook in his mind.

She turned. "Still nothing. Touch my breasts. Feel them. Kiss them."

He did as instructed. They were very firm and heavy in his hands. When he lifted them, the faint scar where they'd been augmented showed. A slot play to the right, a fast shovel pass, moves he rehearsed in his mind.

"Aren't they magnificent? Nothing like Dre's pitiful tits."

"Hers are natural and right for her build. She's beautiful inside and out."

He should have kept his mouth shut. Barb whirled and faced the mirror. She pulled him tight behind her and placed his hands on her overflowing breasts. "Tell me I'm more beautiful than she is."

A line from an old fairy tale movie his sisters loved to watch in the home theater ran through his mind. Mirror, mirror on the wall. It told of a witch who had it in for a beautiful princess. He didn't like the mushy, kissy ending as a kid, but the witch had been awesomely evil.

"Tell me I'm more beautiful than she is, or Dre might have an accident like that snobbish model Josee Riley did with some battery acid."

He shivered. His famous sister-in-law had been saved by nerdy Trinity, but he couldn't be near Dre anymore to protect her. "You are much more beautiful."

"Good. I'll expect to hear that often. Still nothing? I felt that little shiver."

If she expected threats to turn him on, she'd failed again.

"I suppose I'll have to do all the work this time. Lie down on the bed."

He did. She kicked off her heels and mounted him. He did note that every inch of her body was honed to perfection in a gym. Even her pubic hair had been carefully trimmed and dyed to match her hair. "You must work out to maintain such a taut body," he said to delay whatever came next.

Even her laugh had an edge to it. "Yes, in the gym that belongs to the building. Gus made sure I exercised in public with my trainer. Sometimes, he came along just to watch my boobs jiggle. Then when I was still hot and sweaty, we'd come upstairs and have sex. He liked that, too. What do you like?"

"Whatever."

She slid down and took him in her mouth, swirling her tongue, and sucking hard while holding his shaft. He retreated into the world of football again—the trick play he'd rehearsed with Jock, throwing a series of laterals. But the pressure built as his body betrayed him. She knew exactly when to quit and impale herself on his rigid penis. Two or three strong pumps, and he finished. He thought she did, too, as Barb rolled off his body and snuggled in so tightly he felt like gasping for air as her strong scent filled his nostrils and her diamond collar cut into his neck.

"My, it's been such a long time since I was so thoroughly aroused. Did you enjoy it?"

"Yes. You are very accomplished."

"Better than doing it with Dre?"

He knew the game she played now and how to protect the woman he loved. "Much better. She's very inexperienced."

"I thought so. You know there are so many advantages to sleeping with an older woman, their skills acquired over the years for one. I know six ways to do it in a wheelchair. We'll try that just for fun sometime. I still have the one that belonged to Gus. And no need for condoms as I will never accidentally get pregnant like Dre. She was probably setting you up for that."

He didn't answer. A vision of the ring hidden in the bunk bed appeared in his mind. He should take it back to Schifferman's, but not yet. "I have to go now."

"Yes, I'm through with you, but I can teach you so much more. Next time it will go better or else I'll make you take one of my husband's little blue pills. Then you'll be able to keep it up for hours.'

"You won't need to do that." He rolled off the opposite side of the bed and got dressed as he found each piece of clothing. After pocketing his cufflinks, he said, "I'll show myself out."

"Oh, no. That would be rude." Barb rose and led the way, pointing out other possibilities for having sex on the spacious lounges and in front of the trophy cases on the floor. "And you haven't seen the bathroom yet."

At the exit, she gave him a kiss that involved

shoving her tongue halfway down his throat. He held back the impulse to gag. She gave him a little wave. "Until next time," and paraded off naked past the undraped window with a view.

Her driver, who looked great in his uniform, was a handsome, slim young man with Hispanic features but perfect English and addressed as Eduardo, awaited. Occupied with the food in a Grub Hub bag and a girlie magazine which he hastily put away when Rex tapped on the window, he jumped out to open the door. "Have a good evening, sir?"

"Dandy, just dandy. My apartment, please." He thought he heard Eduardo murmur under his breath, "Rather you than me."

He forgot how he got upstairs and into the hot shower where he stayed for a long time washing off her scent. After, he found the bottle of bourbon that had a little dust on its shoulders and poured a straight shot to take the taste of Barb out of his mouth and another to aid in sleeping. Game tomorrow. He had to keep his mind in the game.

Chapter Twenty-Five

As soon as he ran out of the tunnel and through the devil's maw spewing fake smoke, he saw them. His dad sat with Edie, Dre, and Drew in the fifty-yard line box. He flicked his eyes upward. Barb, dressed in brilliant red, stood tight against the window of the owner's sky box, the three blondes next to her, and Mary on the end holding up what appeared to be knitting needles to pass the time. When Barb waved, he gave a curt nod and trotted off to the far end of the field to do his stretches and warmup exercises, away from her, away from Dre.

Dean did the coin toss and started the game, taking the Sinners ahead by two touchdowns despite having two broken ribs taped up under his jersey. Rex waited on the very end of the bench to be called out when needed for a running play or if Dean was shaken up by a sack. He started the second half and could hear Dre shouting his name, cheering him on, along with Drew's childish voice, and had to ignore them. He did his part and so did their defense to win twenty-eight to fourteen.

For over two hours, he hadn't thought of Barb once, but there she was mingling on the sidelines with the reporters interviewing both him and Dean and others who had made great plays. As soon as the reporter moved on to pursue another, she approached like a lioness intent on bringing down prey. She bent his neck down and kissed him on the lips far longer than a brief congratulations called for, loudly proclaiming "My sweet boy is going to win a Super Bowl for me." All that captured on many cameras.

He shook loose and made for the safety of the locker room and the showers where he stayed until most of the players left. X remained, but Dean had gone.

X sat splay-legged on a bench and gave him a hard stare. "Thought you was gonna drown yourself in there, brother. That a cougar scratch you got on your face?"

"You could call it that." Now, he hastened to dress and escape further scrutiny.

"Caressa said she saw you at some charity event, and our new boss was all over you."

"Barb is a lonely woman and wants companionship. If we keep winning, and she stays happy, she might not sell the team to another city."

"So that's what you're doing. What does Dre have to say about it?"

"Nothing. It has nothing to do with her."

"You think? I wouldn't be so sure of that." X rose as if he had completed a play to his satisfaction and left just as Dean returned.

"Hey, the family is going over to Ralph's for dinner tonight. You're coming, right?"

"I don't think so. Tell mom and dad my stomach is bothering me." No lie. Every time he thought of Barb it clenched.

"You didn't play like it."

"Just came on me suddenly."

"Like when Barb kissed you. That would do it for me. Okay, then, get some rest. Take some Pepto. See you at team meeting tomorrow."

His stomach felt worse. He'd just realized that

keeping his deal with Barb would mean avoiding his family and friends, also. They knew him too well, and his mom was especially adept at reading her children.

He had to face her anyhow when his parents breezed in with a container from Ralph's on the Park, a place with a farm to table menu, located in an historic home. The first thing she did was rush to his recliner where he posed in a robe and pajama bottoms for the sake of keeping up the ruse. He watched a Sunday night game played in California. She immediately put a hand on his forehead and declared, "No fever."

"No, Mom, just an upset stomach."

"We brought you some turtle soup. They didn't have chicken."

"Thanks. I'll eat it later. Good game. Want to watch, Dad?" One sure thing, if his dad watched football, they wouldn't be talking much.

"Don't mind if I do. We have to keep a watch on the Niners and the Seahawks. You never know who the Sinners will meet in the playoffs." Joe settled into the other huge, black leather chair and put his feet up.

Out in the kitchen, the microwave dinged. His mom appeared shortly after with the reheated soup. She settled a TV tray she'd unearthed from somewhere over his lap and handed him a spoon. "Eat it now. I want to be sure it stays down before we leave tomorrow."

"Yes, Mama." The rich soup heavy with sherry went down well. No need to say he'd had a sandwich earlier.

"You probably caught some bug from Barb, that harpy. We heard you took her to the Crippled Children's Fund gala."

"She took me. She wanted a companion for the event. It's a good cause. I contributed a nice check."

"So did we but passed on the entertainment. We hear she was all over you."

Rex traced that fact speeding along the family grapevine from Caressa to X to each and every one of his brothers and sisters plus the parents. "It's nothing I can't handle."

"That public kiss should be reported as harassment to the NFL She doesn't own you," his very vehement mother said.

"Actually, she does. Me and the whole team. It was only a kiss. No big deal. She's not as bad as you think." No, far worse—vindictive, cruel, evil. He could not let her know.

"Look, if the NFL has a problem with it, they'll contact her. Now, can we watch the game? Get me a beer, Tink." After all their years together, his dad should have known better.

"You're not sick. Get it yourself. I'm going to get a bath."

As she moved away, Rex called after her. "Use the Pompadour room. The sheets on the round bed aren't clean."

His father took a different approach. "I hope you and Dre are making good use of the Love Palace."

"We are. We were. I don't think it's going to work out between us." He might as well set the stage now.

"All of us thought she was the one for you. If you break it off, make it quick and clean. She deserves that."

"Yes, sir." He thought the fine turtle soup might come up after all.

His dad took a glance at the screen and got up with reluctance. "I'd better go—wash your mother's back or it will be a long drive home in the morning."

****

He didn't sleep well that night. The twisted sheets were a testimony to it. He'd just dozed off when his mother rapped on his door and said, "Open up. We're leaving shortly. I've made you breakfast."

Rising in his saggy pajama bottoms, he let her into his bedroom. She carried the same ancient TV tray loaded with scrambled eggs, dry toast, and a cup of something hot that turned out to be Xochi's tummy tea which she always kept on hand. She kissed his forehead. "Good, still no fever. Don't go into practice until this passes."

"I won't."

"I'm so sorry about you and Dre. Don't drag it out. She was there cheering her heart out for you at the game. Drew, too. This will be hard on the family. We warned you of that long ago."

"I know. I shouldn't have messed with her."

"Is that what you were doing? Messing with her. You know, some of us placed bets on when you'd give her a ring."

"All bets are off now. Thanks for understanding."

His mother brushed the hair off his forehead, that errant curl so like his father's. "I don't understand, but I will try. Get some rest. We love you."

With that she left. His dad poked his head in briefly. "Feel better," he said and went on his way.

He immediately called in sick, then turned off his phone, and spent most of the day trying to sleep. Today, he'd expected to give the ring to Dre. Today, he had to break up with her.

He waited for the knock on his door, or maybe she'd let herself in since she had a key. He cleaned up a little, put on jeans and the black Sinners tee to remind him why he had to do this, but didn't shave. He might as well look like a bad boy to play his part.

The phone rang at seven, the doorman calling to tell him Miss Dre was on her way. He kept the lights on low and confronted her as she came in the door. So beautiful, so concerned. She carried a container, more soup for the sick.

Usually, he would come to her, put that soup aside, and kiss her deeply She gave him a worried smile.

"You must be very sick. Matt told me you missed practice with stomach problems. Delia and I spent all afternoon making chicken soup from scratch. We put in a little hot sauce the way Cajuns like it. Want me to warm it for you? Then, we'll just watch TV or whatever you want since we won't make it to Mariah's for our date night. Drew was very upset when you didn't come for me, but I told him you were ill." She moved toward him, leaving the soup on the counter on the way.

He warded her off with his hands. "No, don't come closer."

"I'm willing to take the chance."

"Don't. Dre, I've moved on. I can't commit to you. You are a wonderful woman and deserve better than me."

She smoothed her devasted features, knuckled away the tears forming in her blue, blue eyes. "Better than Rex Billodeaux, every woman's dream? This is the old it's me, not you kiss off. Right?"

"Not exactly. I need a woman with more sophistication at this point in my life."

"I'm not enough for you, so it is me."

"No, no. you'd be great for anyone except me." Why

wouldn't she go and end this? He couldn't keep lying to her much longer without breaking down.

"Then, it's her, Barb Bienville. At the art gala, she looked as if she wanted you for her dessert, and now that she's a widow, she can. She's beautiful, rich, and I'll bet, great in bed. You have slept with her, haven't you?" She stared him down until he dropped his gaze.

He couldn't deny it and had to keep himself from begging her forgiveness. "She's very adept, not interested in marriage and children. Neither am I right now."

That should do it. If he didn't want Drew, he didn't want her. He'd mouthed the unforgiveable lie.

"Don't you dare use Drew as an excuse. You broke two hearts tonight, and one of those is his. I'll get over this. I will. But I won't forgive you for hurting my son."

Dre stepped close to him now though he backed away. She delivered one, sharp, stinging slap to his cheek, putting all the strength of her arm into it, then turned and walked away. She must never know he hurt more on the inside than out.

Chapter Twenty-Six

Straight-backed and tearless, Dre made it to the lobby. Her car still sat just beyond the doors. She asked for her keys from the concierge. "I won't be staying. He's too ill."

"I'm very sorry to hear that. Let's hope he is well for the next game. But you, are you well? Should I call a cab?"

She wondered what gave her distress away. Watery eyes or the light that had gone out of them?

"No, I will be fine. I will be very fine in no time at all," she lied. If a person repeated a lie often enough sometimes it passed for truth.

Sliding behind the wheel of her old Lexus and putting the car in gear with a hand that still stung from hitting him, she moved cautiously into traffic, not too heavy at this time on a Monday. Once home, she opened the door with caution. The boys would either be in the den getting their television quota or at the kitchen table finishing homework. Delia had left long ago. With the late September evening proving balmy and perfect for romance, Annie and Matt might be outside having a nightcap by the pool, watching the moon's reflection in the water, and sharing kisses as they sometimes did when the boys were occupied elsewhere.

As if someone had thrown a rock into her pond, that would be Rex, all her dreams of having that sort of love and marriage shattered. She crept up the stairs, past the room where Jenny slept and on to her own where she locked the door, went to her shower, and turned on the water. The tears came hard and convulsive and lasted longer than she intended.

Drew knocked on her door and shouted, "Mom, is Uncle Rex okay?"

She threw off her clothes and stood under the water for a minute, enough to soak her hair and wash the tear streaks off her face. Getting out, she grabbed a towel, dried off, and put on her robe. Padding to the door, she said, "Sorry, I was in the shower. What did you say, honey bear?"

"I asked if Uncle Rex was okay. You took him soup and didn't go on your date night."

"He's recovering fast. I wanted to wash away his germs so that none of us would catch what he has."

She might as well get it over with. Drew should be the first to know. He would have no Daddy Rex. "Come sit on the bed with me for a minute."

"Mom, I'm missing TV time. We only have a half hour left."

"This is more important. Rex and I broke up tonight. He has another girlfriend he likes better than me."

"No way! There's no one better than you. Was it me because he didn't want a kid not his own?"

She embraced him in a huge hug. "That wasn't the reason. He wanted someone more sophisticated, worldly. That's not me." But he had cited the fact that Barb didn't like children as one of the reasons for preferring her. Drew must never know.

She thought he'd cry, but instead got a burst of anger. "Uncle Rex has no honor. He let both of us believe he wanted us."

"Honey bear, sometimes things just don't work out."

"Don't call me that. I'm the man of the family now. You won't ever be alone." He wormed his way from her embrace and raced to his own room, slamming the door hard.

To think she'd hoped to give her son a father, and now he felt responsible for her. Damn Rex Billodeaux. She'd forgotten to return his key when she should have thought to throw it at his unshaven face. Taking an envelope from her desk, she got the key from her purse, put it inside, and scribbled his name on the outside. She'd give it to Matt to return.

Drew came back without knocking this time. "Here, I don't want it anymore." He held out the football Rex had given him. Along the seam, he'd carefully written in black marker "Rex Billodeaux's first touchdown for the Sinners" along with the date. Up until this moment it had been enshrined in a special spot among his childhood trophies, mostly for participation in soccer and Little League, a few for spelling bees, and a medal for a first place science fair project.

She nodded, her heart breaking all over again. "I'll see he gets it."

"I'm going to bed early tonight."

"Want me to tuck you in?"

"No. That's for babies." He marched out much as she had earlier from Rex's apartment.

She wanted to go to bed early herself, but forced herself to put on a coverup and go downstairs to find Annie and Matt. They might as well know. Neither watched TV with Daniel and Gabe. As she figured, they were out by the pool with a pitcher of something that looked invitingly cool. Three glasses sat on the table, two half-full. She suspected they already knew.

"Take a seat," Matt offered. "Margarita?"

"Yes, please. I guess you know Rex and I broke up tonight." She took a sip. The drink went down tart and soothing on her throat sore from sobbing.

Annie put an arm around her shoulders and hugged. "Mom and Dad called shortly after you left and told us to be prepared. They waited a long time hoping he'd change his mind. I cannot believe this is my brother falling for that witch."

"He said he needed someone more sophisticated at this point in his life with no expectations of marriage or children." She took another swallow to keep the tears back.

"But he's great with all the boys and Jenny. Now all of a sudden, he doesn't want a family?" Matt's broad forehead wrinkled with disbelief. "There's got to be more to it."

"Maybe, but he is definitely done with me. I know this puts you in an awkward position, Annie. Rex is your brother and will be at all the celebrations the Billodeauxs have. I should start looking for a place of my own so we won't be tripping over each other since I'm not really family. Pour me another drink."

"Oh, Dre, you must realize the Billodeauxs have a very broad interpretation of family. They welcome everyone. I have so many honorary uncles I can hardly keep count, and Mariah is Howdy's mother, but she's claimed us all. The boys are so different but like the Three Musketeers. We can't break that up." Annie squeezed her hand as if she'd never let go.

"I had this idea that Rex and I would find a place to

live near all of you and Dean's family. We'd use your pool and eat pizza at Dean's. That won't be possible now."

Matt spoke up, his voice deep and husky. "But you are part of *my* family. Daniel is Drew's full cousin, and you are my sister-in-law. Gabe and Jenny are his half-cousins. You can't deny that."

"Ex-sister-in-law." She said it with her eyes staring into the limey depths of her glass.

"Nope, there was no divorce. You're stuck with us."

"Matt, I don't know why Melly cheated on you. There is no better man. You've been filling in as dad to Drew all these years. I had no idea he wanted a father of his own until Rex came along. That hurts me more than my own situation. Oh, I want to return the key to the apartment, and Drew is sending back the game ball Rex gave him. Could you give those things to him tomorrow?"

"Damn him," Matt muttered.

"Please give yourself some time, Dre. We have a good arrangement here. Don't let Rex make you throw that away. Wait until the end of the year before making any permanent decisions," Annie pled.

Dre promised, but wondered how she would get through a Billodeaux Thanksgiving and Christmas knowing he'd be there. It hadn't been hard when he barely glanced her way in the past. She wouldn't be able to fade into the woodwork again now that he'd brought her out into the light in so many ways.

She went to her room wanting nothing more than to crawl under the bed covers, pull them up over her head, and fall into a deep sleep. Crying jags took a lot out of a person. But first, she needed to do one more thing for her self-respect. She went to her desk drawer and felt back through all the manila folders where she stored samples of her work for various customers.

She took out the very last, a garish example of a silly, girlish crush, embellished with fancy hearts drawn in red marker, and in the center, written in her best script *Mrs. Rex Billodeaux*. Only teenage girls did dumb things like this. More embarrassing that she'd done it recently.

Inside, she withdrew the playbill from *The Tempest*, a coaster from Mariah's, the ticket stubs from Caressa's nearly fatal concert, and menus from the various places she'd dined with Rex, their selections circled, and Sephy's cherished biscuit recipe that she'd planned to make for him one day. What grownup woman with a child saved such trivial things? She dumped them in the wastebasket by the desk, preserving only the recipe, and tore the folder to shreds. There, maybe now she could rest.

Chapter Twenty-Seven

Rex left a message for Dean not to pick him up for practice. He was feeling better and thought he'd go in his own vehicle to get an early start instead of waiting for him and Matt to pick him up. As proof, he was out on the training field before they arrived. He burned up the place throwing hard passes and practicing routes he could use to make touchdowns. No time for chatter. No time for serious conversations. No locker room remarks about the slight bruise high on his cheek. No thoughts of Barb and Dre for a while.

The situation hit him in the gut when he saw the game ball in his locker and the envelope with the key. He turned down a tepid invitation to go to lunch and instead went back to the apartment to eat the chicken soup, another reminder of Dre. In the afternoon, he did weight training to ward off his feelings.

At least, Barb left him alone most days as she lunched with her female cadre and shopped away her days when she wasn't in the gym flirting with her trainer. She'd made no pact to be true to him, and frankly, he didn't care. The more she played with others, the less she'd want from him. But like clockwork, she called him on Wednesday with her demands for Friday and Saturday nights, time he might have spent with his friends and Dre.

On the schedule, an art opening at a prestigious gallery where his only instruction was to look gorgeous. Saturday night, they would attend a dinner for a lesser charity with a menu of seafood stuffed chicken breast and wine with the meal, but no lobster or open bar. This being New Orleans, even the chicken would be good. He needn't wear a tux, simply a nice suit. Neither event would run late. They'd have plenty of time to be together afterward. Sickening thought.

"And oh," she added. "Nice work on breaking up with Dre. I would have liked to hear her cry, but that slap was satisfying. I also appreciated the way you described me as a sophisticated woman that had no interest in marriage or children. How right you are. She must have been devastated. I wish I'd paid for cameras to be installed."

"You bugged my apartment?"

"Of course. How else could I be sure you are doing as told? A person with my kind of wealth can hire people to do anything—dress up as a maintenance worker doing repairs on the place for instance. Joe and Nell are so amusing. I am sure I'll be just as lively in a bathtub when I reach their age. I mean I could tell what they were doing by the rhythmic splashing of the water."

Now, he had to move out and let his parents have their privacy again. It would be best to be away from all memories of Dre in the round bed, too. He'd been using the blue room since their breakup. After Barb hung up, he tore the place apart looking for the bugs and found one under the curled rim of the Pompadour tub, another hidden behind the mirror over the round bed, a third in the living area, and one disguised among the kitchen magnets his mom accumulated on the refrigerator. Barb hadn't forgotten the master bath. One lay among the ferns on the bidet. Thankful she hadn't paid for pictures, he drowned them all in the sink and put them in his trash.

Motivated, he let his realtor set him up in a furnished luxury apartment in a newly renovated building that had once been a hotel. The best thing about it—no other

Sinners or family members lived there or nearby. She explained that he could redecorate if he wanted. The only thing he wanted to take with him was Dre's engagement ring and the small dragon painting—both had gone missing. Because he found another bug in the ring's place under the mattress, he realized who had them.

He signed a year's lease. Who knew where he'd be next year? Barb could trade him if she liked, and that would be a relief, but not if she sold off the entire team and made his sacrifice for nothing.

At the art opening, he instructed her to buy a splashy abstract that reminded him of a crime scene but attracted Barb. The tickled artist put the blue dot indicating a sale by the picture himself and then led Barb away to introduce her to his friends as a new patron of the arts. They'd already been photographed as a couple by several society reporters when he turned and ran smack into Edie. Of course, she'd be covering the event for *New Orleans Lifestyle.* His twin spared him no mercy other than keeping her voice down.

"How could you dump Dre for *her*? Have you been hit in the head too many times? Don't you dare bring her to Mariah's and expect to sit with us."

"I have no plans to do that."

"Good, because if you do, we'll all get up and leave."

"Edie, no one on the team can afford to aggravate her or she'll sell us."

"Fine if you were only her escort, but she's made it clear you are lovers. You'd do that and crush Dre over football?" Edie gestured to where Barb stood across the room posed in front of her new painting with the artist. "That art is crap and so are you."

His twin sister seized a champagne flute and dashed the contents on his tailored shirt and dress slacks. "I've got to take a picture of her I suppose but not with you. I'll tell her you wet yourself and had to leave."

"I can't leave without her, Edie. Try to understand."

His sister didn't. She raged off as well as she could for a small person and did a fine job of it, got the picture, and disappeared into the crowd.

They left early because of his wet clothes. Edie hadn't done him any favors. More time for fun and games with Barb who desired bathtub sex to prove she could do it as well as his mother, and then sex in her husband's bed against the black sheets.

After the charity chicken dinner the next night, Barb decided to show him how to do it in a wheelchair. She'd worked him up with her hands and mouth as he sat where Gus used to be, then climbed on his lap and swung her long and limber legs up around his neck as she mounted him. His body betrayed him again. With her persistent skills, it always would. Maybe if he got injured…but no, that would sink their chances of a Super Bowl. He couldn't do that.

As he told her, he had to leave early for a flight to Texas to play the Cowboys in a night game. She had no plans to go. Relief swept through him. No outrageous on field kisses caught on the Jumbotron that would appear in every scandal sheet. The team would get back Monday after a certain victory, have a brief meeting, and get some rest. No more Barb for a few days.

He threw himself into game preparation, and the team appreciated that, working well with him, but friendly offers of a beer after practice fell away. His family, quietly furious, especially the women, left him alone for the most part. When a bye week came up in October and they had a few days off to rest and heal, Dean tried to include him in a pizza party at his home.

"Can't. Barb wants me to fly to Paris with her for a couple of days."

"What will you do with only two days?"

"Watch her buy clothes and the usual. Maybe I can escape to the Louvre while she spends money," he said. "Look, tell Dre she should come. I won't be around."

"Convincing her of that might be hard, but I'll try. She hardly leaves the house anymore."

He'd done that to her, turned her back into a wall flower again when she should be flourishing. "She needs the family. I don't mind being the pariah."

"Really? I doubt that, but this affair with Barb hasn't hurt your game, so I'll take your word for it."

"Thanks, I appreciate that."

Not quite halfway through the season, and the team was still undefeated, but he didn't know how much longer he could endure. Two shots of bourbon helped him sleep.

Chapter Twenty-Eight

October in New Orleans turned out to be especially lovely this year. The charming red lycoris that many called naked ladies for their lack of leaves sprang up magically in Garden District lawns. The rain trees native to Australia sent out masses of pink bracts that resembled flowers. Best of all, the humidity dropped along with the lingering heat of summer.

Dre wished she could enjoy it all, but mostly she immersed herself in her work, getting referrals from previous clients, advertising her skills, pleased when she had almost more work than she could handle. Being creative blocked out the thoughts of Rex and put more money in a fund she worked on building to get a place of her own, not an easy task in high priced New Orleans.

When Annie asked if she could take the boys to a birthday party/flag football game in the park by the River Walk, she could hardly turn her down. One day, she had to go out in public again, and this might as well be it. She rather enjoyed the day, sitting in the shade with other moms and watching the guys play supervised by a few dads. After the game, cake and red punch were served, not enough for her car full of sweaty, ravenous kids. She said she'd make hamburgers when they got home, but taking the route that passed the conference center brought them in contact with the ever present Lucky Dog cart. They began clamoring for a hot dog because they were staaarving.

"Okay, okay. I'm going to pull into this loading zone. You have fifteen minutes to dash to the corner and get your dogs. Don't get all the stuff on it if you aren't going to eat it. Here's a twenty. Make sure you get the change."

They burst from the Lexus and ran to assail the Lucky Dog vendor. Though she'd been sitting in the shade earlier, her car had not. The air conditioning hadn't kicked in fully yet, so she got out and left the curbside doors open. She kept her eyes on the boys receiving their treats one by one and on her watch fearing some cop would come along and tell her to move her vehicle.

She didn't see him coming as she took a step farther from the loading zone to get into some shade cast by the building and collided with a man walking briskly by— until she crashed into him.

"Oh, I'm so sorry. Are you okay? You seem a little pale."

"I assure you I don't bruise that easily. It's just that you resemble someone I used to know who died when I was still in high school back in Indiana."

He squinted against the afternoon sun, his eyes very blue, his blond hair defying the gel and shaking loose over his forehead. His features were angular as was his body clad in a well-cut pale-gray summer suit with perhaps some padding in the shoulders. He stood an inch or two taller than her. Not Rex Billodeaux handsome, but he had an interesting face and maybe a hint of acne scars from adolescence.

"Her name was Melinda Ames, a local beauty queen. All the fellows had a crush on her, you know, the older woman who dated a football player. Not me, though. I heard she died in childbirth down here."

Oh God! Cullen Carson, Drew's father all grown up. To lie, to flee, to face the truth. She didn't like any of the options. She glanced over her shoulder to where the boys were still selecting their toppings, knowing Drew would want only mustard and maybe ketchup. Not much time until her son met his father.

She managed to say, "Melly was my sister. She was shot in a crossfire between gangs, but they managed to save the baby. I came down here to help Matt with the child, and I just stayed. New Orleans suits me better than Indiana."

"Andi, you're Andrea Ames." He assessed her head to toe, not in a sexual manner but with amazement. "In high school, you were…"

"A mess, I know."

"No, a Goth, a crazy Goth girl up for anything. Now you're the image of your sister."

"Really, we aren't alike. People have forgotten how beautiful she was."

"You underestimate yourself, but that's not important. I also live here now. I went off to Harvard when I graduated and was assigned a roommate from New Orleans. He used to take me to his home for Mardi Gras, spring breaks, and other occasions. Such a rich culture here and so much acceptance for all. I couldn't go back to Indiana. Jeffrey and I opted to get our law degrees at Tulane. I have a practice in family law now at his father's firm. What are you up to?"

Another glance over her shoulder caught Gabe in the midst of piling on all the toppings, even the peppers he wouldn't eat. She didn't have much time to shake free.

"I got a degree in graphic design from UNO and

have my own small business. I still help Matt with his children. Everyone knew you were bound for Harvard."

"Yes, I left immediately after graduation. Sorry I didn't see you again. You sort of just disappeared."

"I'm sure it seemed that way. Anyhow, great seeing you, but I am parked in this loading zone. I need to load the boys and get home." She wished she'd said something else because Cullen peered at the hot dog toting kids heading their way.

His eyes skimmed over dark-haired Danny and went right to Drew. "Easy to see which one is Melinda's kid. Would you look at that blond hair. However, I feel I owe you an apology and an explanation for why I dropped you. Could we get together for dinner and clear the air between us? Then, perhaps, move on to enjoying this city together. Here's my card."

Dre examined the rather bland announcement printed on good stock that simply said, "Cullen Carson, Family Law." It listed a business and email address and a couple of phone numbers.

"Thanks," she said as the boys arrived. With the car door already open, she started shoving them inside like a pusher for a Japanese train.

Drew leaned over Gabe and said, "Here's your change, M—"

She slammed the door. "Don't get gunk on the upholstery," she said as she slid into the driver's seat and prepared to get the hell out of there.

But Cullen leaned in before she could shut him out and peel away. "Do you have a card?"

He'd only become more interested if she fled. Calmly, she removed her card from her purse. Hers listed only her name, cell phone number, and an email address.

Dre Ames, Graphic Artist, had embellished hers with fanciful flowers. He wouldn't learn her address from it or her peculiar living arrangements.

"Colorful," he remarked. "Seriously, I'll be in touch."

"Sure," she said as if doubting it. "I have to get the guys home or pay for a deluxe detailing on the inside of my car."

"A Lexus, you must be doing all right."

He didn't know much about cars if he thought her ten-year-old model said she was rich. "I make a living. Nice running into you, literally." She turned on the ignition, put the car into gear. He backed away as if she might just do it again with heavy machinery.

Thank heaven, the boys had their mouths full of hot dogs, and Drew hadn't tried to called her mom again. Their appetites outweighed any questions they might ask. At the house, she shooed them to the bathroom to take an early shower. They smelled like a pile of wet puppies with an overtone of cheese, mustard, and relish. She paused to pick a discarded pepper from a backseat cup holder and take a deep breath. It seemed Lucky Dogs were always destined to change her life.

Safe at home at last. Dre went directly to her room and turned on the shower. Now she had two men to avoid in New Orleans.

Chapter Twenty-Nine

Dre might have known Cullen would persist. He'd been the smartest guy in his class if not the most handsome. In those days, he'd been skinny and awkward. Outbreaks of acne periodically marred his fair skin, but above that, he had beautiful blue eyes and lank blond hair always hanging in his face. This did not stop him from being captain of the debate team, a chess master, and class president. She'd wanted a bright father for her child, and he'd unwittingly delivered that.

She'd barely completed her cry in the bathroom when her phone signaled a message.

"Sorry you had to rush off. Please, meet me for brunch at Commander's Palace, eleven o'clock. I've already made reservations. Looking forward to seeing you again."

She wasn't looking forward to seeing him at all. But a window of opportunity opened Sunday morning when Drew went to Mass with Matt and the boys because the Sinners had a Monday night game for a change. Annie, upholding Billodeaux traditions, had started taking Jenny to the Episcopal service, both at eleven. Perhaps Cullen would leave her alone once he had his say. She texted her assent.

Sunday, she left right after the churchgoers and hadn't far to go since the classic and classy restaurant with the strict dress code was nearby in the Garden

District. Her wardrobe had filled with Stacy's help once she began dating Rex. Maybe Stacy was tired of having her loaners dry cleaned all the time. The blue gown she'd worn to see *The Tempest* she might never wear again, but now she had more to choose from and selected a dark green dress with long flounced sleeves, a high neckline, and belted with a front tie that defined her waist as Stacy said. No need for jewelry, and she didn't have much of that anyhow. Low heels would do and the small purse with the essentials she'd learned to pack.

At the restaurant, she'd no sooner given the valet her car keys than she saw Cullen waiting for her under the jaunty blue and white striped awing. Far from being the conservatively clad attorney she'd met yesterday, he wore a white suit, perfectly fine after Labor Day due to the heat, a pink shirt, and polka-dotted tie that incorporated both colors.

He gave her a welcoming smile, and she had to admit his orthodontia had paid off. "Stunned?" he asked as she approached. "Yesterday was business me. This is weekend me. And you are stunning as well. Should we go in?"

Of course they should and get it over with. He held the door for her, helped her get settled in her chair once they were seated, and asked if she wanted a drink. She did badly but needed to keep her wits about her.

"An unsweet tea," she ordered while he got the classic brunch Bloody Mary.

The meal came with a starter, a main dish, and a dessert. She stuck to the rule of not getting anything messy and went for smoked gulf fish mousse, pecan crusted fish, and bread pudding souffle. He selected the gumbo—fearless in his white suit—a fish dish, and the bread pudding. She couldn't help but think that Rex would have gotten the tournedos of Black Angus. When would she forget his preferences?

As she picked at her fish mousse, loading small portions onto crisp chicharrónes, Cullen wasted no time starting the uncomfortable conversation. "I want to say this straight out. I apologize for pushing you into sloppy teenage sex in the backseat of my father's car. I had no care for you or finesse, only desperation to get it done. I am thoroughly ashamed of myself."

She found herself patting his pale, white hand, though she'd thought the same many times. "You were a horny teenaged guy. I wanted to experience sex. It wasn't rape. Could have been better, but it was consensual. I forgive you. Feel better now?"

"Strangely, yes. Good, let's move on to the here and now, Dre Ames. I noticed you'd changed your name from Andrea by your card."

"Yes, I was experimenting with that before I left Indiana, but my mother and father wouldn't go along with it. I didn't want to be cute, little Andi anymore."

"Got it. You are Dre to me." Their fish arrived, but he didn't dive right into it. "Once I saw the card I realized you are quite a celebrity."

"Hardly." Don't go there, please. Don't mention Rex.

"You designed the invitations for the art gala. Jeffrey and I were there, but it was so very dim. We might have met sooner if the stars had aligned."

"Okay, we are aligned now." She pretended to be interested in the pecan crusted fish. "Delicious."

"Yes, so is mine. I've seen you in the papers, both society and those cruel grocery store tabloids. I'm sorry you had a bad breakup with Rex Billodeaux. How he could replace you with a tacky broad like Barbara Bienville, I do not know."

"It wasn't bad, only very quick, sort of like being guillotined, I suppose. He wanted more than I could give him." Please let him not have seen the brief reference to her son in one of those rags.

"I shouldn't have brought it up, but Jeffrey has a penchant for gossip and buys those things all the time. We share a condo, and he litters the place with them."

"Let's talk about you, Cullen. So, family law. You handle divorce cases and such."

"Sadly, yes, but I specialize in child custody battles. Fathers are so often given the short end of the stick. I try to secure their ability to see their children regularly, joint custody if possible. Just last week, I was able to secure a gay couple the right to adopt a child in foster care. That was very satisfying."

"I imagine so. All I do is make book covers on my computer."

"I've seen more of your work than that. You bring beauty into the world."

Well, she had brought Drew into the world, and he was beautiful. Both the fish and company started to have more appeal. By the time they got to their bread pudding finished at the table with warm whiskey cream, she felt at ease with Cullen. She might have made a friend outside the Billodeaux circle, but how could she keep him without confessing he'd fathered a son?

"I'd like to see you again, and I have an idea. Have you ever been to Halloween in City Park?" Cullen took a taste of the bread pudding and closed his eyes to savor it for a moment.

"No, usually we take the kids out to trick-or-treat in the neighborhood. Garden district people give out full-sized candy bars." Steer away from another date.

"Brews and Boos is next Saturday night, adults only. Lots of wild costumes and all the beer a person can put away. The opposite of the art gala, but it benefits the park. Why don't we go together since it isn't on Halloween night?"

"Sounds like fun, but I don't have a costume."

"With your creativity, I'll bet you could whip something up in no time."

"I did wear a Grecian-styled gown to the gala. I guess I could go as a goddess, put on a long wig, and wear some laurel leaves in my hair."

"I've got it. You will be Persephone, goddess of the spring, and I will come as Hades who swept her off to the underworld to be his bride. I have a friend who makes magnificent masks. You should crown yourself with flowers. Don't wear sandals or heels, though. Your feet won't survive the evening, my dear."

She hated to stomp on his enthusiasm, and she'd be wearing a mask. "Okay, but I need to get home. I have a project due on Monday." True, she buried herself in work every day in the week now and took no time off.

"This has been delightful, Dre." He called for the check and refused her offer of a credit card. "My treat, as are the tickets to Brews and Boos. Where shall I pick you up?"

What to do? "I guess at Matt's house. I'll wait on the sidewalk for a fast getaway. If the children get involved, we'll never escape."

"Matt has more than one child, then?"

"Three and a wonderful wife," she answered

honestly. Reluctantly, she gave the address, and they settled on seven to meet.

As she waited for her car to be brought, Cullen stayed under the awning speaking on his cell phone with his back turned away from her. Still, she heard the word "perfect" and the phrase "didn't know that." He disconnected and came to wait beside her.

"Sorry, a call I had to take."

"We all have those."

"See you on Saturday, my goddess."

"Sure." She slipped into her Lexus as soon as the valet driver got out and made another getaway.

Chapter Thirty

"Here goes." Dre modeled her costume for Annie up in her room. While the gown hadn't changed, she'd gotten a long, blonde wig that draped over her shoulders and created a chaplet of silk flowers to put on top of it. More flowers hung in a strand about her shoulders, and she'd found some gold flats to protect her feet in the crowd.

"Cullen is bringing the mask."

"You look wonderful. Again, how well do you know this man?" Annie had turned motherly again. She had raised her in a way from snarky teen through childbirth and college and couldn't help herself.

"I told you we bumped into each other, and he mistook me for my dead sister. You should have seen his face. We're from the same town in Indiana, went to the same high school. He was a year older and off for Harvard before I came down here. Funny how we ended up in the same place."

"Very. I don't like his picking you up at the curb."

"My idea, not his. I don't want Drew to get attached to another man and then have it come to nothing again. I'll introduce you later if we keep seeing each other."

"Maybe it's too soon for you to date again."

"Rex is already in someone else's bed, and I don't intend to sleep with Cullen tonight or any time soon. Remember Adam Malala's advice. 'The best way to get over a lost love is a new love.' "

"But he's Samoan."

"He met his wife that way. Cullen isn't bad looking, taller than me, very polite, not handsy, and sort of funny in some ways. He has a great career that he loves. That's a good start."

"Does he know you have a son? Usually, you tell men that right away to ward them off."

"Not yet, but soon." Heck, she hadn't told Annie the man was Drew's father. If Cullen backed off from that, he'd be punted out of her life so fast he wouldn't know when her foot hit his ass. "Could you make sure the kids are occupied so I can sneak out?"

"They're watching an action movie with Matt. He's not too happy about this either, and Drew will be upset."

"Like I said, when I am sure of this guy, you'll meet him."

"Call if you need a ride home."

She had to squeeze by little Annie to get out of her own bedroom and tiptoe down the stairs. Annie followed all the way to the front door and kept watch until Cullen arrived in a BMW that appeared to have been freshly detailed for the occasion and hurried to open the door for her. She waved a carefree goodbye that she didn't feel.

Cullen had donned a black wig, beard, and toga, a little off kilter with tennis shoes of the same color. He'd placed a golden diadem on his head. He handed her a gorgeous half-mask of white sequins accented with tiny rosebuds and a few puffs of feathers.

"For the goddess of spring. You are fabulous. No one will know who I am until we get to the bash."

"Why is that?"

"You will see." He got them through the traffic, past

revelers everywhere, to a pay lot. They walked to the entrance where another man in a tight black turtleneck and jeans paced with a tail erupting from between his buttocks. He turned and growled at them from a hole in the base of a grotesque mask of a dog with three slavering heads. His face had been blacked to blend into the costume. On his hands and feet, he wore paws with impressive claws. Dre drew back behind Cullen. In New Orleans, you never knew when people were serious or joking.

"Never fear. It is my faithful companion, Cerberus, also known as my roommate and partner in law, Jeffrey Jackson."

"Oh, I see, CC and JJ." About all she could surmise about JJ were his dark eyes and height about the same as CC.

"Never!" they said simultaneously. "Always, Cullen and Jeffrey. No nicknames," Cullen said.

"I will remember that."

Jeffrey growled again but finished in English. "Where have you been? I've had my heads patted too many times, and one person remarked on my nice tail."

"You should be flattered. Someone was trying to pick you up. This is Dre, never Andi."

"Yes, I can see why she is perfect, perfectly beautiful, that is. I could really use a beer. This mask is so hot."

"So is your tail," Cullen quipped as he handed over the three tickets that admitted them to an illuminated oak grove bustling with costumed maskers and busy beer tasting stands. Music of course, there was always music in New Orleans. They picked up three taster cups at the first booth they saw and listened a minute while the craft brewer touted his small batch beer. Moving on to the next stand and the next as they neared the music, Dre lost track of how much she'd had to drink. Usually, two were her limit but how to tell when it was served in tiny cups. She felt mildly buzzed by the time they reached the stands surrounding the band and managed to snag a place to sit and enjoy.

At some point, Cullen left and returned with a sack of soft-shelled crab sandwiches, more beer, and an announcement that he'd sized up the competition which led him to enter them in the costume contest.

"Oh, no! I can't parade across a stage like this," she swore.

"Oh, honey, if I can do you it so can you," Jeffrey said. "In fact, I'd get up and dance with you but I'm clumsy on my paws." He devoured his sandwich, fried legs, and all. "Damn, it's hard to drink in this headpiece. All the beer runs down my neck."

"Good, then you are the designated driver, Jeffrey."

"Unfair, so unfair. You were supposed to be Cerberus."

"I had to match my date, didn't I?" Cullen plucked a crab leg from his sandwich and crunched down on it.

She ate more slowly than the bickering roommates and when finished, Cullen led her out to dance to a slow-paced number. "Jumping around and wiggling are beneath my dignity as Hades, Lord of the Underworld," he explained, but he hadn't progressed much beyond the box step. Neither had she before Rex. At least, he didn't pull her close or feel her up while dancing.

As they returned to their seats which Jeffrey preserved by wide man spreading, a commotion rippled through the crowd. Rex appeared wearing his full gear, helmet, pads, and jersey with his name and number. An aging cheerleader hung on his arm. Oh, Barb had the flat belly to bring off the midriff bearing top bearing a red S on black and the tiny mini skirt, but her large bust overflowed the sides of the outfit, no athlete she. They'd get in her way. From foot to thigh, tall, black heeled boots covered her long legs. Her green eyes spotted Dre from behind a gold mask. She pulled Rex into their path.

"Dre, now nice to see you again. You're wearing the same gown as you did to the art gala. Pity you can't afford something different."

Dre drew herself up, taller than Barb even in flats. "I don't believe in one occasion dresses. They are a waste of money. At least, I didn't steal mine from the Sinsation cheerleaders dressing room."

"Meow," said Jeffrey who had come to join the group. "I mean, bark, bark, bark."

"You probably planned on buying a used wedding dress. So sorry about that," Barb sniped.

Dre held out her hand with her short nails painted pearl pink for this occasion She wiggled her fingers. "He didn't put a ring on it, so no. I hadn't made any plans."

The crowd began to close in, offering Rex whatever they had in hand to sign: napkins, greasy food bags, body parts. "Are you the real Rex Billodeaux?" one asked.

"I don't think I am anymore," he answered but signed the man's T-shirt. His eyes, deep in his helmet and underlined with black grease, were downcast, not looking at anyone directly.

"I own the Sinners and this one in particular, the Sinsations and what they wear," Barb sputtered. "Are these two the best you can do for a date?"

"Hades, Lord of the Underworld, and his vicious

dog Cerberus, yes. He judges the dead and his dog keeps them in Hell. I'm sure they'll see you there."

"Are you threatening me?" Barb's green eyes caked with makeup flared behind the golden mask.

"Not at all. You'll earn your place by your actions." She linked her arm to Cullen's and called, "Come, Cerberus. They are announcing the costume contest." No way would she reveal their identity and expose them to Barb's wrath. She'd stopped going to the sky box to avoid confrontations, though all the Billodeaux women would have defended her. More people crowded into their space to accost Rex.

Once clear of that mob, Jeffrey whispered in her ear as well as he could considering the ungainly mask, "You go, girl. What a beyotch she is. Cullen, I like Dre very much."

"Yes, I'm proud of how she stood up to that harpy. Note the classical allusion."

"Noted."

"Please, I think it was the beer speaking. I really need to pee before we go on stage."

They escorted her to the Porta Potties where she carefully raised her gown to keep from soiling it on the urine drenched floor. Relieved, she grabbed another beer on their way to the stage to build her courage. Cullen explained their costumes. One judge proclaimed her lovely, but they did not win with so many elaborate costumes worthy of Mardi Gras, some scary as hell, that others had worked on for months. Cerberus did get an honorable mention and hung the ribbon from his collar. They went back to drinking and roaming with Dre doing most of the drinking and Jeffrey merely roaming.

Jeffrey remarked, "Hard to believe that was the real

Rex Billodeaux. He's so dynamic on the field and appeared so whipped by that awful woman."

"She's changed him. Ruined him." Dre tossed back another mini beer.

Cullen took her side. "He didn't have the decency to defend you or even to say hello. I'm burning his jersey."

"You're a football fan?"

"Absolutely. We both are. On Sundays, Jeffrey wears Dean's jersey and I wear, or used to wear, Rex's number. If he hasn't curdled the Sinners for you, why don't you come and watch the game with us. We have great snacks."

"I like thisth idea. Give me your address. I'll drive over." She'd been watching the games from home since the breakup but sending Drew with Annie and the kids. Having some company seemed like a wonderful idea. Her legs felt wobbly, and her stomach began to slosh. She burped, covered her lips, and giggled. " 'Cuse me."

"Forgiven. Let me put our address in your phone."

She fumbled to get the phone out of the small purse. Cullen returned the twenty that had floated out with it.

"What time ith it? I gotta be home 'fore midnight."

"Your Annie gives you a curfew?" Cullen asked.

"No, ith not thass."

Very gently, he squeezed her hand. "We know you have a child, Dre. That's wonderful."

"Yeth, a boy named Drew—and he's yours." She poked Cullen's chest and laughed. "Uh oh."

Grabbing the rough bole of a nearby oak, she threw up on its gnarled roots, not the first one to do that this evening. Cullen held the strands of the blonde wig out of the way.

"Gonna hafta get my dress dry cleaned now," she

said as if her previous comment had not shifted all their lives the moment before. Then, she passed out.

Chapter Thirty-One

Dre awoke when the Sunday morning light pierced to the very back of her brain. Splitting headache. Eyes now open, she surveyed the condition of her suite: flower chaplet and boa thrown over a chair, her gorgeous Portia Ramsey gown lying in a soiled white and gold puddle on the floor next to the kicked off golden slippers, and a faint odor of barf pervading the air. She had thought of wearing the designer dress for her wedding but would not give Barb the satisfaction of knowing that. Not anymore. She might donate it to a good cause.

How she'd gotten home and tucked into bed wearing a big sleepshirt she did not know. At least, she wasn't in Cullen's bed sleeping off a drunk after forgotten sex. Maybe, he'd put her in a cab. She sensed he didn't like sloppy drinkers. No more excuses, she had to get out of bed.

First stop, the bathroom for an urgent pee and two glasses of water to get the cotton out of her mouth. Next, to put on a robe and slippers and see if Annie and the kids were still at breakfast. Not that she wanted any. Matt would already be at the Dome getting ready for a noon game.

As she made her way down the stairs, the house seemed oddly silent. No one home? How late was it? A light burned in the kitchen, and there she found only Annie clearing the breakfast dishes into the washer.

Without greeting her, Dre sat down in a chair and rested her head on folded arms on the table.

Annie, also wordless, popped bread into the toaster and turned on the microwave. In minutes, a plate of dry toast strips and a steaming cup of tea sat in front of her along with two aspirin. "Try to eat a little and drink Xo's hangover tea. That and the aspirin will help," said the woman who'd helped her grow up.

"I'm so ashamed. I haven't gotten drunk on beer since high school when I wanted to defy my parents."

"You had a tough night according to Cullen and Jeffrey, a run in with Barb and Rex that you handled with style at the time. After the costume contest, it appeared to hit you hard, and you tried to drink it away." Annie poured herself some coffee and waited for Dre to take a sip of the tea.

"Wow, this is spiked with hot sauce." But she drank some and took the aspirin before saying, "Oh God, Cullen and Jeffrey. You were right. I hardly know them. Anything could have happened. And I think I said, I said…"

"Yes, I know. First, they were perfect gentlemen and carried you to our door. They rapped hoping we'd be up in order not to wake the children with the bell. The one with the clawed feet took them off before coming inside. He didn't want to mar our hardwood flooring."

"Nice of him. Be glad he must have left his gruesome mask and gloves in the car." She nibbled the toast hoping to keep it down.

"They offered to carry you upstairs, but Matt took care of that. I wish he'd carry me up the stairs again sometime. I put your friends in the kitchen since they asked me to stay a moment and went up to get you to bed. By that time you'd thrown up again but made it to the toilet. I'll take your beautiful gown to my dry cleaners tomorrow and hope they can restore it." Annie buttered her piece of toast and spread it with jelly.

"But I told them—a secret I didn't want to let out."

"You should have told us first, Dre. It doesn't matter now. So, Cullen is Drew's father."

"I met him on the street when I stopped for the Lucky Dogs the boys wanted. I wouldn't have recognized him or he me if I didn't resemble my sister so much now. When the boys came running back, he mistook Drew for Melly's child. I wanted to leave it that way for a while until I could find out what kind of man he was."

The silence of the house finally clicked with her. "Where are the kids? Did Drew see me drunk? Did he see his father last night?"

"I sent them over to the Dome with Stacy. And no, Drew didn't wake. I told him you were unwell and staying home today, but no surprise to him since you haven't gone with us since the breakup. Which reminds me, you should expect to have company in about an hour. Better get a shower and clean up."

"Who?"

"Cullen and Jeffrey are planning to watch the game with you. They said they'd take care of you and bring the snacks. Dre, Cullen wants to meet his son and have a part in his life, but he'll keep the relationship quiet until they get to know each other. You can discuss it with him today."

"No, no, no! He's a family lawyer. He's seen me drunk out of my mind and has a witness. What if he tries to get custody of Drew?"

"I didn't get that impression at all. He seems rather understanding and compassionate. There now, go get ready. I'm heading out for the game." Annie took her keys from a hook by the back door, gave Dre a kiss on the top of her head, and left her alone with her thoughts.

She took a shower, scrubbed her short hair to the roots, and brushed her teeth twice, following that with mouthwash. Since her stomach still felt raw, she pulled on a pair of loose sweatpants, a sports bra, and a black Sinners sweatshirt with no distinguishing number on it. She covered her feet in athletic socks, not shoes. Only a little pink lipstick enlivened her pale face. This was not a date, probably an interrogation, so who cared.

At exactly quarter to twelve, her unwanted guests arrived bearing a shopping bag and a covered tray. "Welcome," she said briefly and led them to the large den created out of two smaller rooms on the first floor to accommodate a big screen TV, a warm brown leather sofa and recliner, an old wooden chest used as a coffee table, and lots of room for the children to play with their toys. Lego projects and Jenny's dolls littered the floor. The house still had an old-fashioned parlor and formal dining room, both rarely used. Family life happened here and in the kitchen.

Jeffrey maneuvered around a half-built Starship Enterprise and stepped on a baby doll that squeaked beneath his foot. He set the tray on the chest and removed the foil cover.

"Voila! A charcuterie board designed for a sore belly."

Crackers of various kinds formed an S through a selection of cheeses, red and green grapes, cubes of ham, dried apricots arranged like flowers with black olive centers, fresh strawberries, and frill of thin salami slices. "Beautiful," Dre remarked. "Please sit down."

"No, you sit." Jeffrey pulled one of Corazon's bright afghans from the back of the sofa and draped it over her knees as if she were an invalid.

Cullen came in with two long-necked beers and something bubbly in a glass. "Ginger ale for you. Where are the coasters?"

As beaten and worn as the old chest was, she nearly laughed. "There's a stack in the kitchen by the sink."

He took the drinks with him and returned again with coasters stuck in the pocket of his black shirt and the beverages, arranging them around the board. He didn't sit down. "I have to get my specialty item started."

By the time the coin toss occurred, the aroma of popcorn filled the air. Cullen delivered a large bowl of it to add to the refreshments. "Parmesan coated. It's delish."

That proved true. Picking at food that wasn't too rich or greasy settled her stomach. Cullen got up to refill her ginger ale, and Jeffrey urged her to try the Manchego cheese.

"It's Spanish. I usually put Spanish tuna on the board, too, nine dollars a can but so worth it. I thought not today with a queasy stomach in house."

That was the first time she got to truly study Jeffrey who was quite handsome without his mask and black face, more so than Cullen. He'd worn Dean's jersey in red which set off his black hair combed back off his face and eyes like dark matter set in the universe of his olive complexion. Pressed jeans and tasseled loafers worn without socks completed an ensemble that he made seem elegant. A large Harvard class ring adorned one finger.

Cullen returned with her drink. With his black shirt tucked into deep blue skinny jeans which his tall, thin legs embraced well, he seemed almost vampiric with his pale skin. "Anything else I can get for you?"

"No, thanks. Did you really burn your Rex Billodeaux jersey?," she asked.

"Not yet. It's in the Good Will bag for now. The man is a cad. I won't be seen in it anymore after the way he treated you."

"Hush up and watch the game. Dean is playing the first half," Jeffrey ordered.

As halftime approached, Dre nibbled on a dried apricot. She felt warm and cared for wedged between the two men as if they were her guardians. Not that Matt hadn't always protected her, but with so many children needing attention, most of the loving care went to them. She lavished it on Drew. Again, she uttered words she hadn't intended to. "When I was pregnant, they told me to eat dried apricots for morning sickness. It didn't work."

There it was, the baby in the room. Cullen immediately responded. "I'm sorry I wasn't there for you. Smartest guy in my class, and I thought you'd take care of the birth control because you seemed like you'd been around."

"Stop! Not your fault. I wanted to get pregnant to spite my mother and have someone who'd love me unconditionally, selfish teenage desires that considered no one else. I did not intend to tell you at any time. There is no father listed on his birth certificate because I wouldn't say. You were the only one I had sex with in high school even if I pretended to be experienced. I chose you for your brains. I wanted a bright child, and I got him. No regrets, though motherhood is I harder than I thought."

On the screen, the Sinners trotted off to the locker room one score ahead. Jeffrey rose. "I'll refresh the charcuterie board. You two talk."

"Dre, I want a family. Knowing I have a wonderful son already makes me surer of that. Annie showed me a picture of the kids together and pointed out Drew, the boy I mistook for Melinda's child. He has my eyes, doesn't he?"

"Yes, and your smarts. But I'd understand if you want a DNA test to be sure. Not that I am asking anything of you. However, you should be sure if you want to be a part of his life in any way."

He shook his head. "That's what I'd advise my clients to do, but I feel certain."

She laughed. "You haven't met him yet. I'd like to ease into that. Invite you over and let him get to know you before we break the news. I had no idea how much he wanted a father of his own before Rex. Now, his trust will be hard to come by."

"I understand. Tell me what he likes besides watching football."

"He doesn't play sports well but tries anyhow. His school grades are top notch."

"Other signs I am his dad."

"Yes. He loves riding at Joe's ranch. He wants to play chess but no one else in the family is interested. I've tried a few times. He always beats me."

"Horses, no, but chess would be a good intro for us. We'll figure all of this out, Dre. A person can't have too many people to love."

Jeffrey breezed in with the renewed board and took

his seat just as the players rolled out on the field again. "I took a chance and brought along a can of the Spanish tuna. It's in the lettuce cup. Try a bit on a cracker. Not fishy or oily at all."

"I will in a little while," she promised to please him.

"Cullen, you are glowing with satisfaction. I take it you will get a chance to meet your son. I envy you." Jeffrey flashed him a most winning smile.

"Your turn will come. I'll make sure of that."

Cullen did appear to have more color in his face. Perhaps, he had been dreading this talk as much as she had. She squeezed his hand. He squeezed back. A beginning.

Chapter Thirty-Two

A little more than halfway through the season, and the Sinners had won again despite the baggage he carried besides the football. Saturday night after the encounter at the Boo and Brew, Barb made him pay for an inadvertent compliment to Dre gone awry. She'd allowed him to take off the pads, his jersey, and cleats but wanted him to chase her around the apartment in her cheerleader costume wearing only his tight nylon and spandex game pants minus a jock strap to show his arousal when he caught her. That was not going to happen.

"Barb, I have a game tomorrow. I'm hot and sweaty and need a shower. Why don't we just do it in there and get to bed."

"Umm, I'd like you to take me hot and sweaty and bursting out of your pants on the turf inside the Dome. We could pretend that."

The idea revolted him. His stomach rolled over again as it had been doing a lot lately. He went to her bar, poured a shot, and downed it. There, now maybe he could cope with a few more hours of Barb.

"You're certainly no fun tonight, though I did love the way you totally ignored Dre as if she were the dirt under your feet." Then, she glared at him.

Her mood changes were often mercurial and dangerous. He could read any player in the league, but not her.

"You saw your old girlfriend, and you are thinking of her right now." Instead of running away from him, she coiled close like a cobra about to strike and wrapped herself around him, so maybe a boa, not an asp.

"Sure, she's fresh and lovely but—" He didn't get the words out fast enough to prevent a strike. Her nails, painted red to match her costume, slashed across his back and came away bloody.

Show no pain. That would please her. "I was about to say but not as sexy and accomplished as you are. Having a mangled back isn't going to help me win a Super Bowl for you." He had to keep her mind off of Dre.

"How right you are. Poor boy, let me clean your wounds. She found a clean rag behind the bar, sloshed it with whiskey, and applied it to his back. The sting made him wince against his will. She loved that.

"Perhaps, I misjudged you tonight. Just remember, I now have a completed contract to sell the team to St. Louis for five point three billion, to go up to six billion if you deliver a Super Bowl—unless I decide to keep you here. Don't bother searching for it. I keep it in a safety deposit box since it is such a valuable document. All it lacks is my signature. Moving on, considering the state of your back, you'll have to be on top tonight. Don't worry. I'll help you get it up."

Another evening with a red ring around his dick. Paris hadn't been enough where he'd sat for hours in salons telling Barb how great she looked in every outfit. A fine lunch in a smart café went down uneasily, then sex in their room where she'd insisted on doing it on the bidet. "How French," she'd declared. "Old Gus could never mange this." Easy cleanup, he'd thought.

She let him have the afternoon off in favor of getting a real French manicure and having her roots dyed. He'd taken refuge in the Louvre. Seen all the tourist attractions: the buxom Venus de Milo, the small, dark Mona Lisa, the lavish Winged Victory before he wandered to the hall of mummies and gazed at their colorful cases beside their desiccated and horrific remains. How much like Barb they were, beautiful on the outside, dry and dead inside. More good food roiled in his gut after that, more punishing sex, then a long plane ride home in a private jet with its own bed. He hadn't gotten the rest most of the team experienced during a bye week.

Once, he thought he'd take Dre to Paris on a honeymoon. Matt and his family tended to vacation at national parks or on beaches. He believed she'd never been to Europe. Now Paris was ruined for him—and her unless someone else took her there. Two men, she'd been there with two men at Boo he knew nothing about. That bothered him. She'd never take him back even if he had the chance to escape Barb, but he wanted to be sure she found someone more worthy of her than he.

"Come on. Your mind is wandering again. It's her, I know it's her." That earned him another swipe of her claws on his back, another swabbing with alcohol, and he still had to endure sex with Barb.

The game the next day wasn't his best effort but had gotten the team close to scoring twice. Tom finished both drives off with field goals. Their fierce defense kept the other team from scoring all except once, and they'd triumphed thirteen to seven. He knew the men played hard to give Dean his last Super Bowl. They didn't play for him.

Dre didn't watch with Joe and Edie or from the sky box anymore. He tried to keep his eyes away from the sight of Barb in low-cut red pressing her boobs against the glass in hers and hoping to make it into the television feed.

He'd come in early and suited up before the rest of the team to hide her handiwork of the night before and waited to be the last person in the showers, but not long enough. As Huddleston came out wrapped in a towel, he tried to cover his back with the same, but big not so bright Hud stopped by his locker to talk, unusual these days when most of the team ignored him except in practice and on the field.

"Man, those are some scratches," Hud observed.

"Barb was feeling feisty last night." He draped his towel over his shoulders.

"So, you and Dre are really, really over, huh."

"Yeah."

"Mind if I ask her out?"

"It's not up to me. Try if you want, but I don't think you have much in common."

"She likes football, right?"

"Yes, but also Shakespeare and art." The thought of Hud's huge paws on her body upset him in ways he could never reveal.

"I didn't get here by not trying. I'll ask her. I figure if you broke her in she'll be great." Hud's Neanderthal brow wrinkled. "Is she a scratcher?"

"You'll have to find that out for yourself if she gives you a chance." His hands knotted on the ends of the towel. He had the urge to wrap it around Hud's neck and squeeze.

"Okay. Just wanted to make sure you were cool with it."

Truth be told, Hud wasn't his favorite teammate. He'd plotted to get Ty kicked off the team and said some ugly things about Edie as well. He'd heard about all this from the family since he'd been out of town at the time. Ty had forgiven the man who could throw a mean block and was an asset to the team, but he'd never warm to him. No one talked trash about his twin.

Finally, finally, Hud lumbered away toward his pile of street clothes. Rex fled to the showers, the last one in. The next two opponents were on the east coast. They'd be on the road for a couple of weeks, and he'd get some relief from Barb. Lately, she'd taken to throwing lavish game day parties at her place, inviting new friends she'd made in various organizations and boasting about "her boy toy", Rex Billodeaux. The thought made his stomach grind again.

He stuck his head under the hot water and let it scour his sore back. It burned, burned, burned.

Chapter Thirty-Three

Dre met Cullen for lunch twice before the weekend. Mostly, they talked about Drew's childhood. She confessed her alienation from her own family but said Annie and Matt had filled in the gap along with Joe and Nell who acted as loving grandparents. In turn, Cullen admitted to his family's disappointment with his staying in New Orleans. He went home for some holidays, always glad to return to the much less tense Big Easy. They'd both found their place in the world. She liked him more and more.

They decided that he would come to the game day family get together since Annie was hosting this one. Better to meet Drew on familiar territory.

"Is it all right if I bring Jeffrey for backup? Sure, I go before judges all the time, but meeting your friends en masse is intimidating."

"Mostly the group is women and children. But if Jeffrey brings his charcuterie board and his general gorgeousness, he'll be welcome."

"That's how he wins people over."

"We usually stick to bowls of mild chili and hot dogs for the kids. Lots of corn chips. Stacy will put out some fruit and vegetable trays for the sake of our good health. Bring what you want to drink."

Now that Sunday had arrived, Dre kept wiping her sweaty palms on her Sinners sweatshirt while awaiting

Cullen's arrival. She'd told Drew a special friend was coming over to join the party. Who? The man who'd taken her out last Saturday. Drew frowned.

"I know I should have told you that I had a date, but he was wearing a scary costume. I didn't want you to be afraid." Her son did not buy that weak excuse.

"We're not babies. We know that stuff isn't real."

The doorbell rang and in walked Cullen and Jeffrey burdened with snacks again. Under one arm, Cullen carried a beautiful inlaid box that he set out of the reach of Jenny and Jude's twins before unloading the food in the kitchen where the chili bubbled on the stove and the large bag of corn chips had already been raided. Drew trailed them waiting for an introduction.

His mother jumped in with both feet. "Honey, this is Cullen Carson, the man I went out with last week and his friend, Jeffrey. They wanted to meet you."

"Yeah, you're the guy who made my mother sick. You didn't take good care of her. Don't ever call me honey. I'm Drew, short for Andrew because we're Drew and Dre."

Cullen apologized. "Yes, I'm sorry about that. We did bring her safely home and took care of her last Sunday."

"What are your intentions toward my mother?"

Oh no, the same question he'd asked Rex. Dre took a deep breath and waited for Cullen's answer.

"Right now, friendship. We knew each other back in Indiana and just recently reconnected. Time will tell how it goes."

"Oh, I do like this boy," Jeffrey said. "I'd hate to come up against him in court."

Meanwhile, Drew's wingmen, Daniel and Gabe,

came to stand right behind him. Stacy's three teens, attracted by the drama, formed a third line of defense. They would have rather been elsewhere with their friends, but suddenly the day had gotten more interesting.

Cullen tried again. "I understand you like to play chess. I brought my board along."

"We got one, but no one will play with me."

"Because you always win," Daniel said, getting right to the point.

"And it's slow and boring," added Gabe.

Cullen smiled in a way Dre hadn't seen since his high school matches which she'd scouted when looking for a father for her child. It said he'd win. Would that upset Drew?

"I'll most likely win at first. But I can teach you a few moves you might like, maybe at halftime."

Drew shrugged. "Halftime might be too short, but okay. The game is starting." He turned and walked into the den. His pals went with him.

The teens remained as Jeffrey unveiled his tray twice the size as the last one and more elaborate. "Charcuterie, anyone?"

"That's better than mom's veggie trays any day," said Wynn, the only girl in the group. Her elder half-brother, Beck whispered in her ear to which she answered, "I don't care and neither should you. May we have some now?"

"*Certainement.*"

"That's certainly in French, DJ," she told her less sophisticated younger brother. They descended on it like locusts on a Mormon field. Wynn filled her plate with strawberries cut into floral shapes and topped with something creamy. Her brothers went directly to the pepperoni and salami rings and the cheese chunks. Jeffrey urged Wynn to try the Manchego which she did.

Stacy came in and shooed them out of the kitchen. "Leave some for the rest of us. Come on, you'll miss the kickoff."

The guests were given the honor of either end of the sofa with Dre, Annie, and Jude sandwiched in between. Stacy curled her yoga and Pilates limber body onto a large floor cushion. The teens dragged beanbag chairs from the other end of the room and slouched into them. The three boys lay on their stomachs with the sofa afghan under their bellies. Jenny and her same-age cousins set up a party with juice boxes and a bowl of corn chips on a small table.

"Xo isn't coming?" asked Dre who wanted the psychic sister to read the two men's auras and make sure nothing bad lurked there.

"No, she doesn't like to drag her brood from Chapelle when the team is on the road and they can't see their daddy in person. Besides, I think she's expecting again," Stacy said.

"No! When is she going to stop?" Jude, who'd already stopped with her twins, asked.

"Really not our business. Oh, and Edie messaged her regrets. She has to cover some society event for the magazine and is ticked off about it. Lorena and Alix flew to see the game with Mikey and Mia along. Me, I wouldn't travel with two-year-olds. Their choice. Sarge and Jessie will watch with Mom and Dad at the ranch. Trin and Josee are in Europe again. Is that everyone? So just us." Stacy sipped her drink of choice, red wine, from a glass set beside her.

Actually, the last omissions pleased Dre. All those people meant lots and lots of opinions, loving and well-meant but still annoying. She felt gradual introductions to the many Billodeauxs would go better for Cullen, and her for that matter.

Using their now usual two-quarterback system, Dean played the first half with assists from Rex in running plays and one where he was hoisted over a pile of bodies into the end zone to score. A weak cheer went up for that performance, but not from her or the men or Drew.

"I thought we weren't cheering for Uncle Rex after what he did to my mom." Drew pouted.

"We're cheering for the Sinners, dear," Annie said. "Not any one person."

Jude, using her doctor's eyes, remarked, "There's something off about Rex. He's playing hard but not with his usual energy. He should have spiked that ball in the end zone, and he just walked away."

Sitting next to her, Jeffrey offered, "Too much beyotch, I believe." He failed to observe that little Jenny stood by his elbow.

"What's beyotch?" Jenny asked, her big, brown eyes completely sincere.

"A very bad lady."

"Okay. You're pretty."

"Why thank you. You're very cute yourself."

Jenny beamed until Gabe said, "Men are handsome, not pretty."

"Oh, but I think I am." Jeffrey made himself even more attractive with a dashing smile.

Jude elbowed him. "You're good at this."

Cullen sat quietly until halftime when the group

266

lined up at the stove for a bowl of chili or a hot dog with mustard, ketchup, chili, or all three. Annie doled out the chili according to age and the likelihood of how much mess each child would make. Stacy stood by the fruit and vegetable trays and made sure the kids no matter their age took some. When they were all served, the adults got their bowls augmented with cheese shreds, corn chips, and delicacies from the charcuterie bowls like the Russian eggs the teens had ignored. They emptied the last of the wine into glasses and took their seats again, all but Cullen who ate fast and asked Drew, who had just finished his mustard dog in four big bites, if he cared for a quick game of chess.

"I guess so."

Cullen cleared a space on the old chest and opened his inlaid box. He removed the pieces of onyx and alabaster and let Drew choose his color, white. They arrayed them on the reverse side of the box that served as a board. Cullen sat on his end of the sofa, and Drew knelt on the floor. Tense, Dre pretended to eat while watching them both. Cullen won in just two moves. Devastation crossed her son's face.

"He whooped my ass! I fell for the Fool's Mate. I didn't think he'd try that because he wants me to like him."

She wanted to pull him into her arms and comfort him, but first had to do her duty as a mother. "Language, Drew, and grammar for that matter."

"All the guys say it."

"Yeah, Mom, all the guys say it," Cullen echoed with a slight smile on his rather thin lips.

"Don't undermine me."

Cullen held up his hands in surrender. "Never. It's

true I won't simply let you win, Drew. I know lots of gambits I can teach you. Soon you'll be unbeatable by kids your age."

Drew held out a fist. "Respect," he said. Cullen bumped with him and cleared the board as the game started again. Dre let out a breath she didn't know she held.

The Sinners won again, thirty-five to twenty-one, and continued their march toward a perfect season and the Super Bowl. Clean up began in the kitchen, but Cullen and Drew stayed behind playing a second game of chess.

"Dre, you should know he always leaves me with the dishes even though I do most of the cooking," Jeffrey informed her as she bagged leftover veggies.

"If that's his worst trait, I can live with it. Just look at him with Drew, both so intent on that game I barely understand."

"Cullen is a good man. He won't hurt you the way Rex did."

"I believe that." Because she would not let another man get that close again. She could settle for fondness rather than passionate love if Drew was happy.

Her son burst into the kitchen. "I lost again, but I'm learning a lot, Mr. Cullen says. Can he come to our game party at Aunt Stacy's next weekend so we can play some more?"

"You bet, honey bear. I mean Drew."

Behind her son, Cullen smiled like a man keeping a happy secret he couldn't wait to divulge.

Chapter Thirty-Four

He dreaded the upcoming family Thanksgiving, an event he'd always loved, and felt saddened when he couldn't get home from up north for the holiday. Rex disconnected from his mother's phone call. She rarely bullied people into coming. They always had enough turkeys and hams, baskets of biscuits and French bread, dozens of side dishes brought by guests from an unexpected artichoke casserole all the way down to ziti in tomato sauce plus the Cajun favorites like rice dressing, baked beans, and mac and cheese. Sometimes, Edie's roommate from India brought special dishes not made with beef or pork, but she'd returned to her native land after graduation. He'd miss the dessert table with its choice of both pumpkin and sweet potato pies and so many cakes, chocolate, red velvet, coconut, and one shaped like a turkey that Xo always baked for the kids. Junior now made Mawmaw Nadine's special bread pudding in much larger quantities since she'd gifted the recipe to him in her will.

None of that this year. His stomach burned just thinking about the feast. But his usually laid back mom insisted he at least put in an appearance for a few hours despite the long drive of three hours from New Orleans to the ranch and back. He'd be required to share a meal with Barb in her condo that evening. Sickening thought, as he would be the dessert.

He'd explained to Mama Nell that the lonely widow with no family of her own wanted his company. His mother, who usually invited everyone, hesitated before saying, "You can bring her along."

"No, no, I can't. To be honest, she'd ruin the day for everyone else. The team members hate her, and if she ran into Dre it could get ugly." No way would he let Barb sully a Billodeaux thanksgiving as she did everything she touched.

"Dre won't be here. She and Drew are celebrating Thanksgiving with her new boyfriend. We're losing her, Rex."

"Maybe it's for the best." His gut twisted again. "Is he good to her?"

"I haven't met him yet, but Annie and Stacy say he's a lovely man who plays chess with Drew. Nice looking, according to them, and an attorney. Evidently, they knew each other back in Indiana, same hometown, and recently discovered they both lived in New Orleans now. They have a lot in common."

"That's great." He had to get off the subject of Dre before he spilled it all to his mother, and hence to the whole clan. "I'll come for a while but must leave early."

That settled it.

On Thanksgiving day, he drove his classic red Corvette, taken out of storage for the occasion, home to Chapelle. He could always talk cars with the guys and give the girls short rides, anything to keep them away from the topics of Barb and Dre. Intentionally arriving as dinner was being served, he kissed his mom on the cheek and blended into the line of guests filling plates to overflowing. Taking only one tablespoon of each dish usually required two trips. He didn't go unnoticed for long. His sisters swarmed him. Their younger children were already seated in the kitchen supervised as usual by Xo.

"Hey, hey, let me get something to eat. Then, you can grill me like the leftover ham. I brought the 'Vette if anyone wants a ride." He put a slice of turkey on his plate, bypassed the tureen of gravy sitting on a warmer, and went on to a spoonful of rice dressing, the mac and cheese, and a biscuit.

"You still eat like a child. Take some salad and come sit down with us," Stacy ordered.

He ignored her. "Where are you sitting?"

"We have a table out on the gallery. It's mild today, a little breeze, but no mosquitoes," Annie said. "We need to tell you something important away from the crowd."

He glanced around the room. No sign of his dad who was always a huge presence in any space. Also lacking were their large husbands and Teddy who stood out in his wheelchair. "Where are the guys?"

"Out in the barbecue pavilion having some sort of meeting, but us first. If that's all you're going to take, let's go." He thought Edie, short as she was, might attempt to frog march him to their destination.

"I'll get a beer for you," Lorena offered. "You'll need it."

That got him moving in their direction as they passed through the crowd like his linemen poking a hole in the opposition for him to run through. Out on the gallery, their half-eaten meals and beverages cluttered the table, but a space had been saved for him.

Lorena, his tall, volleyball playing, Olympic medal winning sister, put a beer in front of him. "Drink, you'll need it."

"Eat first," Jude badgered. "You've lost weight, and I don't like your coloring."

Without much on his plate, he finished swiftly, took a pull on his beer, and said, "Okay, what?"

"You know the guy Dre is dating?" Annie said.

"I only saw him once at the Boo and Brew, tall, pale, blue eyes, dressed up like some kind of Greek god. If that's the guy, she's only been seeing him about a month. Mom says he's an attorney. That's about it."

"But she's known him a lot longer." Annie patted his hand.

This couldn't be a good sign. He chugged more beer. "Yeah, from Indiana, right?"

Tall, blue-eyed, smart, from Indiana. The pieces began to fall into place like a good play, only he wouldn't like the outcome.

"He's Drew's father. Dre never told him, but then there he was, the horny teenager all grown up, nice to her and her son from the get go. They're going to tell him today." Annie now had both of his hands captured in her warm grip.

He pulled free and stood up. "Nothing I can do about that now."

"Break it off with Barb. Ask her forgiveness before she decides it's in Drew's best interest to marry the guy. We know he wants a family," Stacy verified.

The memory of telling Dre he didn't desire kids right now, knowing that would be the last nail in the coffin of their love, came back all too strong. He thought he might be sick over the gallery rail if he didn't escape soon. "She won't be able to forgive me. I made sure of that."

"But why?" asked Alix, the athletic former Sinners'

punter Tom had married.

"I can't say, but you of all people know about taking one for the team. I need to leave."

"Please, stop and see Xochi in the kitchen before you do. She's been worried about you," Annie implored.

"Okay, I'll go out that way and tell her I'm fine, just wonderful."

He heard their mingled feminine voices saying as he strode away, "We tried. We tried."

In the kitchen, he found Xochi surrounded by small children, handling them with her usual aplomb. She sat back a bit from the table, and the roundness of her belly betrayed another pregnancy.

"I guess I should say congratulations," he said. Make it about her, not him, but Xo's dark, compassionate eyes were already studying him in the way they did when she read an aura. She didn't speak right away until one of the kids asked for more milk. Pouring it from a pitcher into a sippy cup, she snapped the lid back on and handed it to Alix's Mia. At least, he thought that's who she was with her strawberry blonde hair.

"I'm not as far along as I look. It's twins this time, but sometime in March or April you'll be an uncle again. Sit down. Here, have some bread pudding. JJ didn't touch it. And a glass of milk. That would be good for you."

"Nothing wrong with me, Xo." To prove it, he dug into the bread pudding, meringue-topped and creamy beneath, the best bread pudding in the world. It brought back memories of his plain-spoken mawmaw and many happy gatherings. His arrangement with Barb had severed so many ties with his family already. When would it end and how?

273

The small, child-sized portion didn't last long. He drank the milk to wash it down, and all the while she studied him, her tan face marked with concern but glowing with impeding motherhood. "You are sick in both mind and body, Rex. Once you burned with a bright yellow flame, and now that is a dirty brown smudge. Barb Bienville is poison to you. You must get away from her."

"You must mind your own business. I'm leaving." Before he could flee, she caught his hand.

"Let me give you this." A sudden warmth filled his body like being bathed in the light of a sunny spring day. His stomach stopped gnawing. He felt—better.

"Thanks for whatever that was." He'd heard she could heal but hadn't experienced it before. Never needed to. He'd always been strong, healthy, sure of himself, until now.

"It won't last long, Rex. Set yourself free."

He didn't answer but made for the door, running away from his too loving family. He intended to go straight to the parking area and turn back to New Orleans. Rest up because Barb didn't expect him before early evening. The sight of the men gathered in the barbecue pavilion turned his head. Yes, they were eating and drinking, but Trin, his nerd brother, held a calculator in his hand, thumbing away on it. He swerved their way and paused by the screen door, his approach muffled by the fallen pecan leaves on the path, his form shadowed by the evergreen live oak that overhung the small building.

Conor Riley, his dad's best friend from the old days, spoke. "Joe agrees to put in the thirty percent required for team ownership. I'll put in a billion. I'm sure we can raise the rest. We appreciate that Trin and his wife and Teddy are willing to make up another billion. We're still short."

"Mostly Trin, but I wanted to help," Teddy said in that mellow announcer's voice the networks paid him a million dollars a year to use, but not near what the players earned.

"We can't ask my dad. All his money has gone to his church and the needy, and I'm out because I'm still playing like most of the guys at this table." Junior nodded toward Dean, Mack, Tom, Ty, and Jock.

"Would Ned and Paula Bienville put up a share? They'd love to stick it to Barb because they didn't get the team," Dean suggested.

Rex stepped inside and slammed the screen door to get their attention. "Don't bother asking them. If Barb gets a whiff of their involvement, any deal will be off. She wants to hurt them and the city for snubbing her. Right now she has a contract to sell the Sinners out of state for over five billion locked in a safety deposit box. The only thing that might change her mind is getting her involved with high class society in New Orleans. You'd do better to get Stacy to wrangle an invitation to the Rex ball for her. I know you go sometimes."

"We aren't members, only invited guests, but we'll see what we can do."

"Good. I've gotten her onto some committees and made her a patron of the arts."

"Is that what you're doing, son, all that you're doing?" his dad asked as if it hurt him to say.

The glow that Xo had instilled in him began to fade. Nausea returned. "I need to go back to New Orleans to celebrate Thanksgiving with her."

"Mate, I don't know how you can stomach that," Jock said, and the others muttered their agreement.

He didn't reply, just left, fading away into the shadows under the trees.

Chapter Thirty-Five

Dre should have known Thanksgiving with Cullen and Jeffrey would be a culinary extravaganza: arugula salad, duck a l'orange with a mix of white and wild rice with almonds, and creamed spinach with mushrooms, all prepared by Jeffrey. She'd volunteered to bring a bread and a pumpkin pie, but Sephy's biscuits and the reliable recipe from the Libby's label on the canned pumpkin seemed very humble beside it even in a homemade crust and embellished with daubs of Cool Whip and a turkey cutout.

She waxed proud over her son's adaptability and ability to converse with such sophisticated men. When asked if he liked duck, he'd replied, "Sure. Daddy Joe goes hunting and brings back ducks and geese. We all get some only they don't get served with orange slices. This is good though."

About the spinach, he said, "It's lots better in this white sauce."

He shoved down enough arugula to satisfy her prompting to try it. Rice in all forms was a regular part of his diet, so no problem there, but he did eat the majority of the biscuits. Her pie reaped praise, and Jeffrey inquired about the recipe. "Like the biscuits, an old family secret," she told him.

The adults sipped a German Riesling with coffee afterward while Drew stuck to milk with a promise he

Lynn Shurr

could have a Coke during the afternoon football games. Before they adjourned from the antique mahogany dining table bearing a fruit cornucopia to the living area with a TV large enough to please anyone, Cullen stood to make a final toast. This was it. Here it came.

"I'd like to give thanks this day for reuniting with an old friend and for bringing Drew, a son I never knew I had until recently, into my life. I hope in time we can form a real family together."

"Amen to that," said Jeffrey.

"Honey, I mean Drew, how do you feel about that?" she asked.

"Oh, I figured it out a while ago. We have the same shade of blue eyes. He's smart like me, and I think I will be tall, too. What really gave it away was both of you being from the same town and school in Indiana. I was only waiting for you to tell me."

That earned a "Bravo" from Jeffrey. "May I be your uncle?"

"I have lots of honorary uncles, so yeah."

With that, Cullen and his son adjourned to the sofa to watch football together. Dre stayed back to let them bond. "I'll help with the dishes."

"See, I told you he always forgets about them. How I envy Cullen right now. He has a genuinely nice half-grown son who accepts him. What a dream. I'll do the duck pan, so sticky. You take the pots. The china must be hand-washed and dried along with the silver in clean water. We picked out the patterns together, but if you'd like something else that would be fine."

"Why would I do that? I like the wide gold band and the silverware is simple and tasteful. It's not for me to say." Well, that was puzzling.

They joined Cullen and Drew on a pale-gray sofa accented with red pillows once they completed the chore. An eclectic collection of original art adorned the walls: French quarter sketches, Louisiana landscapes, and a few abstracts. The immaculate room had never known the ravages of children, especially boys. Dre doubted if any feet had ever rested on the glass-topped coffee table. They watched two games, had second servings of pie, and headed home before it got too late.

In the quiet of the car and the light traffic on this holiday less raucous than rest, she quizzed her son on their day. "Did you like Thanksgiving with Cullen and Jeffrey?"

He stared out the side window without glancing her way. "Yeah, it was okay."

"But not like being with your cousins at the ranch, right?"

"Yep. The food was good but kinda strange. I'd rather have turkey and rice dressing and lots of cake for dessert."

She might as well level with him before Christmas. "I don't think we will be going to the ranch for holidays anymore."

Now, he turned a glum face her way. "Because of you and Uncle Rex breaking up?"

"Yes, we'd still be welcome, but it might be embarrassing to run into him there. He's part of the Billodeaux family, and we're only honoraries. We shouldn't make their party awkward."

"So we can't pretend they're our family anymore."

The sadness he emanated wrung her heart. "You will always be welcome at the ranch and can go with Matt and Annie if you want."

279

"Then, you'll be all alone."

"I'll probably be with Cullen. He makes me feel cherished. He'll be a caring father to you."

"Cherished, is that the same as love?"

Her son always had good questions. Perhaps, he'd follow Cullen into the law. "No, not exactly." Nor was it passion. They hadn't kissed yet, but she doubted she'd feel it throughout her entire body as she had with Rex. That was behind her. Her best life ahead might be a quiet one of mutual respect and perhaps another child or two. Cullen had hinted that he'd want more if she did. She'd like that. He'd made Drew, and a few more the same would be wonderful.

She parked in her usual space and noted Matt's SUV wasn't in his. She knew he'd have a practice tomorrow for a home game Sunday, and they wouldn't stay over at the ranch. With luck, she and Drew would be asleep and not have to hear all about the big Billodeaux bash.

Chapter Thirty-Six

Waiting for Coach and Dean to give their usual pre-game pep talks, Rex sat on a bench fully suited up except for his helmet. He could use some pep after that horror of a Thanksgiving Eve with Barb. He'd stowed his Covette in its storage space as soon as he got back to the city. No way did he want it spoiled by being commanded to take Barb for a ride. He'd always planned to go with Dre to some secret spot and make love. Another dream destroyed.

He'd downed some Tums and swilled Pepto-Bismal from the bottle. It turned his shit black but made him feel better. He'd taken a nap to prepare for an evening with Barb.

Her driver, sympathy on his face, had picked him up as usual. Wearing a slinky negligee, she awaited him at a candlelit table with the wine already poured and salads topped with feta on ornate plates with golden chargers beneath them. Despite a greeting that included rubbing herself against him for an extended time without arousing him, he managed to eat the stuffed Cornish game hen with wild rice, and roasted brussels sprouts. No pumpkin pie, but a pecan flavored with bourbon for dessert. He would rather have had the bourbon in a shot glass. She made sure he knew she'd had the whole thing catered because Barbara Bienville had no need to cook for any man. Fine with him.

She checked her diamond encircled wristwatch as if impatient. "Bedtime," she declared. His stomach was a seething ball of misery, but he might as well get it over with, get back to the apartment and rest up for tomorrow's practice. Again, she rubbed all over him, only this time he responded immediately and urgently without having the least urge to do so. She insisted on leading him by erect penis to her bedroom where she gave him the command to get out of his clothes and lie down. She came to coil beside him.

"Very nice," she judged his erection. "I've been thinking why should I have to do all the work every time. You've been resisting me."

He could not deny that.

"So, I crushed one of my husband's boner pills and put it in your wine. It's a fairly strong dosage as Gus had a lot of trouble getting it up after he turned eighty. Even then, he only managed one shot. But you, so young and healthy. You should be good for three or four ejaculations throughout the night. Happy Thanksgiving."

As if he felt thankful for what she'd done to him. He didn't reply, simply closed his eyes and let her straddle him. He came quickly but the erection didn't go away at once. She was able to satisfy herself.

"Next time I arouse you, you'll be on top. We won't have to wait all that long."

"Barb, I have practice in the morning. Big game on Sunday."

"But it seems such a waste. You'll leave when I let you go."

After a fourth time, she did. He'd had little sleep and a bad practice, but she didn't call for him again that weekend. From now on, he'd only drink tap water at her place—or the alcohol of his choice from her bar.

The men began to gather for the pep talk. Lucky him that Hud decided to sit next to him instead of shunning that seat like the rest of the team.

"Hey."

"What do you want, Hud?"

"Nuttin'. I called Dre. She said she was flattered, but she's seeing someone. You know that? Did you set me up on purpose? Because if you did, don't expect me to protect you out there today."

"Thanks for the warning, but I didn't know until Thanksgiving Day when my family told me. Good for her. She deserves better than me."

Hud struggled to work that out, his face contorting in the process. "You kiddin' me? You can have any woman you want. You can throw away a prime babe like Dre. Why you with that b—"

Coach came in and began to wind them up for a win. Dean threw out a few cautions about what to expect from a team of this caliber. "I know our place to win the division is already assured, but let's go for that perfect record. The Super Bowl is scheduled for New Orleans this year. How great would that be?"

Rex put his hand in for the group hurrah and went out to take his place on the end of the bench until needed. He was summoned more often than usual for running plays and after the half took over for Dean. Late in the fourth quarter, the Sinners stayed ahead by one score. His job now mostly amounted to short passes to get downs and run off as much time on the clock as possible to prevent the opponent from getting the ball. He set up another play and drew his arm back for a short pitch to Mack who was supposed to take a slide as soon as he had the down. The ball barely left his fingertips when the opponent's big center came busting through a hole in his defense and butted him in the stomach. He went down on his back. Whistles blew. Flags flew.

Not the first time he'd had the breath knocked out of him, but now he gasped for air. The pain in his middle felt like an internal grenade had gone off inside him. He pushed up with both arms and fell to the turf again. Something trickled down his chin. Blood. Had he bitten his tongue? Too much blood for that. The team gathered around him He reached out a hand to big Jock Brown.

"Help me walk off."

"We got you, mate. Hud, get his other side."

In truth, they carried him, his feet barely moving, until the trainers swarmed him, put him on a stretcher for a ride out of the arena. The pain didn't quit, not in the ambulance or at the hospital though they'd given him a shot of something on the way to take care of it. Once they put the IV in, it started to recede. Good stuff.

"Mr. Billodeaux, we're going to put you under for an endoscopy and take a look at your stomach."

He swore he heard his always acerbic sister, Jude in the background saying, "Bet you fifty it's a perforated ulcer."

He nodded. "Go ahead."

When he came out of it, she'd won her bet. He needed a laparoscopic procedure to put a Graham Patch on the hole in his belly. It seemed simple enough. Transfer the fatty tissue from another part of his stomach to the hole and suture it in. No external cutting.

"When will I be able to play again?"

"Jesus, is football all you care about?" Short and furious, Jude stood nearby in her white coat.

"It's all I have left. You're not going to operate on me, are you?"

The lead doctor cleared his throat and answered, "Four to eight weeks depending. Expect a four day stay in the hospital afterward. And no, Dr. Bullock will not be doing the procedure. She is too close to you."

"But you better believe I'll be watching."

"Do it as soon as you can. We have playoffs coming up. The Sinners won today, huh?"

"Yeah, the guy who hit you drew a penalty, automatic first down, game over. Same score as when you left the game."

"Good. Doctor, I'm ready whenever you are."

When it was over, he found his mother by his bed and his dad guarding the room from all intruders except Jude who came in an official capacity to check on him and unofficially, to chew him out.

"You were ill, I told you. Xo did her woo-woo stuff and said you were sick in mind, body, and spirit. Did you listen to us? No. If you'd gone for a checkup, you wouldn't be here now.

"They would have pulled me from the game. It was going to be a tough one. The team needed me. What do you care? You won fifty dollars and proved you were right."

"That bet was a joke, but I do enjoy being right. Listen, do what the doctor tells you, and you'll heal faster. Don't be a stubborn ass." She left after giving that medical opinion.

One by one, his other siblings visited for short periods of time. No matter how angry they were about Dre, they were there for him. Dean told him not to worry about the next game. Just get well. Same for the others who played. His dad allowed a smattering of Sinners not related to him in the door. Hud swore it wasn't him who failed to defend the quarterback.

"I was across the field blocking for Mack." Tears came to that big mug's squinty eyes.

"I know. That was the play. Don't worry about it."

"Next game will be hard without you."

"Tell the guys I'm sorry I didn't take better care of myself."

His room filled with flowers and balloons that he directed to be donated to local nursing homes. Fans crashed the Sinners site sending get well messages. They didn't know what a shit he really was. And now he felt like it, too.

Around the time he would have been expected at Barb's on a Monday, he woke from a doze. He'd been sleeping on and off, letting the antibiotics for the H. Pylori bacteria and painkillers do their job. The food wasn't worth waking up for—soup, crackers, apple juice, though the ice pops went down well. What woke him? Barb's strident voice outside the door and his dad's audible-calling answer that echoed down the hallway.

"Let me in. I need to check on my investment. I own that boy."

"No-you-don't. Get out of here."

His mom went to the door and opened it enough to stick her head into the fray. "Leave, or I am calling security. Think how that will look in the tabloids. The lobby is brimming with reporters."

Barb's stiletto heels turned and picked their way down the tiled floor toward the elevators. His parents had made it clear they would be staying with him at the bachelor pad for the duration of his recovery. He felt safe for the first time in months.

Chapter Thirty-Seven

What a Sunday it had turned out to be. Drew asked to watch the game from the sky box as if he knew his days to do this were limited. He took off with Annie and his cousins while she'd gone to Cullen's condo to be spoiled by their care. Would she rather have wine than beer? A different topping on the popcorn? More air conditioning or less?

Dre kept watching for a glimpse of Drew, and she thought she'd seen him once when the cameras focused on the glass where Stacy stood cheering her husband on. A brief view of Barb all in red made her shiver and brought on the question about the temperature in the condo. Even at the end of November, heat was rarely needed in New Orleans, but the ever-present humidity still had to be chased away.

Cullen caught on quickly. "I doubt if we could afford a sky box, but certainly four season tickets will be within our grasp."

"We'll talk about it next year."

"I'm happy you think there will be a next year for us."

The game itself had been touch and go, exciting to the last plays as Rex slowly worked the team down the field. Then, the disastrous hit that landed him in the hospital. Closeups of Rex bleeding from the mouth, being helped off the field, made her rise from her seat and stifle a sob.

"We know you still have feelings for the man, but you must never crawl back to him, Dre. Verbal abuse is as bad as physical. He has his family and the team to look after him."

Cullen took her hand and coaxed her back on the sofa.

"Our breakup has caused a rift among the Billodeauxs, and it is my fault. I wasn't enough for him. I need to accept that. But he hurt Drew, and that is unforgiveable. I am working on new living arrangements, trying to take us out of their lives so they can still have Rex over without any awkwardness."

Cullen and Jeffrey exchanged glances. Jeffrey got up and went into the kitchen. In the background, the game ended with a win. Viewers, stay tuned for additional information on the status of Rex Billodeaux. Cullen turned off the TV.

"Dre, this might not be the best time to ask, but I have a proposal for you."

She half-expected him to whip a tasteful diamond ring from somewhere on his person, not in his skinny jeans for sure. No ring appeared. Good, she wasn't ready to make this decision yet. Perhaps, next year for that and season tickets. But he went on with what he wanted to say.

"Jeffrey and I have been discussing how well you and Drew fit in with us. If I married you, we would of course try to get a Garden District place where Drew would be comfortable, and you could have your own wing while Jeffrey and I would stay in another."

"I don't understand. Are you proposing a marriage of convenience? Isn't that what it used to be called?"

"A beard," Jeffrey called from the kitchen. "Our beard."

"Our families and close friends know we are a couple. We keep it low key because of his father's law firm. I'd marry him if could, but my parents aren't as accepting as Jeffrey's. He isn't welcome in their home when I go to visit. They call him that boy from New Orleans who made me queer when I always was."

"I suspected Jeffrey was gay. But—but you were all over me in high school. You made a baby with me."

"Was it the overdone charcuterie boards?" Jeffrey said, peeking around the corner.

Cullen shook his head. "Not now, Jeffrey. I was desperately trying to prove I was not homosexual. Once I left Indiana and met Jeffrey, I admitted the truth to myself. We have been together ever since."

Jeffrey came out of the kitchen if not the closet. "We do want to make a family. In fact, we've been considering a surrogate, comingling our sperm, and doing it by artificial insemination. If you want another child and are willing, we'd go that route. I believe we could all be very happy together."

"In a loveless marriage?" What did it matter? She wouldn't love again after Rex.

"Oh, no, we do love you and Drew. We care for you, just not in that way. I know other gay men who have good marriages with women and also have children. Most are older. It's the way they dealt with the Catholic church and society when gay love was forbidden, though it has always existed," Jeffrey assured her.

"We'd pay for Drew's tuition at his current school and see that he had opportunities to attend any college of his choice. You could continue to develop your career in your own studio." Cullen piled on the benefits of an alliance.

It might be for the best, her way out of the caring Billodeaux family, but still nearby for Drew's sake. "This is a lot to take in, especially today. I need to discuss it all with Drew, especially the gay part."

"We could help you with that," Jeffrey suggested.

"No, it's always been Dre and Drew. I'll speak to him soon but give me a while to consider your— proposal. I think I should leave now."

"You've had a shock. Let me drive you. Jeffrey can follow in your car."

"No, I'll drive her. You follow. I don't trust you with the Beamer in post-game traffic."

Cullen rolled those beautiful blue eyes. "His father gave that car to him when he graduated from law school. Still doesn't have a scratch on it. He needs to get over it."

They let Jeffrey drive the BMW to Matt's home, maybe no longer hers soon. She beat the family home, retreated to her room, and waited. The house filled with noise again after the dinner hour. Her loved ones were home. She didn't go downstairs, but Drew sought her out.

He seemed sad rather than elated as he usually did after a Sinners' win. He came to lie down beside her on the bed, a rare occurrence anymore. She put her arm around him and waited some more, not knowing how to begin.

Her son spoke first. "I know he's a jerk, but I'm worried about Uncle Rex."

"It's not bad to be concerned about another person, even if you don't like him anymore. That's called compassion. Pray for him if you want. I will. Say, how would you feel if I married Cullen?"

Drew wriggled away a few inches. "Isn't he gay with Jeffrey?"

"You know this how?"

"Beck said he thought so, but they are both still good guys so it shouldn't matter. I knew that, too. Once when we were at the ranch and I was still little, I heard that word, homosexual, and asked Mama Nell about it."

Of course, Mama Nell never lied or shrank from a discussion. "What did she say?"

"That some men love other men and wanted to be with them as if they were married. There are women who like women, too. I don't think I want to be gay."

"Oh, honey bear." He didn't correct her. "They are born that way and often know very early that they are different. But it does make their lives harder."

"I mean, I don't think I am. There's this girl in chess club. We always play together, and I sorta like her, Mom."

"I'd love to meet her. Maybe we could have her over for a movie night." She'd gotten way off track. "In our case, Cullen and Jeffrey would still be together, but we'd form a family, and that would be easier if I married your father. We'd live near here, and you could attend the same school, and visit your cousins. Not too much would change. Let's consider it. No hurry."

Her son appeared to have drifted off to sleep in her arms, or maybe he was faking. She didn't rouse him in any case. They had best think about it until Christmas at the very least.

Chapter Thirty-Eight

Walk, that was all the exercise they allowed him, and it drove Rex Billodeaux crazy. Soon, they promised some light weight work, and how did he feel about yoga? Today, he walked briskly down Canal Street, denied himself a forbidden coffee, and sipped on water. Much as he appreciated his parents' care, he had to get out of the apartment. So, he rose before they did, had toast, and set out before the sidewalks became crowded with tourists and dog walkers.

As he approached Schifferman's jewelry shop, he noticed a silver-haired man unlocking the front door—Leslie.

"Hey, Les," he greeted, and the small man turned on him.

"How could you?"

"How could I what?" Dare to get sick, but most likely consort with Barbara Bienville.

"Give Miss Dre's ring to *her*. She came slinking in here with it still in the box to have it appraised. I explained our policy of no returns on custom work. It was all I could do not to shoo her from the shop."

"But I didn't—"

"Good day, sir." Leslie swept inside to dwell among his gems like a guardian dragon and would have slammed the doors if possible, but Schifferman's closed with a discreet sigh.

Rex moved on, sipping his water, doing some deep breathing to quiet his stomach acid. He crossed to the other side of the street and doubled back to the bachelor pad where by now his mom would be making some bland breakfast for him. How he craved a spicy burrito. The chauffeured Caddie cruised alongside, seeking a space to pull over but settling on double parking to the chagrin of early morning drivers trying to get to work. Barb's driver hopped out.

"Mrs. Bienville wants to see you immediately."

"I don't want to see her. I'm still recuperating."

"I wouldn't defy her today. She's in quite a snit."

"Thanks for the warning, Ed."

They'd developed a friendship of sorts with the driver telling him that old Gus had directed him to report if Barb went anywhere besides the hairdresser, nail salon, or dress shops in case she broke their prenup. His personal opinion was that she'd gone nuts since gaining her freedom and might come for him next when she was through with Rex. If only that were true.

But this day had to come. Maybe he could still broker some kind of deal to save the Sinners even if he wasn't up to acrobatic sex of any kind. He took a place in the back while Eduardo risked his life returning to his seat as traffic flowed by.

On the way, he breathed slowly in and out, trying to practice some of the relaxation techniques Ty taught him to center himself. Name three things you see: Mariah's Place closed for the morning where he'd been with Dre, the marble lobby of Barb's condo, Gus' amazing collection of sports memorabilia now showing notable gaps as his widow sold off the treasures. Name three things you can smell: breakfast, the longed for coffee, and Barb's cloying perfume ruining both. Name three things you feel: fear that he'd let the team down, worry that Dre might marry her son's father, the faint hope that someday she'd understand and forgive him. Name three things you hear: glass breaking as Barb flung her china coffee cup against a wall where it splattered and broke, the shattering of the plate she aimed at him which missed but sent eggs benedict sliding to the floor, and Barb's voice shrieking. It didn't help.

"What good are you to me now? You can't play football and are of no use to me as a sex toy. Bad enough, but you have broken our bargain and squealed to your father about me."

The early morning light did not flatter a face enraged and distorted with anger. Not made up for the day, every flaw showed. Her breasts hung low without support. Her snarled hair appeared more rusty than red, and her plumped lips drew back to reveal teeth that still had toast crumbs in their crevices. He did give thanks that he'd never seen her in the early morning before.

She thrust a paper in his face. "Delivered by special messenger at this ungodly hour. A letter from the NFL that I have broken rules both written and ethical—as reported by Joseph Dean Billodeaux. I am abusing my quarterback according to him."

"I had nothing to do with that. I did not complain to anyone."

"What are you going to do about it?"

"Deny it of course."

"That won't be enough. We must convince them of your love for me—by using this."

She held out the Schifferman's box. He knew what it contained. Barb snapped the box open, took the emerald cut diamond from its silk lining, and jammed it on her finger as far as it would go until stopped by a bony knuckle. "We are now officially engaged."

"Not with that ring. I'll go along with a sham engagement, but not with that ring." He grasped her arm and pried the ring from her finger, stowed it in a pocket.

"I promise if you bruise me, I'll call security to take you away in handcuffs. Then, it will be you abusing me, not the other way around. What's that sound? Your reputation circling the drain."

He'd always been able to think fast on his feet. "I said I'll go along with it. I'll get you a ring more suited to your hand. It should be larger and have more diamonds. Other good things are ahead for you. Stacy is getting you an invitation to the Rex ball. The Sinners will win the Super Bowl right here in New Orleans. You can throw a victory party like no other, and the team will go up in value."

"I took that cheap ring to Schifferman's for an appraisal. I suppose Dre only rated a forty-five-thousand-dollar diamond, but that officious little man behind the counter still wouldn't give me a refund when I told him I was unhappy with it. I have bigger and better in my safe—along with the contract from St. Louis. I'll pick one out and announce our engagement, which we've kept a secret from the world. If this doesn't work, you'd damn well better win the Super Bowl for me. Dean has dropped the last two games without you to assist."

"I'll be back by the first of the year if they let me. The Sinners are so far ahead in games won that we'll still take the division and have home field advantage for the playoffs. Losing me has thrown the team off, but Dean will get them together again, I guarantee." He used one of his father's favorite phrases. Somehow, it gave him hope.

Barb pointed her nails at him. They were chipped and one was broken. She'd probably been entertaining her trainer for all he cared. Picking up an ornate, silver stand lighter she kept around to impress guests, she flicked it open and held something small she'd pulled from a nearby drawer to its flame. Dre's tiny portrait of a dragon spewed fire for real and disintegrated over a plate of half-eaten toast.

"Make sure she is out of your life, or no one will believe our engagement. Then, other things might catch on fire. Get out of here. If this doesn't work, bye-bye Sinners. I hope you love Budweiser."

As he turned something hit him on the back of the head, the ring box. He scooped it up and kept right on walking.

At the apartment, his mom did have breakfast and a scolding ready for him. "Where were you? I was so worried."

He couldn't eat that food, not now. "How about a protein drink, my antibiotic pill, and an antacid instead?"

His dad sat at the table eating scrambled eggs doused with hot sauce and bacon along with a cup of strong, dark roast coffee which only made Rex more furious with envy. "I wish you hadn't sent that complaint to the NFL. Barb had her driver scoop me up while I walked. She's talking about selling immediately to St. Louis. I had to placate her any way I could. You won't like it."

Joe put down his steaming mug. "I know how she has been using you. I'm collecting statements, gathering witnesses to testify before the other NFL owners to vote her out as unfit to have a team, believe you me."

"Before you can finish she'll sign and mail that contract. I had to promise to become engaged to her to stop it."

The pan his mother had been washing clattered in the sink sending bits of scrambled eggs into the air. "No, no, never." Her always sharp eyes noticed the bulge of the ring box in his shirt pocket. She snatched it. "Is this the diamond you intend to give her?"

"No, that is the ring I intended for Dre. Barb will supply her own as mine wasn't good enough."

"You *were* serious about Dre. I knew it all along. Do you know how much you'll hurt her with this announcement?"

"That's over now, gone, lost forever."

His dad exchanged a glance with his mom in one of those mystic moments of communication they shared. "Pack your bags, son, while I finish breakfast. We're going back to the ranch where she can't get at you anymore."

"I'll get your meds and make you a protein drink to go."

He found himself obeying. Stripped of his phone and riding in the back seat of their car with the kiddie locks employed as if they feared he'd open a door and throw himself into traffic, which seemed like a not so bad idea, but another appealed more. Soon he'd be behind the iron gates of Lorena Ranch with its high security and peaceful acres far, far from Barb.

Chapter Thirty-Nine

Dre knew something brewed in the kitchen other than a pot of tea when lunchtime arrived. The boys were in school, Jenny in day care, Matt in training, and yet the door opened and closed, opened and closed. She went downstairs to heat some soup, all she felt like eating lately, and found the Billodeaux women she felt closest to gathered as they did for any family crisis. Was she the crisis? Did they tell her today she wouldn't be invited to the Christmas gathering because Rex was at the ranch still recovering? No problem. She'd already agreed to spend that day with Cullen and Jeffrey, and Drew would be with her.

"Sit," said Annie. "Have some nice hot tea."

"Please, don't worry. I'll be spending Christmas with Cullen."

"It's not that." Edie had a look on her pixie face as if she'd just killed Santa. "Here, *New Orleans Lifestyle* fresh off the press. I wanted to get to you first and explain. Barb paid big bucks for this article and required that I write it just like she did for her game day party with its gross beer fountain and enough beluga caviar to account for the deaths of a dozen sturgeons. The guests were a strange mix of socialites and her old friends. I interviewed as few as possible and got out there when she started boasting about Rex being her boy toy. She told my editor I'd done such a fine job on her shindig that she wanted me again. She likes to hurt people, and that's why she truly asked for me. Here." Edie rolled back the slick cover to the rear of the magazine where various paid announcements were placed.

In glossy color, Barbara Bienville stared at her with a hand prominently displayed on her big chest. A huge diamond haloed with more diamonds and attached to a wide band encrusted with many small stones shone on her ring finger.

Rex Billodeaux and I are so pleased to announce our engagement which we have kept secret for many weeks waiting for football season to end when we could throw a proper party much bigger than my modest game day celebrations. With his recent illness, we felt we could not wait. My happy thirty-year marriage to Gus Bienville proved that winter/spring romances could work very well. Of course, ours is more of a fall/summer romance, but we expect the same happy outcome. A wedding date has not yet been set.

"She wrote that dreck herself. Fall/summer romance, ha! She's old enough to be his mother." Edie fumed.

Standing behind Edie, Stacy snorted. "She's lying. Rex didn't choose that ring. Gus gave that gaudy piece of work to her for their thirtieth anniversary the week before he died. She flashed it at me up in the sky box. Next thing you know he's dead, and she can't wear it because she's supposed to be in mourning. Though, I'm surprised she didn't."

"I asked her a few more questions to fill out the article."

Of course we met through the Sinners. I so admired his skill on the field and urged Gus to sign him. After the funeral, he was such a comfort to me. One thing led to another. Now we are in love.

As for having children, I suppose with enough hormones I could manage, but we'd prefer to adopt poor orphans. However, I don't believe we need anyone else in our lives to be ecstatic together.

Ours will be the wedding of the year. I give New Orleans Lifestyle exclusive rights to cover it.

"Orphans, my ass. She probably eats them with her mother of pearl caviar spoons," Edie huffed. "Rex loved Drew. I know he did. Does."

All eyes turned toward Dre. She supposed that they expected tears, but Rex had made it very plain that he wanted a more worldly woman who did not desire children. He hadn't said he loved Barb, but then, he hadn't told her that either. She sipped the tea, some herbal remedy Xo possibly made to quell hysteria. She did not feel anything in the ice-cold block of her heart. When it thawed she might, but not now, surrounded by her friends.

The front door opened and closed again letting in yet more people who cared about her. Who next? Jeffrey rounded the kitchen doorway first with Cullen a step behind.

"We came as soon as I showed Cullen the article. Oh, my dear. We would never hurt you like this with such a gauche announcement. Ours would be loving and elegant."

Cullen took her cold, cold hands and rubbed them. "Dre, will you accept our proposal now? You will always be cherished."

Annie, in whom she had confided the entire situation was quick to speak. "Now is not the time to make such an important decision."

"I second that," said Stacy.

"No, I've been thinking about this for a couple of weeks. I accept your proposal, Cullen. Edie, will you write the announcement and see that it runs in *Lifestyle* and the other papers?"

"I will, and it'll be better than this swill. I'm sorry my brother is such a pig."

Jeffrey held up his phone. "Let's pose you in front of the fireplace in the den. Something nice to go with the article."

"I should change my clothes. I'm in jeans. My feet are bare."

"But your top is adorable. I'll take it from the waist up. Come along."

Cullen, as always during the week, wore an impeccable business suit. He placed a gentle arm around her waist and stared into the camera. She did the same. The flash went off.

The picture would appear beneath the heading *Ames/Carson to Wed* with the usual names of their parents, their hometown, colleges attended, and current employment juiced up a little by Edie's description of Dre as the noted graphic artist who had done the design work for the Artists Alliance Gala and citing Cullen as a well-known family attorney excelling in his compassion toward children. She added in their meet cute story of running into each other near a Lucky Dog cart, unaware that both were living in New Orleans now. A friendship renewed turned to love. They planned a small wedding in June.

Dre signed off on it. For now, she wanted no mention of Drew. Time enough for that when Cullen announced his groomsmen as their son and Jeffrey.

Chapter Forty

Rex completed a walking circuit of the ranch and ended at the family gym where Sarge waited to direct him in some light weight work and a few yoga poses that would help his core but not stress it, the Apanasana or wind-relieving pose and the cat/cow position among them. He'd do them for now but couldn't wait to get back to crunches and some real ab work.

His parents had sealed him in a Barb proof bubble, no phone, no outside contacts. They screened any incoming calls as reporters tried the ranch numbers and even lurked outside the gates to get photos of him out and about, shouting questions through the bars. How are you feeling? When will you get back to playing?, which was the worst of all, when will you and Barb marry? He soon learned to alter his path away from the road. Knox Polk requested the police to clear the road as all the parked cars were a traffic hazard.

His dad issued regular reports on his recovery to soothe the fans after Dean's two losses, but as Rex had promised his nemesis, the team settled down and won the next. The last game in January would be a piece of king cake with extra frosting on top their opponent was so weak.

Sometimes, he went into the woods and sat in the glade, listened to the bird songs, smelled its mossy scent, watched the wind stir the gray strands of Spanish moss in the trees, and remembered being there with Dre and how she felt beneath him. He'd briefly considered trying an escape over the fence and into the cane fields, hitchhiking back to New Orleans, and telling her all, but that had never worked in his teen years and wouldn't now. Instead, he lay back and simply remembered being in love, then berating himself for not telling Dre sooner.

As he went through the gate to the pool house where the gym was located, Knox Polk intercepted him. "Someone left an envelope for you on the gate and drove off in a black Cadillac."

"Give it to me."

"It's at the big house, your father's orders, but I thought you should know."

"Thanks, Knox. I'm a little tired of being babied."

"Thought so." Always a man of few words, their ranch manager went back to being vigilant in protecting the family.

Sarge waited in the gym and when he cancelled, she reprimanded him for slacking off. An athletic trainer with only one foot, she could still kick ass. Usually, she wasn't one for talk either, but had been almost chatty about the boy she and Mack were adopting from his guardian grandparents, mother dead from an overdose, father unknown, and what they could do for him to get him out of that wheelchair.

"Something came up. We'll reschedule for after lunch but before Shasha gets home from school. Okay?"

"This time, but you know the importance of keeping to a schedule. Maybe, I'll come have lunch with you and make sure you return."

"No need for that unless you want some of Corazon's gumbo."

"I do. I hope you aren't fretting over the Christmas gathering coming up. If your parents haven't said, Dre and Drew aren't coming. They are going to be with her fiancé and his friend, Jeffrey."

He stopped dead. Sarge nearly stumbled over him but caught herself in time. "So sorry. I thought you knew. Let's get you to the house. You probably need your meds."

"Yes, nothing like a handful of antacids for lunch."

Garlands festooned the entry way and staircase as they went in the front door and made their way to the kitchen. His mother's decorating crew had arrived to erect the towering royal spruce that perfumed the air with its evergreen fragrance. Her usual poinsettia frenzy filled the den and dining area with color. Christmas was coming, but without Dre.

His parents sat companionably drinking coffee on this slightly brisk day and spoiling their upcoming meal with slices of Corazon's chocolate chip pumpkin bread, another sure sign of the holiday approaching. A large brown envelope, unopened, lay between them on the table like a serving of something far less enjoyable. His name was scrawled on it with a black marker. He was no handwriting analyst, but he could tell it had been written in anger.

"Oh, you're early. Should I heat up a can of chicken soup?" his mother said as if the envelope were invisible, and Corazon's gumbo didn't simmer on the stove.

"I came for my mail, and I want gumbo."

"Your mail is mostly get-well wishes that we turn over to the Sinners' PR department to answer. They send a signed picture and a short, typed message. We still pay the bills on the apartment, and your medical expenses are being covered by the Sinners' management. You have nothing to worry about."

"Except that." He pointed to the envelope as if someone had smeared the table with shit.

"Told you we should have burned it unopened," his dad said.

"We hadn't made up our minds before you barged in."

"Enough!" He seized the envelope and ripped it open. "Shall I read it aloud? It begins 'You Rotten Bastard.' Could be from Barb or Dre."

"Dre would never say that about you," his mother objected. "She still cares."

"I suppose that's why she's engaged to marry another man."

"My bad," Sarge admitted. "I thought he knew."

"We figured it would come out at Christmas but wanted to give you another week to recuperate before then, son. Read on. We know it's from Barb," his dad urged.

I received another letter from the NFL today. Despite our engagement which they suspect to be a sham, testimonies continue to flow in about how I treat you. Even that dimwit, Huddleston, said he saw you with deep scratches that you admitted I gave you. It affected your play. Dean claims after meeting with me alone, you became morose and alienated yourself from friends and family due to psychological abuse. Matt Keaton says I caused you to break up with your girlfriend under duress. I had to fire my driver whose affidavit was the most damning of the bunch. All true of course, but you were sworn to secrecy and obviously broke your word to me not to tattle.

Therefore, I feel no need to keep mine not to sell the team until the end of the season and to keep it in New Orleans. The agreement with the consortium in St. Louis has been signed and delivered. I can do that special messenger thing, too. As the NFL was going to call an owners' meeting after the Super Bowl to oust me as unfit to have a team, I have to get my money's worth and quickly.

You and your friends will never be Sinners again. I am keeping the rights to the name and the team merch which will become highly collectable. More for me. I almost hope you lose the Super Bowl, but that extra billion in my pocket will buy me a grand place in Paris if you still have the will to win.

If you are not aware yet, your former girlfriend is now engaged to the queer father of her son. My investigator did a very fine job of learning all the details. Perhaps she thought being in a gay throuple with Jeffrey Jackson is better than being with you. You weren't all that great in bed. Gus did better in his eighties.

I could say I wish you well, but I don't. I hope your career tanks, and Dre never forgives you. Don't expect to see me again. I'll be in Paris.

Your former lover, Barbara Bienville

He'd braced his arms on the table to keep his hands from shaking, but the tremor in his voice could not be disguised. Her barbs went deep, the loss of the Sinners and Dre. He'd still have a team by another name far away from her and Drew, maybe for the best. They would never forgive that he'd put saving the team first. The personal insults didn't matter at all. He hadn't tried to be a good lover.

He shook the pages in his dad's face. "This why I

didn't want you to interfere. I agreed to be her companion and anything else she wanted if she'd consider keeping the team in New Orleans. I thought if I could introduce her to the right people she wanted to meet and get her involved with the city, she'd reconsider selling out of state. But she had a sadistic side I didn't count on."

"No surprise to me," his mom said. "I didn't know how you could bear her—and then that harsh breakup with Dre. She had to be behind it."

"She demanded the breakup, had the apartment bugged to make sure of it."

"While we stayed there?" his mother asked.

"Yes. She said she planned to be as good as you and mom in a bathtub when she reached your age.

His dad seemed a tiny bit pleased. "Yeah, we still got it going on."

"Not now, Joe. Let our son tell his story."

"The man she hired found Dre's engagement ring and gave it to Barb. After that, I couldn't say a word about Dre without some sort of retaliation. She promised that she'd have acid thrown in Dre's face if she even suspected I had contact with her again. I had to make Dre hate me. I told her she wasn't enough woman for me and that I didn't want kids. I knew that the last part would end us forever—for her own sake. She might be better off with Cullen even if he is gay."

He put his face in his hands and laid his head on the table. "Now I've lost everything, my self-esteem, the Sinners and any chance they will respect me enough to let me lead them, and worst of all, Dre and Drew who can never forgive me." Tears he tried to hide ran out between his fingers.

Lynn Shurr

Sarge hugged his shoulders. "You think I didn't cry when I lost my foot and my military career? You believe the veterans I work with don't cry about their losses and how hard it is to climb back up from the pit they're in— because they do. Let it all out and begin to heal. A good workout this afternoon will help. As for forgiveness, I took Mack back after he messed up."

"As did Stacy when Dean fathered a child with Ilsa. When Lorena felt betrayed by Jock, she finally believed him. Forgiveness there for all of us if we ask for it. But no gumbo for you until the doctor gives you an okay. I'll heat that soup now." His mother got up and turned away to the stove.

Raising his head, he thought he noticed a tear on her cheek. He'd made his mother cry, another thing not to be proud of. He couldn't look his dad in the eyes, but Joe's voice got through to him.

"It took your mother to teach me there was more to life than sex and football. After your playing days are over, there is still love and family. Now, we're filing this letter with the NFL. I'm getting a pen and paper. You'll write your side of the story. That woman may have run a sneak play around us, but she'll never own a team again, I gua-ran-tee you me. There's a slim chance the deal will be cancelled, but don't get your hopes up." His father in full game is on mode took a pen and legal pad from a shelf near their old-fashioned land line.

"I signed an NDA. I have no hopes."

"Screw that. If she sues us, we'll sue her right back. Here, start—writing." His dad thrust the pen into his hand.

Her eyes still tearful, his mother turned. "That's self-pity speaking, Rex. You finish your recovery and

310

then you will rebuild. Meanwhile, think about what you are going to say to Dre to win her back."

"Yes, ma'am," he replied as if he were still a child who had done wrong. He felt like one.

Chapter Forty-One

Christmas day with Cullen and Jeffrey, so different from the ranch gathering, but they'd tried very hard to make it special. Perhaps a roasted goose, whipped potatoes with a touch of truffles, and green peas with pearl onions wasn't exactly kid food, but Drew ate it. Now, he'd been given the honor of flaming the plum pudding for dessert, a huge responsibility. Dre smiled at the ceremony they made of it. This might be the start of new traditions for her and her boy.

With the air-conditioning turned up to allow for it, an electric fire flickered in their small hearth. A modest-sized tree hosted over-sized designer ornaments but also a group picture of the four of them together in a small frame, a nice touch that reminded her of the tree at the ranch decorated by experts and then covered in the homemade decorations created by two generations of children. Perhaps, many more would follow.

Was she in love? No. Was she happy? Perhaps not, but content with her decision. She believed she could live her life this way, though Cullen and Jeffrey kept adding more incentives to their proposal. If she felt she wanted a lover at any time, they'd condone it. If the situation proved unsustainable, Cullen would draw up a fair divorce settlement giving her alimony according to each year their marriage had lasted. He wanted to adopt Drew and change his name to Andrew Ames Carson. Their desire to have another child outshone all the rest. In the artificial light from the fireplace, the tasteful diamond solitaire ring they'd given her sparkled on her ring finger. She hadn't wanted it, but at least they'd honored her wish to keep it small.

They'd spent most of the day watching Christmas movies, *It's a Wonderful Life*, *A Christmas Story*, and *Die Hard*, Drew's favorite, alternating those with football games whose announcers couldn't stop talking about the clandestine sale of the Sinners to a group of St. Louis buyers. Barb, clothed in gold and with a smug smile, had done a press conference to boast about the five billion-dollar plus deal she'd made. No tasteless engagement ring flashed on her finger, but she did give the reporters the bird as she also said, "The engagement is off. Rex wanted it, but I don't need a man to tell me what to do. *Bon chance*, suckers. I'm off to Paris." They'd watched it once, then changed the channel each time it appeared again.

The analysts preferred showing and reshowing the collapse of Rex Billodeaux on the field. Though his recovery was assured, when would he be able to play again? With these two shocks, could the Sinners make it through the challenging playoff games to come with or without their second quarterback?

They turned off the TV to have their late dinner. She helped Jeffrey put the meal on the table while Cullen played a solemn game of chess with Drew. No more noise or interference to mar their day. After the main course, Jeffrey soused the plum pudding with brandy sauce and handed Drew a barbecue lighter to keep him at a safe distance. With one flick, the liquor caught fire in a moment of blazing blue glory much like her love affair with Rex. Then, it was gone.

The doorbell rang. Who had the nerve to disturb them on this holy day?

"I'll get it," Drew said, racing from the dining room before anyone could stop him.

The door opened. An all too familiar voice said, "Merry Christmas."

She rushed to her son's side with Cullen and Jeffrey practically stepping on her heels.

"Oh, I don't think so," said Cullen to Rex.

She didn't believe all four of them could have pushed him outside. He looked well again, buff and rested. Wearing worn jeans and a blue chambray shirt because no one at the ranch had to dress up on Christmas day if they didn't want to, Rex also had his cowboy hat slanted down low shading his eyes. He carried a burlap sack like some a kind of Cajun Santa. He held it out but didn't release it to anyone of them.

"My mom and dad wanted me to deliver some presents. Say, could we sit down for a few minutes? It's a long drive, and I turned back twice before I got the nerve to come here."

"Some nerve," echoed Jeffrey, but Cullen nodded and led the way to the living room where he gestured to a side chair before placing her on the sofa between himself and Jeffrey.

Rex drew out two packages in Christmas wrap and handed them to Drew who shook the boxes. "Legos!" her son said with the first joyous smile she'd seen on his face all day. The smile faded as fast as the flames on the now forgotten plum pudding. "I'll text them a thank you in case I don't see Mama Nell and Daddy Joe again."

"I've told you that you will," Dre countered at once.

"Believe your mom. Once they make a person part of the family, they don't let go. Doesn't matter how they got there. This is for Jeffrey and Cullen." He sat the foil wrapped loaf on the glass coffee table since neither reached out for it. "Corazon's chocolate chip pumpkin bread with the recipe on the back."

Jeffrey picked it up and sniffed as if he searched for bombs. Satisfied, he studied the recipe. "How nice of her. I'll see she gets a handwritten note of thanks."

"Drew, I want you to have this forever. I know you can't forgive me for hurting your mom, but this will always be your game ball. Someday, you might recall the good times instead."

Rex sank back into the pads of the chair as if Drew might throw the football in his face. He didn't, only turned it over on the table so that the carefully lettered message showed. No thanks were forthcoming. It appeared Rex didn't expect any.

"That's a very valuable ball, son. Say thanks," Cullen prompted.

Dre thought she caught a slight cringe in Rex's posture as Cullen asserted his parental rights. Good.

"Yeah, thanks."

"This is for you, Dre." He opened a Schifferman's box and presented her with a ring she knew must be a custom piece.

"I had it made for you. The stone across the top represents Drew and the spaces were left for other children. A few days before I planned to give it to you, I made a deal with the devil's mistress to keep the Sinners in New Orleans. I'd do whatever she wanted of me for that. One of those things was to break up with you. What I said about you not being enough when you were everything to me was a lie. So was the other. I had to drive you away." He tilted his head toward Drew.

Dre listened, but said, "Thank you, but I already have an engagement ring." This man had the power to destroy her again when the first wound still smarted. He'd put football before their love.

"Not one as gorgeous as this. We wanted to go bigger, but she wouldn't have it," Jeffrey said.

"It's yours, Dre, no matter how you want to wear it. You can sell it for Drew's education, maybe."

"Cullen has already promised he'll take care of that." She refused to make this easy for him. She would not run into his arms simply because he seemed ashamed and forlorn beneath the brim of his hat.

"Barb swore if I so much as mentioned your name she'd…" Again a glance at Drew. "She'd do to you what Josee's old boyfriend did to her."

"I remember that! All the tabloids wrote about it. That evil beyotch," Jeffrey said with all the vehemence he saved for the villainesses in his favorite soap operas streamed for later viewing.

"Jeffrey, why don't we take Drew into the kitchen to slice the plum pudding and give Dre and Rex some space." Cullen stood, but he'd gone very pale. "Come along, Drew. You'll love it."

"But my mom shouldn't be alone with him."

"I'll be fine. That's a Drew/Dre promise." She put all she could in her voice to reassure him. Be strong, Dre, be strong.

Once her son was gone, Rex leaned forward and moved a hand toward hers. She took it away and left the ring. He removed his hat, but his eyes still seemed shadowed. Twisting its brim, he tried to look her in the eye and failed.

"Every time I was with her taking one for the team I felt as if I cheated on you. She could tell my mind wasn't on her and made it worse for me. If you want the gory details, I wrote out all the abuse to go with the letter she sent me before leaving town to attach to the NFL file, but I'd rather you didn't. You won't have any respect left for me if you do." He stood as if ready to retreat.

"Once I asked you if you felt like damaged goods for getting pregnant at such a young age, and you said no—because you had Drew. Now I'm damaged goods, but I don't have the son I wanted or you. All I've got left is football and when that is gone—nothing.

"My mother said forgiveness is always possible if a person asks for it, but I don't believe that. What I did to you and Drew is beyond forgiving. I have to leave."

Her numb heart began to feel again. His agony reached out to her. "I didn't hear you ask."

"You mean you could? Dre, will you forgive me?"

"Yes."

"Will you accept this ring with all my love?"

"Yes." Other words were beyond her.

He took her hand and removed Cullen's diamond, replacing it with his own. He swiped the back of his hand across his eyes and moved to pull her close. How good his body felt, how natural and true. Their kiss was interrupted by a gasp from the dining room where Jeffrey and Drew placed plates of plum pudding.

"That was so beautiful, I almost changed sides," Jeffrey gushed.

Rex focused on Drew. "I'm asking you to forgive me, too."

The answer wasn't quick in coming. "I guess so—if

Mom does."

Cullen joined them. "I understand, but I still want to be a part of my son's life."

"I agree. You will be. I guarantee." Rex crossed the room to shake Cullen's hand.

"Well, I've set an extra place. Shall we have dessert? We also have coffee," Jeffrey invited.

"You had me at coffee. I'm allowed to have an occasional cup now."

While the atmosphere wasn't relaxed, it was civil. Dre felt grateful for that. When Jeffrey got the Mardi Gras baby he'd put in the pudding instead of the traditional silver coin, he said with sadness, "I guess this won't happen now."

Cullen closed his hand over the plastic baby still in Jeffrey's palm. "I promise it will. We'll find a surrogate. We'll have children. Drew is only the first."

Eyes watering, Jeffrey asked, "May I still be your guncle, Drew?"

"Sure. I'd like that. You're funny."

Forgiveness and hope, love and laughter. The best of all Christmas gifts.

Chapter Forty-Two

The Sinners' last regular season game came the first weekend of the new year. Rex dressed out in full pads with extra protection across the stomach though he knew Coach didn't plan to use him unless an emergency occurred. The weak team they played expected annihilation, and they would get it. Coach and Dean still delivered a pep talk as the atmosphere in the locker room hung dark and heavy with the knowledge that the Sinners would be no more by February. He asked to speak. This took almost as much courage as asking Dre for forgiveness.

"I want to say I'm sorry. I tried to save the Sinners by making a deal with Barbara Bienville. I thought I could do it alone, but I failed to save the team. Coping with her took a toll on my health. I take full responsibility for those two losses at the end of the season, but I'm back. We can still win the Super Bowl if we all pull together."

Leave it to Hud to say, "Why should we bother to put another billion into Barb's bank account? Why risk getting hurt for her?" A few guys in the back muttered, "Yeah."

"Do it for Coach and Dean who are taking their retirements. Do it for the city of New Orleans and all of our fans. Most of all, do it for our team, the last of the Sinners who want to go out on top."

The yeahs turned to yeas. He repeated this booster throughout the playoffs as one by one teams fell before them. Having the home team advantage didn't hurt one bit. Their fans came out more raucous and outrageously dressed than ever. Somewhere among them in costume were Cullen and Jeffrey. They'd worn black with Scream masks out of mourning for the lost team. He'd made sure they got Super Bowl tickets.

On the day of, Dre and Drew sat with Joe and Edie in the fifty-yard line seats, exactly as it should be. He presented his fiancée with the game ball from a touchdown he'd run in just for the heck of it. Ty did the same for Edie when he ran an interception fifty yards for a score. Everyone got a piece of the very large pie as the numbers climbed. Matt and X ran for touchdowns. Tom made two field goals. Dean, as if his shoulder didn't hurt, threw three long ones that scored. The ferocious defense kept the opponents to fourteen points, nothing close to the fifty-five put on the scoreboard by the Sinners. This rout didn't make for a great Super Bowl, but at least the half time show featuring Caressa and a bevy of New Orleans musicians provided some good entertainment.

When the red and black confetti stopped falling, the interviews and presentation of the seven-pound Vince Lombardi trophy were done, the champagne soaked athletes hung up their Sinners uniforms for the last time. They headed to Mariah's Place to continue the celebration. Despite the continued reveling in the streets with a car or two set on fire, Mariah still closed promptly at two a.m.

"I'm getting too old to be up all night," she said with tears marring her heavy makeup as she gave each of "her boys" a hug before going upstairs. She left behind the core of the team and her long-time bartender to take care of their needs with the door locked to anyone else. Their women had left around midnight. Dean called for a last round. Rex felt a pang of sadness.

"You know I'm taking my retirement along with Coach. How about the rest of you?" Dean asked as he sipped bourbon.

Junior Polk spoke up first. "Me, too. With twins on the way, I want to be home for Xochi. I'm thinking of opening another restaurant called Junior's in Breaux Bridge right near the I-10. We'll suck those tourists in with our crab cakes and the best bread pudding in Louisiana."

"Most of us sitting here still have a few years on our contracts so during that free week we earned before going into playoffs, a bunch of us went to St. Louis to check out housing and schools. We found a new development up on the bluffs, gated community, with plenty of lots for sale," Matt said. "We can build side-by-side to Rex and Dre. That way the boys can still be close. I plan to put in a pool though we won't get the use of it as much farther north. You're all invited to swim."

"We figure we'll settle on the other side of you, mate. Lori says she can get a coaching job anywhere with those two Olympic medals, maybe open a school for volleyball training, but right now she's concentrating on having another little ripper for Mikey to play with. We'll keep our units here and put them out to let. A good investment. We'll be back for our anniversary at the ranch every year," Jock revealed.

"Mack?" Dean questioned.

"I have a contract to fulfill, but I can't take Sarge away from the ranch, not with a new handicapped child coming to live with us. It's her happy place. I guess I'll get a condo. She'll visit when she can."

"How about we build a guest wing onto our house and put you up there with walk in showers for your kids when Sarge brings them to see a game? You should be with family. Me and Lori got used to you living under us," Jock offered.

"Afraid I'll stray or go back to drinking?"

"Righty-O, mate, righty-O." Jock grinned and tossed back what remained of his drink.

"Okay, I'll take you up on that offer and chip in for the cost."

"Tom?" Dean continued.

Rex knew they'd always been close from childhood on. This would be hard on both of them.

Tom kept it light. "I'm not quite as ancient as you, bro. I still have some leg left. We're selling the condo and maybe we'll build in the same neighborhood as the rest of the guys. With Alix expecting our second, a boy this time that she wants to name Anders after grandfather, we'd like more room and a yard. She wants them to know their cousins from Wisconsin since it's a little closer. Not looking forward to having her mom and sisters visit, but I'll cope. Don't worry. We'll be visiting at the ranch often."

"X?"

"First we have a wedding at the AME in Chapelle with the Rev presiding. Our mamas love that idea but moving to St. Louis not so much. We can't budge them. Like Matt, I still have a contract, but Carie and I are thinking of looking downtown for a place. She'd like to open a club like Mariah's where we can all hangout again, and she'll sing when she wants. Gonna be weird being the Pioneers. Brown and gold are not my colors. I just know the mascot will end up being some guy in a coonskin cap."

Dean shook his head sadly. "Probably. Ty?"

"You know I'm a city boy. Edie says she can get a job at a magazine like *Lifestyle* easily, so we'll settle in the urban area, maybe near X and Carie. My granny and mama aren't keen on losing us, but their lives are in New Orleans—and I won't have to be around my father much which is good."

"Who's left? Rex, you have anything to add?"

"A wedding in early June at the ranch. We'll hang around there until the St. Louis house is built. Dre wants a studio and says she can work anywhere—but we need to have a guest room for Cullen and Jeffrey. Drew, that kid, he says he doesn't want anyone arguing over him. I'll be his athletic father, and Cullen will be his intellectual father. He's going to call us both dad and doesn't want to be adopted. He'll continue to be Andrew Ames. Oh, Dre promised to donate her eggs when Cullen finds a surrogate. Then, the child will be Drew's half or full sibling."

"That's something else," X said and finished his drink.

"I think it's very, very Billodeaux. Dre learned from us, and now she'll be one. This is the end for me." He stood. "Time to go."

The rest filed out the door to waiting rides the bartender summoned, but Dean and Rex lingered for moment. Dean embraced his brother. "I know you'll take good care of the team."

"That's a promise." The last of the Sinners glanced back at the checkerboard floor where he and Dre once danced and left the building.

Thank you for purchasing
this publication of The Wild Rose Press, Inc.

For questions or more information
contact us at
info@thewildrosepress.com.

The Wild Rose Press, Inc.
www.thewildrosepress.com